W9-CTP-114

AND THEN THE ENEMY
WAS UPON THEM!

Emerson flew the *Banshee III* like one possessed. He slammed in full power and shot so fast down a corridor between two Feds that they couldn't train on him. Then he hit the attitude jets and angled up, actually clipping the antenna on another Fed as he flashed by.

Emerson's group had almost broken out above the enemy pack when a missile snaked past the *Banshee III*. It just missed them, but it blew *Bad Mac* to atoms. And that was when Emerson's gunner froze, knowing the Feds had just murdered the woman he loved. Emerson slapped control of forward screen arms to another crewman and yelled for him to take over. They were almost out and could see their reinforcements streaking in behind the few Fed fighters still in their way, but in that maze of fire, it was too late. Numbing concussion rocked *Banshee III*, and she spun away into darkness. . . .

THE WAR YEARS
3
★ THE ★
JUPITER WAR

FEATURING
GREGORY BENFORD

EDITED BY
BILL FAWCETT

A ROC BOOK

ROC
Published by the Penguin Group
Penguin Books USA Inc., 375 Hudson Street,
New York, New York 10014, U.S.A.
Penguin Books Ltd, 27 Wrights Lane,
London W8 5TZ, England
Penguin Books Australia Ltd, Ringwood,
Victoria, Australia
Penguin Books Canada Ltd, 2801 John Street,
Markham, Ontario, Canada L3R 1B4
Penguin Books (N.Z.) Ltd, 182-190 Wairau Road,
Auckland 10, New Zealand

Penguin Books Ltd, Registered Offices:
Harmondsworth, Middlesex, England

First published by Roc, an imprint of New American Library,
a division of Penguin Books USA Inc.

First Printing, August, 1991
10 9 8 7 6 5 4 3 2 1

 Roc is a trademark of New American Library,
a division of Penguin Books USA Inc.

Printed in the United States of America

Contents

Prologue:
Old Tune, New Words

The first recognized act of the Jupiter War was the destruction of the *Johnny Greene* by Confederation fighters, but no modern war really starts with bullets. As befits any media event, the Jupiter War started with words. Words that had been building in intensity for more than two decades. The consistent failure of the Earth's nations to form a working planetary government virtually forced every nation to choose sides. In 2041, for the first time in six hundred years, Switzerland joined the United Nations, now a military alliance. What had once been merely a debating society during the twentieth century had turned by the rapprochement of the super powers into a body whose main purpose was to enable the four major powers, the States, Europe, Russia, and Japan, to continue their dominance of the rest of the world. After the failure of the economic aggressions of a failing Japan, the international body evolved into an active military and economic alliance. An alliance whose purpose, once Japan became a desolate backwater, was to ensure that the less powerful nations of the Southern Hemisphere and Middle East continued to supply them with raw materials.

As their abundant resources propelled the nations of the Southern hemisphere to importance, old grudges against the "exploiting" powers radicalized the nations of the Southern Hemisphere. Controlling an ever greater part of the world's dwindling resources, the nations of South America, Africa, and Arabia used the massive wealth they were accumulating to modernize their countries, and their armies. Together they formed the Confederation of States, whose expressed purpose was little less than the domination of their former "oppressors." As these nations grew in both economic and military strength, they began looking for ways to flex their newfound muscles. The older countries, fading in both importance and economic strength, sought to reassure themselves by asserting their own power whenever the opportunity to do so safely arose. Soon minor skirmishes, mostly at sea, constantly threatened to erupt into a greater conflict.

A worldwide war in the twenty-first century was not a viable alternative. Beyond the suicidal destructive strength of fusion bombs was the even greater power for destruction of the myriad of custom diseases held in every nation's arsenals. There were simply too many ways to die, and with the Confederation's newfound prosperity, too much for either side to lose. Grudgingly, peace continued. During the fourth decade much of this competitiveness was directed into the space programs of the two alliances. As the space between the Earth and Moon became cluttered with military hardware, the leaders of both sides discovered that any war directly above the Earth would inevitably prove as destructive to the planet as any other. When each side could shift thousands of men anywhere on the planet in a matter of hours, no "brushfire war" would remain limited. The contradiction of near-complete peace and a near-constant state of high military preparedness continued for the rest of the first half of the century. The pattern was both familiar and frightening. The world was the home of just too much fear, too much distrust, and an overwhelming amount of lethal weaponry. Forced by circumstances, the nations comprising each alliance had virtually ceased to have meaning. By 2032 the world consisted of two mega-nations and a number of backward neutrals who were completely unable to affect the situation.

In space the outposts of each side continued the animosity. The nations of the United Nations had staked their claims to the Moon and Mars long before the Confederation became a factor. With the energy of a new convert, the Confederation threw its resources behind the exploitation of the asteroids. Awakening to this new challenge, the United Nations turned its still considerable resources to the settlement of the resource-rich moons of Jupiter. Permanent settlements were established by both sides in 1038.

Part of the New Year's Celebration in 2054 was a Peace Festival in almost every capital of the United Nations. Most of these festivals were marked by the most massive displays of military strength seen that century. The Russian leadership of Stalin would have felt quite at home viewing the French display, in which it took over seven hours for all of the units to file past the reviewing stand. The military displays were more appropriate than the announced theme for these celebrations. In reality, freed of the constraints placed on their forces near Earth, both sides had long maintained a low-level conflict. In many ways the moons of Jupiter were ideal for confrontation. Rich enough to be worth fighting over and highly photogenic, this area was also distant enough to give both combatants' populations a false sense of security.

There is no reliable record of the first incident. By 2051 each side was losing an average of two ships per month. Virtually all of the fighting occurred in space. They were fighting over the resources of the Jovian moons, and it made no sense to destroy the only means of exploiting them. Then again war is hardly a matter of sense. It took only the one incident to escalate the conflict irreversably.

DREAD MOON

by Gregory Benford

1

Airboys had it easy, Russ thought. He did not have much time to think this, because he and their ship, the *Asskicker II*, were falling pretty nearly straight down onto the Ganymede ice fields. Philosophy would have to come later. If ever.

But atmospheric pilots did have it easier. Air gave your airfoil some lift. Absence of air—that is, pure space—at least let you turn easily, let you swivel and fire attitude rockets without trouble.

In between was *this*—the thin, howling scarf of gas boiled out of Ganymede by men. Just enough gas to make trouble, but too skimpy to use for much aerodynamic lift.

It wrenched and slapped at *Asskicker II*. Russ fought them down through the skimpy skin of atmosphere, using the air's rub to brake.

"Secured?" he called.

"Aye!" came shouts. From Zoti and Nye and Kitsov and Columbard, all strapped in, watching their subsystems.

They sounded scared. Usually in this raw war death came fast, and nobody had time to really get their guts snarled up.

But when the snake had hit *Asskicker II* they'd patched the punctures, stopped the engine runaway, saved the electricals. Salvaged a few minutes, maybe.

Certainly they hadn't salvaged the mission. The ship had been venting methane from the aft tanks, a giant fart. They could not possibly complete the dive around Ganymede and lay their egg on Hiruko Station.

The Feds had probably seen the blowout and figured they were dead. So Russ and Columbard had let
their ship tumble into Ganymede's upper air, arcing
around the rim of the moon so that the main Fed
cruiser couldn't see them.

"We gotta get down!" Columbard called.

"Yeah, yeah," Russ answered. His copilot knew the
zigs and zags of space nav, but knifing down through
this shrieking air rattled her.

"Got one-nine-zero sec till we come out from behind Ganymede," Columbard said rapidly. "The
Feds—"

"Nosing in," Russ said.

He fired their remaining engines. The methane flared
and sputtered and then growled, angry as a damaged
hornet.

The sudden hard thrust threw his stomach into his
throat. He gulped, eyes watering.

They dipped and banked and the speckled ground
was coming up like a big hand, swatting them.

"Slam it!" he called.

Columbard gave them max power. Russ saw a blue-
white peak slice by them like a snowy hook. He tried
to find a level spot. *Asskicker II* had to come down
vertically and had never been designed for more than
scooping through the upper layers of atmospheres, to
feed its ramscoops.

Damn this soup! he had time to think—and then
they hit.

Hard.

And bounced.

And split.

Their reserve air blew out, *whoosh!*, taking debris
with it. Russ felt a painful jab in his side and then they
flipped over.

Shouts, shrieks.

A bone-jarring, splintering crash.

His board went solid red.

Power gone, armory down, life support . . .

Columbard's tracer showed red. Then blue.

Outside, Ganymede was a broad, dirty-gray plain.

Russ found that a shattered strut was poking him in the ribs. One more centimeter and it would have punched through his skinsuit.

He would be sucking on the whole solar system, trying to inhale it—like Columbard.

He found her in the tangle, legs crushed and her eyes wide open, as though looking into some fresh truth he could not see.

2

Russ flexed his four-fingered clamp-hands and surveyed the landscape. They were on the nightside of Ganymede, though pale crescents of the other moons sliced the darkness, and Jupiter hung like a fat, luminous melon above the distant horizon. He counted three distinct shadows pointing off at angles, each differently colored.

"Maybe these'll help us sneak by optical pattern-recog detectors," he said to Zoti, pointing.

"Shadows?" she asked, puffing up a slope even in the light gravity. She carried a big supply pack. "Think so?"

"Could be." He didn't really think so but at this point you had to believe in something.

"Better get away from here," Zoti said.

"Think the Feds got a trace on us?"

She shook her head, a tight movement visible through her skinsuit helmet. "Our guys were giving them plenty deceptors, throwing EM jams on them—the works."

Russ respected her tech talents, but he never relied on tricks alone. Best thing was to get away before some skimmer craft came to check for the wreck.

"We'll hoof in three minutes," Russ said.

He looked back at the crushed metal can that a big blue-black ice outcropping had made of *Asskicker II*. It didn't look like a fabulously expensive, threatening bomber now, just a pile of scrap. Nye and Kitsov came up the hill, lugging more supplies.

"Got the CCD cubes?" Russ asked Nye.

"Yeah, I yanked them." Nye scowled. He never

said much, just let his face do his complaining for him.

"Think they've got good stuff?" Russ asked.

"Some fighter stuff," Nye said. "Then a big juicy closeup of the snake that got us."

Russ nodded. Snakes were the thin, silvery missiles that their Northern Hemisphere tech jockeys couldn't knock out. "Well," he said, maybe that'll be worth something."

Kitsov said, "Worth to Command, could be. To Natwork, no."

Zoti said, "Natwork? Oh—look, *Net*work can't use anything that's classified. A snake shot will have TS all over it."

Russ asked, "TS?"

Zoti grinned. "They say it means Top Secret, but as far as we're concerned, might as well be Tough Shit. Means we make no loot from it."

Russ nodded. He hated this mercenary shit. If everything had gone right, *Asskicker II* would have lobbed a fusion head smack onto Hiruko Station. Earthside network royalties for the shot would've gone to them all, with Russ getting twice the share of the others, since he was captain and pilot.

Had that made any difference? You could never really be sure that some subconscious greed hadn't made you rush the orbit a little, shade the numbers, slip just a hair off the mark. Could that be what had let the snake through?

He shook his head. He'd never know, and he wasn't sure he wanted to.

"Still think we'll see a single yen out of it?" Zoti asked him. He realized she had interpreted his shaking head as disagreement. They would be reading him closely now. The crew wanted reassurance that they weren't doomed and he was the only authority figure around. Never mind that he'd never led a ground operation in his life.

"I think we'll get rich," Russ said, voice full of confidence he had dredged up from somewhere. He wondered if it rang hollowly but the others seemed to brighten.

"Is good!" Kitsov said, grinning.

"It'll be better if we get out of here," Russ said. "Come on."

"Which way?" Nye asked.

"Through that notch in the hills there." Russ pointed.

Nye frowned, black eyebrows meeting above his blunt nose. "What's that way?"

"More important, what *isn't* that way," Russ said. "We'll be putting distance between us and Hiruko Station."

Nye's forehead wrinkled. "You sure?"

"We don't have any nav gear running. I had to sight on the moons." Russ said this confidently but in fact he hadn't done a square, naked-eye sighting since tech school.

Zoti said tentatively, "How about a compass?"

"On ice moon?" Kitsov chuckled. "Which way is magnetic pointing?"

"That's the problem," Russ said. "No magnetic field. Let's go."

They moved well in the low gravity. None were athletes but they had kept in shape in the gym on the voyage out. There wasn't much else to do on the big carriers. Columbard had said that Zoti got all her workout in the sack, but then Columbard had always been catty. And not a great enthusiast in the sack herself, either. Not that her opinion mattered much, Russ thought, since she wasn't around anymore to express it.

A storm came sweeping in on them as they climbed away from the wreck. It was more like a sigh of snowflakes, barely buoyant in the thin, deadly methane air. It chilled them further and he wondered if they would all get colds despite the extra insulation they all wore over their combat skinsuits.

Probably. Already his feet tingled. He turned so that his bulky pack sheltered him from the wind. They'd all get frostbite within a couple of days, he guessed.

If they could survive at all. A man in a normal

pressure suit could live about an hour on Ganymede. The unending sleet of high-energy protons would fry him, ripping through delicate cells and spreading red destruction. This was a natural side effect of Jupiter's hugeness—its compressed core of metallic hydrogen spun rapidly, generating powerful magnetic fields that whipped around every ten hours. These fields are like a rubbery cage, snagging and trapping protons spat out by the sun. Io, the innermost large moon, belched ions of sulfur and sodium into the magnetic traps, adding to the sleet. All this rained down on the inner moons, sputtering the ice.

Damn it, he was a sky jock, not a grunt. He'd never led a crew of barracks rats on a mud mission.

He kept his mind off his bulky pack and chilled feet by guessing what the Feds were doing. The war was moving fast, maybe fast enough to let a downed bomber crew slip through the Fed patrols.

When Northern Hemisphere crews had held Hiruko Station they'd needed to work outside, supervising robot ice-diggers. The first inhabitants of Ganymede instead used the newest technology to fend off the proton hail: superconducting suits. Discovery of a way to make cheap superconducting threads made it possible to weave them into pressure suits. The currents running in the threads made a magnetic field outside the suit, where it brushed away incoming protons. Inside, by the laws of magnetostatics, there was no field at all to disturb instrumentation. Once started, the currents flowed forever, without electrical resistance.

He hoped their suits were working right. *Asskicker II*'s strong magnetics had kept them from frying before, but a suit could malf and you'd never know it. He fretted about a dozen other elements in a rapidly growing list of potentially deadly effects.

Already he had new respect for the first Hiruko crews. They'd been damn good at working in this bitter cold, pioneering against the sting and bite of the giant planet. They had carved ice and even started an atmosphere. What they hadn't been so good at was defending themselves.

No reason they should've been, of course. The Southern Hemisphere had seen their chance and had come in hard—total surprise. In a single day they had taken all Ganymede. And killed nearly every Northerner.

The bedraggled surviving crew of *Asskicker II* marched in an eerie dim glow from Jupiter. Over half of Ganymede's mass was water-ice, with liberal dollops of carbon dioxide ice, frozen ammonia and methane, and minor traces of other frozen-out gases. Its small rocky core was buried under a thousand-kilometer-deep ocean of water and slush.

The crust was liberally sprinkled by billions of years of infalling meteors. These meteorites had peppered the landscape, but the atmosphere building project had already smoothed the edges of even recent craters. Ancient impact debris had left hills of metal and rock, the only relief from a flat, barren plain.

This frigid moon had been tugged by Jupiter's tides for so long that it was locked, like Luna, with one face always peering at the banded ruddy planet. One complete day-night cycle was slightly more than an Earth week long. Adjusting to this rhythm would have been difficult if the sun had provided clear punctuation to the three-and-a-half-day nights. But even without an atmosphere, the sun seen from Ganymede was a dim twenty-seventh as bright as at Earth's orbit.

They saw sunup as they crested a line of rumpled hills. The sun was bright but curiously small. Sometimes Russ hardly noticed it compared to Europa's white, cracked crescent. Jupiter's shrouded mass flickered with orange lightning strokes between the roiling, somber clouds.

Ganymede's slow rotation had been enough to churn its inner ocean, exerting a torque on the ice sheets above. A slow-motion kind of tectonics had operated for billions of years, rubbing slabs against each others, grooving and terracing terrain.

They leaped over long, strangely straight canyons, rather than try to find ways around. Kitsov proved the best distance man, remorselessly devouring kilometers. Russ watched the sky anxiously. Nothing cut the blackness above except occasional scruffy gray clouds.

They didn't stop for half a day. While they ate he ran an inventory on air, water, food. If their processors worked, recycling from the skinsuits, they could last nearly a week.

"How much food you got?" Nye wanted to know while Russ was figuring.

"I'm not carrying any," Russ answered levelly.

"Huh?" Like most cynics, Nye was also a little slow.

"I'm carrying the warhead."

"What!" Nye actually got to his feet, as though outraged.

"Regs, Sergeant," Russ said slowly. "Never leave a fusion head for the enemy."

"We got to survive out here! We can't be—"

"We are," Russ said. "That's an order."

Nye's mouth worked silently. After a while he sat back down, looking irritated and sheepish at the same time.

Russ could almost sympathize with him, perhaps because he had more imagination. He knew what lay ahead.

Even if no patrol craft spotted them, they couldn't count on their carrier to send a pickup ship. The battle throughout the inner Jovian system was still going on—he had seen the flashes overhead, far out among the moons. The Northern Hemisphere forces had their hands full.

He looked down at his own hands—four clamp-fingers with delicate tools embedded in the tip of each. Combat pilot hands, technological marvels. Back on the cruiser they could detach these ceramo-wonders and his normal hands would work just fine.

But out here, in bitter cold and high sucking vacuum, he couldn't get them off. And the chill seeping into them sent a dull ache up his arms.

The pain he could take. The clumsiness might be fatal.

"Get up!" he called. "Got klicks to go before we sleep, guys."

3

They spotted the auto-truck the next day at noon.

It came grinding along beside a gouged trench. The trench looked man-made but it was a stretch mark. Ganymede's natural radioactive elements in its core had heated the dark inner ocean, cracking the ice shell.

But the strip beside the natural groove was a route the automated truck used to haul mined ores.

Or so Russ figured. He did know that already, after just over a day of hard marching, his crew was wearing out fast. Zoti was limping. Maybe she *had* spent her gym time on her back. He didn't give a damn one way or the other, but if she slowed them down they might have to leave her behind.

But the truck could change all that. He stopped, dead still, and watched it lumber along. Its treads bit into the pale blue ice and its forward sensors monotonously swept back and forth, watching for obstructions.

Russ was no infantry officer. He knew virtually nothing about flanking and fire-and-maneuver and all the other terms that raced through his head and straight out again, leaving no residue of useful memory.

Had the Feds put fighting machines in the trucks? The idea suddenly occurred to him and seemed utterly logical. He could remember nothing in the flight briefing about that. Mostly because the briefing officer expected them to either come back intact or be blown to frags. Nobody much thought fighter-bombers would crash. Or have surviving crew.

Could the truck hear his suit com? He didn't know.

Better use hand signals, then. He held up a claw-hand. Nye kept walking until Kitsov grabbed his arm. They all stood for a long moment, looking at the orange-colored truck and then at Russ and then back at the truck again.

One thing was sure, Russ thought. If the truck was carrying a fighting machine, the fighter wasn't so hot.

His crew made beautiful targets out here, standing out nice and clean against the dirty ice.

He waved with both arms. *Drop your packs.*

Somewhat to his surprise, they did. He was glad to get the bulk off his shoulders.

The truck kept lumbering along, oblivious. He made broad gestures. *Pincer attack.*

They closed the distance at a dead run. The truck didn't slow or turn.

They all leaped the deep groove in the ice with no trouble. They cleared the next forty meters quickly and Nye had reached the truck when a small popping sound came from the truck rear and Kitsov fell.

Russ was headed for the hatch in the front so he couldn't see the rear of the truck at all. The popping came again and Nye fired his M18 at something, the whole clip at once, *rrrrrrrtttt!*

The popping stopped. Russ ran alongside the truck, puffing, Zoti beside him. Nye had the back of the truck open. Something came out, something all pipes and servos and ripped aluminum. Damaged but still active. Zoti brought up her M18. Nye hit the thing with the butt of his M18 and caved in an optical sensor. The fighter didn't stop. It reached for Nye with a knife that suddenly flipped up, standing straight out at the end of a telescoping arm. Zoti smashed the arm. The fighting machine tumbled out and went face-down on the ice. Russ shot it in the back of its power panel. It didn't move anymore.

"Damn!" Nye said. "Had a switchblade! You ever—"

"Get in front!" Russ yelled, turning away.

"What? I—"

"It's still armed," Russ called, already running. If Nye didn't want to follow orders that was fine with him.

They had all nearly reached the front of the truck when the fighter went off, a small *crump.* Shrapnel rattled against the truck.

"Think it's dead now?" Zoti asked, wide-eyed.

"Leave it," Russ said. He walked to where Kitsov lay facedown.

The man had a big hole in his chest and a bigger one in back. It was turning reddish-brown already. The thin atmosphere was sucking blood out of the body, the stain spreading down the back and onto the mottled ice. It made a pool there which fumed into a brown vapor.

Russ looked at it, his mind motionless for a long moment as he recalled Kitsov once saying some dumb reg made his blood boil. Well, now it was.

Russ knew that even the skimpy gear on *Asskicker II* could have kept Kitsov running long enough to get back to the cruiser. Out here there was utterly no hope.

Two days, two crew. Three remaining.

And they had maybe six days of air left. Plenty of time to get their dying done.

4

Russ wondered what shape and size of man had designed the forward seat. He peered out through a smeared viewport, barking his knees against the rough iron. The auto-truck had been fashioned from Ganymede ore and nobody had bothered to polish rough edges. The seat bit into him through his skinsuit and somehow the iron smelled bitter, as if some acid had gotten in at the foundry.

But, far more important, the cabin was *warm*. The Ganymede cold had seeped into them on the march and they kept the interior heaters on high, basking in it.

He watched the rutted terrain ahead closely. There had been no sign of activity during the day they had ridden in the auto-truck. The truck was sluggish, careful, dumb. It had stopped twice to pick up ore canisters from robot mines. The ore came out of a hole in the ground on a conveyor belt. There were no higher-order machines around to notice three stowaway humans.

Russ got out of the seat, having to twist over a ceramic cowling, and jerked a thumb at Nye to take over. They switched every half hour because after that you couldn't stay alert. Zoti was asleep in the back. He envied her. He had caught some down-time but his nerves got to him after a few hours.

"Helmet," he called. Russ pulled his on and watched Nye zip up. Zoti slept with hers on, following orders. The simple pleasure of the cabin's cozy pressure was hard to give up.

He climbed out the broken back hatch. Nye had riddled it but the pressure seal inside self-healed. Russ used handholds to scramble onto the corrugated top of the truck. He could see much farther from here. Watching the rumpled hills reassured him somehow. Scrunched down below, staring out a slit, it was too easy to imagine Feds creeping up on them.

Overhead, Jupiter eclipsed the sun. The squat pink watermelon planet seemed to clasp the hard point of white light in a rosy glow, then swallowed it completely. Now Europa's white, cracked crescent would be the major light in the sky for three and a half hours, he calculated. A rosy halo washed around the rim of Jupiter's atmosphere as sunlight refracted through the transparent outer layers.

He wished he could get the crazy, whirling geometry of this place straight in his head. The Feds had knocked down all navsats, and he couldn't stay on the air long enough to call for a position check with the carrier.

This truck was carrying them away from Hiruko Station, he figured. It would be reassuring to get some sort of verification, though. No pickup mission would risk coming in close to Hiruko.

He took out his Fujitsu transponder and tapped into the external power jack. He had no idea where the carrier was now, so he just aimed the pistol-grip antenna at the sky and got off a quick microwave "mayday" burst. That was all the carrier needed to know they were alive, but getting a fix on them would be tough.

Job done, he sat and watched the slow swirling dance of the sky. No flashes, so maybe the battle was over. Only for a while, though. Neither side was going to give up the inner moons.

Russ grinned, remembering how just a few years back some of his Earthside buddies had said a real war out here was pointless. Impossible, too.

Too far away, they said. Too hard.

Even after the human race had moved into the near-Earth orbits, scattering their spindly factories and cylinder-cities and rock-hopping entrepreneurs, the human race was dominated by nay-saying groundhogs.

Sure, they had said, space worked. Slinging airtight homes into orbit at about one astronomical unit's distance from the sun was—in retrospect—an obvious step. After all, there was a convenient moon nearby to provide mass and resources.

But Earth, they said, was a benign neighborhood. You could resupply most outposts within a few days. Except for the occasional solar storm, when winds of high-energy particles lashed out, the radiation levels were low. There was plenty of sunshine to focus with mirrors, capture in great sheets of conversion wafers, and turn into bountiful, high-quality energy.

But Jupiter? Why go *there*?

Scientific teams had already touched down on the big moons in the mid twenty-first century, even dipped into the thick atmosphere. By counting craters and taking core samples, they deduced what they could about how the solar system had evolved. After that brief era of quick-payoff visits, nobody had gone back. One big reason, everyone was quick to point out, was the death rate in those expeditions: half never saw Earth again, except as a distant blue-white dot.

Scientists don't tame new worlds; pioneers do. And except for the bands of religious or political refugee/fanatics, pioneers don't do it for nothing.

By 2050 humans had already begun to spread out of the near-Earth zone. The bait was the asteroids—big tumbling lodes of metal and rock, rich in heavy elements. These flying mountains could be steered slowly from their looping orbits and brought into near-Earth rendezvous. The delta-V wasn't all that large.

There, smelters melted them down and fed the factories steady streams of precious raw materials: manganese, platinum, cadmium, chromium, molybdenum, tellurium, vanadium, tungsten, and all the rare metals. Earth was running out of these, or else was unwilling to pollute its biosphere to scratch the last fraction out of the crust. Processing metals was messy and dangerous. The space factories could throw their waste into the solar wind, letting the gentle push of protons blow it out to the stars.

For raw materials, corporations like Mosambi and Kundusu grubstaked loners who went out in pressurized tin cans, sniffing with their spectrometers at the myriad chunks. Most of them were duds, but a rich lode of vanadium, say, could make a haggard, antisocial rockrat into a wealthy man. Living in zero-gravity craft wasn't particularly healthy, of course. You had to scramble if a solar storm blew in, and crouch behind an asteroid for shelter. Most rock-hoppers disdained the heavy shielding that would ward off cosmic rays, figuring that their stay would be short and lucky, so the radiation damage wouldn't be fatal. Many lost that bet.

One thing they could not do without, though, was food and air. That proved to be the pivot-point that drove mankind still farther out.

Life runs on the simplest chemicals. A closed artificial biosphere is basically a series of smoldering fires: hydrogen burns with oxygen to give water; carbon burns into carbon dioxide, which plants eat; nitrogen combines in the soil so the plants can make proteins, enabling humans to be smart enough to arrange all this artificially.

The colonies that swam in near-Earth orbits had run into this problem early. They needed a steady flow of organic matter and liquids to keep their biospheres balanced. Supply from Earth was expensive. A better solution was to search out the few asteroids which had significant carbonaceous chondrites—rock rich in light elements: hydrogen, oxygen, carbon, nitrogen.

There were surprisingly few. Most were pushed painfully back to Earth orbit and gobbled up by the colonies. By the time the rock-hoppers needed light elements, the asteroid belt had been picked clean.

Besides, bare rock is unforgiving stuff. Getting blood from a stone was possible in the energy-rich cylinder-cities. The loose, thinly spread coalition of prospectors couldn't pay the stiff bills needed for a big-style conversion plant.

From Ceres, the largest asteroid, Jupiter loomed like a candy-striped beacon, far larger than Earth. The rockrats lived in the broad band between two and three astronomical units out from the sun—they were used to a wan, diminished sunshine, and had already been tutored in the awful cold. For them it was no great leap to Jove, hanging there 5.2 times farther from the sun than Earth.

They went for the liquids. Three of the big moons—Europa, Ganymede, and Callisto—were immense iceballs. True, they circled endlessly the most massive planet of all, 318 times the mass of Earth. That put them deep down in a gravitational well. Still, it was far cheaper to send a robot ship coasting out to Jupiter, and looping into orbit around Ganymede, than it was to haul water up from the oceans of Earth. The first stations set up on Ganymede were semiautomatic—meaning a few unlucky souls had to tend the machinery.

And here came some of that machinery now.

Russ slid back and lay down on the truck's flat roof. Ahead a team of robos was digging away. They had a hodgepodge of tracks and arms and didn't look dangerous. The biggest one threw out a rust-red stream of ore which the others were sampling.

One of the old exploration teams, then. He hoped they'd just ignore the truck.

"What'll we do?" Nye whispered over comm.

"Shut up," Russ answered.

The truck seemed to hesitate, deciding whether to grind over to the robos. A small robo noticed this and came rolling over on balloon tires.

Russ froze. This robo looked intelligent. It was probably the team leader and could relay an alarm.

Still lying flat, Russ wormed his way over to the edge of the truck roof. He brought his heavy pilot's hands forward and waited, hoping he blended into the truck's profile.

The robo seemed to eye the truck with swiveling opticals. The truck stopped. The robo approached, extended a telescoping tube. Gingerly it began to insert this into the truck's external socket.

Russ watched the robo's opticals focus down on its task. Then he hit it carefully in the electrical cowling. His hand clanged on the copper cowling and dented it. The robo jerked, snatching back its telescope arm.

The robo was quick. It backed away on its wobbly wheels, but just a little too fast. They spun. It slewed around on the ice.

Russ jumped down while the robo was looking the other way. It might already be transmitting an image. He hit the cowling again and then pried up the copper sheet metal. With two fingers he sheared off three bundles of wire.

The robo stopped. Its external monitor rippled with alarm lights. Russ cut some more and the alarms went off. MECHANICAL DAMAGE, the robo's status digitals said.

The other robos just kept on studying the soil.

Zoti was coming out of the rear hatch when he climbed back on the truck. "Back inside," he said. "Let's go."

They got away fast. Those robos had been easy only because no Feds had gotten around to reprogramming them.

Soon enough, somebody would. They were in for a long war out here. He could feel it in his bones.

Trouble was, Earthly interests swung plenty of weight—and mass—even out here. The old north-south division of wealth and ability was mirrored in the solar system, though warped. The Southern Confederation Feds wanted a greater share of the Jovian wealth. So they had seized a few Northern Hemisphere ice-eating bases, like Hiruko Station. Those robos now labored for the Fed factories waiting in near-Earth orbit for the ore.

The shock of actual war, of death in high vacuum and biting, unearthly cold—that had reverberated through Earthside politics, exciting public horror and private thrills.

Earth had long been a leafy preserve, over-policed and under-armed. Battle and zesty victory gave the great publics of the now-docile planet a twinge of exquisite, forbidden sin.

Here was a gaudy arena where civilized cultures could slug it out, all the while bitterly decrying the beastly actions, the unforgivable atrocities, the inevitable horrific mischances.

And watch it all on 3D. In full, glossy color.

The economic motivations sank beneath the waves of eager surrogate participation. Unfortunately, the two were not so easily separated in the Jovian system. The first troops guarded the automatic plants on the moons. Thus they and the plants became first targets for the fleets that came accelerating into the system. Bucks blended with blood.

Hiruko Station was the first to fall to the Feds. Now the only way to root them out was to blast the surface, hoping the ice mines would escape most of the damage. That had been *Asskicker II*'s job.

Russ wished he could get news of the fighting. Radio gave only meaningless coded buzzes, flittering through the hiss of the giant Van Allen belts. News would have distracted him from his other preoccupation: food. He kept remembering sizzling steaks and crisp fries and hot coffee so black you had to sip it slow.

Already he had to be careful in dividing up their rations. Last meal, Nye and Zoti had gotten into a petty argument about half a cereal bar. They knew there wasn't much left, even with the packs of Kitsov and Columbard.

He rode along, not minding the cold yet, thinking about fried eggs and bacon. Zoti came topside. She had been copilot and she shared his dislike of the cramped, blind cabin, even if it was warm. They were used to fighting from a cockpit, enveloped in 3D graphics, living in an all-seeing electronic world.

"I could do without this mud-hugger stuff," Zoti said on short-range suit com.

"Mud, now that I'd like," Russ said.

"Yeah, this ice gets to me. Brrrr! Pretty, though."

Russ studied the gray-blue valley they were entering. Gullies cut the slopes. Fans of rusty gravel spread from them across the rutted, rolling canyon floor. It did have a certain stern beauty. "Hadn't noticed."

"Wouldn't mind living here."

He blinked. "Really?"

"Look, I grew up in a ten-meter can. Rockrats for parents."

"How you like this grav?"

"A seventh of a G? Great. More than I ever got on a tether."

"Your parents ever hit it big?"

"Last time I was home, we still measured out our water in cc's."

He waved at an ice tower they were passing. He hadn't been able to figure whether they were eroded remnants or some kind of extrusion, driven by the oddities of ice tectonics. "So to you this is real wealth."

"Sure." She gave him a quizzical glance. "What else is better'n ice? You can make air with it, burn the deuterium for power, grow crops—even swim."

"You ever done that?"

"In grav? Naw—but I sneaked into the water reserve tanks at Ceres once. Strangest thing I ever did."

"Like it better than zero g?"

She nodded enthusiastically. "*Every*thing's better in gravs."

"Everything?"

"Well," she gave him a veiled glance. "I haven't tried everything yet."

He smiled. "Try Earth normal sometime."

"Yeah, I heard it's pretty bad. But grav keeps everything steady. It *feels* better."

He had wrenched his back carrying the fusion warhead and felt a twinge from it as the truck lumbered through a depression. "Not so's I'd notice," he said moodily.

"Hey, cheer up. This's a holiday, compared to fighting."

"This *is* fighting. Just slow-motion, is all."

"I love it, ice and gravs."

"Could do with some better rations." It was probably not a good idea to bring up food, but Russ was trying to find a way to keep the talk going. For the first time he was feeling differently about Zoti.

"Hell, at least we got plenty water."

The truck lurched again and Russ grunted despite himself. "Maybe we should carve out some more?"

"Sure," she said lightheartedly. "I'm getting so I can spot the pure water. Tastes better'n cruiser supply."

"Wait'll we get onto the flat. Don't want this truck to speed up and leave you behind."

"Take it off auto." They had already nearly left Zoti once when she laser-cut some water ice.

"Don't want the risk. We override, probably'll show up in a control system back at Hiruko."

"I don't think the Feds have had time to interface all these systems. Those Dagos don't know zip."

"They took Hiruko pretty easy."

"Snuck up on it! Listen, those oily bastards . . ." And she was off on a tirade. Russ was a Norther, too, born and bred, but he didn't have much feeling about political roots that ran back to lines drawn on Earth's old carcass. He listened to her go on about the filthy Feds and watched the lurching view, and that was when he saw the bat.

It came over the far ice hills. Hard black against the slight haze of a yellow ammonia cloud, gliding when it could, jetting an ivory methane plume when it couldn't.

"Inside!" he whispered.

They scrambled off the truck roof. Zoti went in the rear hatch. He looked over the lip of the roof and saw the bat veer. It had seen them. It dove quickly, head-on toward them.

The M18s were lashed to the roof. There wasn't

time to get Zoti back out so he yanked an M18 free—
making sure he got the one loaded with HE—and
dropped off the back of the truck, slipping and landing
on his ass. He stooped far over and ran by kicking
back on the ice, so that he didn't bounce in the low
gravity. He used the truck for cover while he got to
the shelter of some jagged gray boulders.

It made one pass to confirm, sweeping in like an
enormous thin bird, sensors swiveling. He wedged down
among the rocks as it went over. It banked and turned
quickly, coming back. Russ popped his helmet telescope out to full extension and saw that it carried
rockets under the wings.

It lined up on the truck's tail and swooped down. It
looked more like a kite from this angle, all airfoil and
pencil-thin struts.

The bat was looking at the truck, not at him. He led
it a full length and opened up with the HE shells.
They bucked pretty bad and he missed with the first
two rounds. The third caught it in the narrow fuselage.
He saw the impact. Before he could grin a rocket fired
from under the right wing and streaked straight for
him, leaving an orange trail.

He ducked. The rocket fell short of the truck but
close to him. The impact was like a sudden jar. He
heard no sound, just found himself flat on his back.
Mud and ice showered him.

The bat went on, not seeming to mind the gaping
hole in its thin fuselage, but it also didn't rise anymore. Then it started a lazy pitch, yawed—and suddenly
was tumbling end over end, like a thrown playing
card.

It became a geyser of black fragments against a
snowy hill.

5

Russ had caught all the right signals from her, he
thought.

It was dumb, he knew that, and so did she. But
somehow the tension in them had wound one turn too

many and a mere glance between them set all the rest in motion.

Sure enough, as soon as Nye left by the forward hatch to reconn over the hill, Zoti started shucking her skinsuit. Then her thin green overalls.

He wasn't far behind her. They piled their clothes on the deck and got down on them. He suggested a sitting position but she would have none of it. She was feverish and buoyant in the muted phosphor glow of the cabin, swiveling on him with exuberant soft cries. Danger, sweat, piercing cold—all wedded into a quick, ferocious, hungry battering that they exacted from each other, rolling and licking and slamming among the machine-oil smells and rough iron rub. Fast and then, mysteriously, gravely slow, as though their senses stretched time in pursuit of oblivion.

It was over at last, and then maybe not, and then definitely not, and then, very fast this time, over for sure. They smiled at each other through a glaze of sweat and dirt.

"Lord!" she gasped. "The best!"

"Ever?" Frank disbelief.

"Sure. . . ." She gave him a sly smile. "The first, too."

"Huh? Oh, you mean—"

"First in real gravity, sure."

"Gravity has a way of simplifying your choices."

"I guess. Maybe everything really is better in gravs."

"Deck of an auto-truck isn't the best setting."

"Damn straight. We'll give it a try in some place better."

"You got a date." He got to his knees and started pulling on his blue longjohns.

Automatically he reviewed their situation, shifting back into reality after a blissful time away. He replayed events, trying to see it whole, to look for problems, errors.

They had been forced to override the truck's controls. The bat had undoubtedly reporting something, maybe even direct vid images of them. So Zoti and

Nye had conferred over the board and got the truck off its designated route.

They left the marked track and ground gears to work their way up among the jagged hills. An hour later two bats came zooming over. By that time Nye had gotten the truck back into a cave. They had left the snow two klicks back, picking their way over rocky ridges, so the bats had no tracks to follow.

They sat there edgily while the bats followed a search pattern, squaring off the valley and then other valleys, gradually moving away.

That had given Russ time to think and get hungry and eat. They didn't have much food left. Or time. Unless the Norther fleet kept Hiruko busy, the Feds would have time to send a thorough, human-led search party.

So they had to change tactics. But keep warm.

Hiruko probably had this truck identified by now.

Which meant they needed another truck. Fast.

Once they'd broken the code seal on the truck's guidance, they had access to general tracking inventory. Nye had found the nearest truck, about fifteen kilometers away. They had edged out of the cave when an ivory fog came easing in from the far range of rumpled mountains.

The truck moved pretty fast when its cautious nav programs were bypassed. They approached the target truck at an angle, finally lying in wait one hill over from its assigned path.

And when Nye went out to reconn the approaching truck, Russ and Zoti had taken one swift look at each other, one half-wild glance, and had seized the time.

Nye came back through the hatch as Zoti tucked her black hair into her neck ring.

"It's coming. No weapons visible." Nye looked from Zoti to Russ, puzzled.

Russ realized he was still flushed and sweaty. "Good," he said energetically. "Let's hit it."

"Better hurry," Nye said, his face narrowing again as he concentrated on tactics. "It just loaded up at a mine."

"Okay. Come out and help me on with my pack," Russ said.

Nye looked surprised. "You still gonna carry that warhead?"

Russ nodded. "Regs."

"Look, we gotta *move*. Nobody'd expect—"

"You want to pay for it when we get back?"

Nye shrugged. "Your hassle, man."

"Right," Russ said evenly.

The second truck was moving stolidly down a narrow canyon. It had the quality of a bumbling insect, dutifully doing its job.

"Flank it?" Zoti asked as they watched the truck's approach.

"Okay," Russ said. "You two take it from the sides, just after it passes."

"And you?" Nye asked sarcastically.

"Hit it right where the canyon necks in. See? I'll come in from the top."

It had finally occurred to him that the light gravity opened the choices of maneuver. He leaped from the nearest ledge, arcing out over the canyon and coming down on the top of the truck.

Zoti and Nye fired at the rear hatch, rounds skipping off the thick gray iron. A fighting machine, Class II infantry, popped out the front hatch.

It clanked and swiveled awkwardly. It had heavy guns built into both arms and started spraying the rear of the truck, chipping the metal corners. It hadn't registered Russ yet. When it did a small gun popped out of the machine's top and fired straight at him. He shot the machine three times and it tumbled over and broke in half.

Russ didn't get to see it fall. A heavy round went through his shoulder. It sent a white-hot flower of agony through him and knocked him off the truck. He landed on his neck.

6

"Actually," Nye said with a sly sort of humor, "that shoulder may not be the worst news you got."

Russ was not in a terrific mood. Nye's wit went unremarked. "What?"

"I got a readout on this truck's itinerary. Didn't have to bust into the command structure to do it, either." Nye grinned proudly.

"Great." His neck hurt worse than his shoulder. The truck's rumbling, shifting progress sent jabbing pains all down his spine. The bandage over his shoulder wound pulled and stung. Aside from this he was merely in a foul mood.

"We're going to Hiruko Station," Nye said. "Drop off the ore."

"Well, that doesn't matter," Zoti said. "We'll just jump off somewhere."

Russ nodded blearily. His mouth was dry and he didn't feel like talking. "Right. Steal another. Play musical trucks with the Feds."

"Better hurry. We're less than twenty klicks from Hiruko."

"What?" Russ barked.

Zoti's mouth made a precise, silent O.

"Looks like you had us pointing the wrong way all along," Nye said, his humor dissolving into bitterness.

Russ made himself take a breath. "Okay. Okay."

There didn't seem much more to say. He had probably screwed up the coordinates, gotten something backward. Or maybe the first truck took a turn that fouled up his calculations.

It didn't matter. Excuses never did, not unless you got back to the carrier and a board of inquiry decided they wanted to go over you with a microscope.

Zoti said carefully, "So close . . . they will pick us up easily if we leave the truck."

"Yeah," Nye said. "I say we ride this truck in and give up. Better'n freezing our tails, maybe get shot at, then have to give up anyway."

"We bail out now," Russ said.

"You hear what I said?" Nye leaned over Russ, trying to intimidate him. "That's *dumb*! They'll—"

Russ caught him in the face with a right cross that snapped Nye's head around and sent him sprawling.

For once his pilot's hands proved useful. They were heavy and hard and in his weak condition gave him just enough edge. Russ was sitting on the floor of the truck cabin and he didn't want to bother to get up. He also wasn't all that sure that he even could throw a punch while standing, anyway. So when Nye's eyes clouded and the big man came at him Russ kicked Nye in the face, lifting his boot from the deck and catching Nye on the chin. Nye fell facedown on the deck. Russ breathed deeply and waited and let his neck stop speaking to him. By that time Zoti was standing over Nye with a length of pipe. He waved her away.

"Now, I'm going to pretend you just slipped and banged your head," Russ said evenly. "Because we got to get out of here fast and I don't want to have to shoot you for insubordination or cowardice in the face of the enemy or any of those other lawyer's reasons. That would take time and we don't have time. So we just go on like you never did anything. Got that?"

Nye opened his mouth and then closed it. Then he nodded.

"Do you . . ." Zoti hesitated. "Do you think we *can* get away?"

"We don't have to," Russ said. "We just have to hide."

"Hide and freeze," Nye said sourly. "How's the carrier gonna—"

"We won't hide long. How much time will it take this truck to reach Hiruko?"

"Three, maybe four hours. It's going to a smelting plant on the rim of the first bubble. I—"

"Close enough for government work," Russ said.

He felt infinitely tired and irritable and yet he knew damn well he was going to have to stay awake until all this was done.

Zoti said, "Are you sure you can . . . ?"

Russ breathed in the stale cabin air. The world veered and swam.

"No, matter of fact, I'm not."

7

The fusion warhead went off prettily on the far horizon. A brilliant flash, then a bulging yellow-white ball.

Nye had rigged the trigger to go if anybody climbed through the hatch. He further arranged a small vid eye and stuck it into the truck's grille, so they got a good look at the checkpoint that stopped the truck. It was within sight of the rearing, spindly towers of Hiruko Station. The town was really rather striking, Russ thought. Some of the towers used deep blue ice in their outer sheaths, like spouts of water pointing eternally at Jupiter's fat face.

Too bad it all had to go, he thought.

The three of them were lying beneath an overhang, facing Hiruko. They ducked their heads when they saw a Fed officer scowl at the truck, walk around it, then pop the forward hatch. He looked like just the officious sort Russ hated, the kind that always gigged him on some little uniform violation just as he was leaving base on a pass.

So he couldn't help grinning mirthlessly when the flash lit the snow around them. The warhead was a full 1.2 megs.

Of course, it was supposed to be a klick-high air burst, delivered from orbit. Designed to take out the surface structures and Feds and leave the mines.

This was a ground-pounder. It sent a shock wave they watched coming toward them across the next valley. He didn't have time to get to his feet. He rolled out from under the ledge. The wave slammed into their hill and he felt a soft thump nearby. Then the sound slapped him hard and he squeezed his eyes shut against the pain in his neck.

When he opened them Zoti was looking into his face anxiously. He grinned. She sat in the snow and grinned back saucily.

He looked beyond her. The hill had folded in a little and the ledge wasn't there anymore. Neither was Nye.

If it had just been snow that fell on him they might

have had some chance. He had gotten partway out from under the ledge, nearly clear. But solid ice and some big rocks had come down on him and there wasn't any hope. They dug him out anyway. It seemed sort of pointless because then all they could think to do was bury him again.

The bomb cloud over Hiruko dispersed quickly, most of the radioactive debris thrown clear off the moon.

They sat in a protected gully, soaking up what sunlight there was, and waited. As a signal beacon the fusion burst couldn't be beat. Carrier ships came zooming over within an hour.

A survey craft slipped in low on the horizon a little later. Only when it was in sight did Zoti produce the rest of their food. They sat on a big flat orange rock and ate the glue-like bars through their helmet input slots. It tasted no better than usual but nobody cared. They were talking about gravity and its myriad delights.

Hardware

The weapons that were used in the Jupiter War were generally refinements of those that had been in use for almost a hundred years. The lack of any effective source of massive power prevented any beam weapons from being of more than marginal value. The scarcity of Transuranics also limited the number of atomic weapons drastically. In spite of these limitations, man's ingenuity at devising ways to kill and maim provided a wide range of weaponry. Primary among the ship-to-ship weapons were missiles. Most contained not explosive, but shrapnel. Since the speed of most ships made an actual hit in the traditional sense a rarity, proximity fuses that strewed a ship's projected path with steel balls traveling at several thousand relative miles per hour had been established as the most effective weapon.

Shrapnel missiles more often disabled rather than destroyed an opponent, and were inversely effective to the distance they were fired at. This meant that most serious confrontations consisted of ships literally diving at each other, firing from the first moment possible in hopes of destroying the other first. Once the range had closed, explosive shells had more chance to hit and were exponentially more destructive.

The combat effectiveness of a ship was directly proportional to the amount of ordnance it could carry and the speed with which it could spew the missiles out. The vulnerability of a ship was also similarly related to its speed and cross section combined with its ECM. Since the distances involved within the Jovian system are comparatively small, small ships could contain a high proportion of weapons to drive and life-support systems to fuel and drive. Unfortunately such ships were of only limited value in protecting the long routes from each side's asteroid bases. In order to use these fighter-style combat ships over greater distances carriers were employed. Since a ship on a planet was incredibly vulnerable, and begged for an attack that was likely to destroy the base as well, these carriers later became even larger to enable them to serve as mobile combat bases for several months at a time.

Propulsion at the beginning of the Jupiter War was supplied by a highly efficient form of reaction drive, for fuel methane was refined—though ironically, it was never possible to employ the methane atmosphere around Jupiter as a source of fuel. Larger ships, carriers, and freighters, were capable of housing a fusion reactor. This provided power for both the early forms of beam weapons and to refine fuel for the smaller ships. New forms of propulsion were continually experimented with, but until very late in the conflict none proved reliable.

As the fusion technology improved under the stimulus of war, a new class of ship evolved. This was the cruiser. The cruiser was the smallest ship capable of carrying and employing a fusion generator. Approximately ten times the size of the largest fighter, the cruiser had to make up with ECM and offensive power what it sacrificed in agility and cross section.

On a personal level, propelling a piece of solid matter into your enemy's body was still the most effective way to kill one another. If anything, the vulnerability of space suits made slug-throwing weapons even more appealing. Innovations were needed to enable such weapons to fire in an airless environment, but most of these had been achieved during the skirmishes on Earth's Moon during the 2020s.

Computers, while immense aides to navigation, proved ineffective in combat. They could supplement, but never succeeded in replacing, a human gunner for making decisions in combat. The trend of developing computers to simplify and augment, rather than replace, human operators that dominated the twenty-first century meant that war still was a matter of men facing men over the barrel of a gun, or missile tube.

ODD MAN OUT

by David A. Cherry

Brant Emerson floated in the dark, attached by a tether to his fighter, *Banshee III*. He had been working for hours with an arc welder just aft of the command module and needed a break. His gaze followed the path his ship was on, down the gravity well to its bottom, Jupiter, thousands of kilometers away and, at his velocity, all too close.

Behind the reflective shield of his visor, a wisp of dark brown hair was out of place and channeling sweat from his brow to the corner of one eye. His sharply chiseled features, a pleasingly odd mixture of Celt and Cherokee, scowled in irritation as he adjusted the temperature setting on his suit.

His helmet com crackled with static. Must be one of the crew trying to reach him suit-to-suit. Bright move. He wondered how long it would take whoever it was to remember the level of radiation out here and try ship com.

Emerson had shipped into this war from Earth, where he had taken his military training, like the rest of his crew. Unlike them, he was a rockrat brat, born on the rickety station that miners had pieced together near Ceres. Jupiter was part of his backyard, and he was more familiar than they with its environs, one of the most notable elements of which was its magnetosphere.

A gigantic planet-wide ocean of liquid metallic hydrogen thousands and thousands of kilometers deep gave Jupiter a magnetic field far stronger than anything else in the solar system except Sol itself. And Sol's winds fed it continuously with a plasma of particles streaming in at over five hundred kilometers per second. The bow front, where those winds broke against the magnetosphere, was a particularly pleasant region —the magnetosheath, where solar-driven particles released their energy and drove the plasma to temperatures twenty times hotter than the sun.

Instinctively, Emerson plotted the sunward side of Jupiter. Good. It was hours away, and he would be done long before he had to worry about the solar wind kicking up and pulsing the sheath back his direction.

He knew he was more paranoid than his earth-born crew about exposure to various forms of radiation, but no one in his right mind went EVA in the Jovian gravity well if he could avoid it. The lecture that covered it in basic was optimistic, stressing innovations in suit-shielding. But that was mudside PR, government hype. And everyone with sense knew it. New suits might help, but things like that still came from the lowest bidder—good ol'guvment issue. Little enough to pit against the maelstrom of Jupiter's magnetosphere.

Even inside the sheath it was no picnic. Not much of the solar wind broke through to the magnetosphere but it was enough, combined with junk spewed up from Io, to create radiation belts up to a million times more intense than anything near-earth orbiters had to face from the Van Allen Belts.

On Earth there were sayings about people too stupid to come in out of the rain. In space there were similar sayings, but the rain was far more deadly. And it was always raining. Near Jupiter it was worse.

Still, a little shower of highly charged particles wasn't going to worry him much at this point, as long as it didn't knock out the com or interior temperature controls on his suit. He had a job to do, his duty, and he was going to see it through.

That had always been part of his problem. Maybe he was too competent. He was a natural pilot, and he almost always outscored everyone else on any test, any subject. They kept moving him up the ladder, putting him in charge. He never had time to make any friends along the way. He was always "new meat." He had been alone so long. He would have given a lot for just one friend right now.

His helmet com crackled again, reminding him of the three lives tucked safely inside beneath him: his crew, his responsibility. He looked back the way they had come, back toward the battle and their base ship, the carrier *Triumphant*, though he knew there was nothing to see from this distance. They could have been friends. Almost were, until that last moment.

"Babydoll? This is Papa." Varick's voice had crackled through the helmets of sixteen fighter crews making up Babydoll Wing. "The cat's outta the bag. Time to secure and heat 'em up."

Emerson gave the interior of *Banshee III* a quick once-over and scanned his boards as he flipped the prelims. His copilot, Williams, was checking the secondaries. Williams, short and solid, didn't actually look like a bulldog, but his tenacity and temperament invited the comparison. He had a take-charge attitude and the abilities to go with it. There was intelligence in those sharp blue eyes and a force of personality which lent him a stature that belied his lack of height. A top pilot in his own right and unquestioned leader of the crew, despite Emerson's superior rank, he was Emerson's greatest asset in battle—with the second highest kill tally in the wing—but his most devoted adversary off duty.

It was nothing personal. Emerson knew that. He was just new and in Williams's way. To Emerson it was a familiar scenario, the story of his life. But that was no consolation. It made his loneliness and isolation all the harder to bear, especially since at his last posting—a backwater job with a small fighter squadron escorting tankers to orbital factories near earth—he had just started to make a few friends, fit in, have *someone* he could talk to. But duty had called, as it always did, and taken all that away.

He had been too efficient for his own good in defending the tankers, and when *Triumphant* had needed an ace pilot to fill a sensitive slot in its top fighter wing, the computers at HQ had selected him to receive the honor.

Behind him, Thompson and Prock were at their stations manning rear armament and going through their own checks. Thompson was tall, lean, and handsome with a caustic wit and a calm self-assurance that some might take as arrogance. Emerson had been around him enough to know, however, that he was merely pragmatic and honest about his competence. Prock, the country boy from Oklahoma who had started out to be a Baptist minister, was no less competent but far more quiet and unassuming. Emerson hoped for a chance to get to know them better, but so far they had sided with Williams in shutting him out.

Banshee hummed as she came up to power. There was the usual friendly banter among the crew as they anticipated the coming action, and as usual, it excluded him. They never crossed the line into actual insubordination, although they came close. That would be a win for him, in their minds, and they would not stand for that. Or maybe on some level they had developed a kind of grudging respect for him. He was never sure. But the tension was always there, every look, every verbal exchange bringing home the same message: outsider, stranger, failure. You are not welcome here.

He had thought of transferring to another ship but there were no openings, and besides, that was the coward's way out. Too easy. No, he would just have to keep trying, be the best pilot he knew how to be for them. They would open up eventually. Maybe the coming action would draw them all a bit closer.

The whole wing had drifted to these coordinates the day before and lain in wait, cold as so much flotsam, for just this moment. Information wrung from a captured Fed fighter crew had led *Triumphant* to figure it could intersect the Fed carrier *Perez* to the northeast and bring the battle right over Babydoll's head. And it had worked, in a way.

Triumphant had caught *Perez* loafing and had the advantage of surprise and speed as it came in blasting, launching four wings of fighters to keep the *Perez* fighters bottled up inside while *Triumphant* slashed by and banked for another run.

It was daring tactics, some would say desperate, to risk a carrier in close-up maneuvers with another base ship like that, but *Triumphant*'s commander was counting on its unexpectedness to carry the day. If it all worked according to plan, they could take out or capture *Perez* with all its chicks on board, and Babydoll could come in for mop-up detail. If not, Babydoll was the commander's ace in the hole.

Unfortunately, the info from the captured Feds had left out one prime detail: *Perez* was not traveling alone. It was in tandem with another carrier, the *Bolivar*. And when *Triumphant* let loose its fighters against the *Perez*, *Bolivar* was free to send out its fighter wings. That set up a mad scramble as *Triumphant*'s ships swarmed the *Perez*, trying to inflict as much damage as possible before *Bolivar*'s fighters could launch and close.

Emerson and the rest of Babydoll Wing sat in their cold ships watching it all on screen. "Get ready, guys," Williams called on intra-ship com. "The Feds are almost on 'em, and they'll be splitting out to bring 'em our way any minute."

"Not just yet they won't," muttered Emerson.

Williams gave him a look of scathing derision and glanced back to share his amusement with his buddies. All three had crewed *Banshee III* for a year with its former pilot, Bob Varick, before he had been moved up to fill a slot in *Gravedigger* as wing leader. They had been a tight clique. They didn't see it as fair that Varick had been moved up without them, and it was insult to injury when, instead of Williams moving up to pilot *Banshee* as expected, Emerson had been dumped on them. He might have been a hot pilot way off in the backwater, but he was green as far as they were concerned; and his being a "nice guy" and all didn't cut squat with them. Just his being there was a slap in their face.

"Right, Emerson," snarled Williams. "Are you crazy?

Wouldn't you bug out with fifty jillion Feddies fixin' to fry your tail?"

Emerson chose to ignore the sarcasm and looked over to Williams, guard down intentionally to convey a willingness for friendship. "Yeah, but they're between the *Perez* and the Fed fighters," he said, as if that should explain it.

"So?" smiled Thompson.

"So?" sighed Emerson. "So if I were commander, I'd keep our boys and girls in there a while. We're already hurting *Perez*, and she doesn't dare open a launch bay for fear we'll throw something inside that'll take out a bunch of fighters in a chain reaction that'd blow out a good portion of her shell. We stand to lose a few ships, but the incoming Feds will have to be real choosey on their targets 'cause if they miss us they're apt to hit *Perez*. That should give our guys the time and edge to thin out *Bolivar*'s flyers quite a bit before we have to disengage."

"Yeah," sneered Williams, "and then our guys'd be all cut up, and *Perez* opens up with four fresh wings. Those are *our* people out there dying." Williams shook his head. "You're cold, man."

Emerson was getting fed up with their attitude. Didn't he have a right to an opinion? Couldn't they at least once consider something he said instead of attacking it? He didn't figure it would do any good to antagonize them further, so he just stared at the screen and thought to himself, it's a cold situation out there no matter what, Williams. You'd rather run now and face full, fresh complements from both carriers at the same time? Care to figure up the body count on that?

They sat in silence, watching the scene unfold on the screen exactly as Emerson had called it. The commander on *Triumphant* kept his flyers in so close to *Perez* that its gunners had a hard time tracking them, whereas to them *Perez* was a wide-open target. A few were lost in the initial attack from *Bolivar*'s fighters, but *Perez* took a lot of fire from them, too, so the Feds did become more cautious and the Northern Hemisphere forces were more than able to hold their

own. It was bloody. All in all, both sides had lost
nearly half their ships by the time *Bolivar* itself moved
up and *Triumphant*'s fighters peeled off for home.

With the advent of the second Fed carrier, *Triumphant*
had scrapped its plan for a second run at *Perez* and
had stationed itself above and past Babydoll Wing to
bring the retreat right over their heads. They waited
until their sister ships and the remnants of the pursuing
Bolivar wings had gone over. *Bolivar* itself was hanging close to the damaged *Perez*, and *Perez* was spitting
out fighters as fast as it could. To their credit, they
kept their cool and circled *Perez* to form up properly
before heading after the *Triumphant*. When they finally came it was in a square, two wings in front, two
wings following close behind.

It was about then that Varick had given the call to
"heat 'em up." And before the Feds had time to react
to the sudden appearance of Babydoll's heat signa-
tures, the wing was headed up full throttle toward the
underbellies of the *Perez* wings.

Varick was good. He had timed it right. The Feds,
still a long way from *Triumphant*, were in tight formation and had their instruments trained dead ahead on
the only action they were aware of. The confusion of
dealing with the damage back at the Fed carriers must
have helped out, because there was never any evidence of warning from the carriers to their fighters
that they were under attack from below.

"Babydoll on the call. Split and fire. Split and fire.
Mark! Give 'em all you got!" Varick called the play
like a quarterback. And Babydoll's diamond formation split like a starburst into sub-wings, four groups of
four, each headed for one of the Fed wings, each
dead-on with all forward ports blazing.

Banshee III was flying right side of its own little
diamond formation, with *Criptkicker*, their sub-wing
leader, to the fore, *Bad Mac* to the left, and *The
Valkyrie* bringing up the rear. At the last possible
instant, on a word from *Criptkicker*, they veered off
into a loop that would take them back down to form
up with the rest of Babydoll. As they did, the rear

gunners opened up to give the Feds a parting present. The G-forces were tremendous. It was the kind of crazy, gutsy stunt that only Babydoll Wing could do really well. Emerson doubted that even Varick had been sure of this call until the last second, when he had seen that the timing was right and the tight Fed formation was going to hold for them. But it had been quick, smooth, and deadly. Their last sight of the Feds as they went into their loop had been a real reward for all their long hours of waiting: all four Fed wings engulfed in fiery chaos as damaged ships were rammed by those behind them in a devastating chain reaction.

Then *Criptkicker* became a ball of flame and shrapnel. Emerson and the others avoided most of it, but a good-sized piece of *Criptkicker*'s shell gouged into *Bad Mac*.

Emerson, now the sub-wing leader, boosted to form the head of a triangle with his remaining ships and contacted *Bad Mac*'s pilot. "Jackson, this is Emerson. What's the damage?"

There was a pause. Then, "It's a r-r-real mess in here. A strut holed us like a bullet. In one side and out the other. Went right through O'Riley. Missed Graham but nicked her suit, so we lost her to vacuum. Nelson and I are on suit air, and he's pretty shaken up. Me too. I keep fading in and out." Another pause. "I don't think we're gonna make it."

"Jackson, listen. You're still on course, still in formation. You're doing fine."

"Luck and instinct."

"How're your boards?"

"A lot of red lights. Some secondaries are working. Most of the ones I really need are. But Nelson's out cold now and I'm not much better. I can run, but I can't shoot too. Not much. I've got no rear shooters. I'd better sit this out."

Williams reached over and gripped Emerson's arm. Gave him a look. Emerson read it and understood. Bev Jackson and he spent their off-duty time together. They were close. She was hurt. He wanted her back. Not in some stinking Fed cell.

Emerson gave Williams a nod. "Jackson? You stay with us. That's an *order*! You just follow me and *The Valkyrie* will guard your tail. Right, Kees?"

"You got it, Brant. Jackson, honey, you just trust your backside to ol' Kees." That was Kees van Derventer in *The Valkyrie*.

"Okay, guys. Get me home and the drinks are on me."

"That's the spirit."

Williams traded Emerson a look of gratitude and patted him on the shoulder. Emerson had a warm glow inside. Maybe he had just made a friend.

While all that had been going on on their way back down to reform, another channel on Emerson's com had been buzzing with Varick filling in the sub-wing leaders with rapid-fire updates. "Form up Big D on meet; V45N line 240E to base, okay Babydoll? We lost two. *Texas Miss* cut too close and caught scrap. *Criptkicker* caught a snake on the rollover. Anybody else elected?"

Emerson spoke up, a sub-wing leader now, and entitled. "*Bad Max* tagged scrap but can fly. Only Jackson is functional, but we will cover for her."

"Thanks, *Banshee*. Anyone else? Okay. Watch your screens. We scratched about twenty-eight from the race, but the rest got through and are on their own loop back to us."

I know all that from my screen, thought Emerson.

"What you *can't* see on your screen, unless you are on broad range, is that *Bolivar*'s fighters are on their way back too. They either got a recall or had second thoughts about taking on our forces near *Triumphant*."

Emerson switched to broad scan.

By then Babydoll had reformed and found itself at a strength of fourteen, with two enemy carriers behind them, nearly sixty Fed fighters between them and home base, and no element of surprise left.

"Where the deuce is the rest of *our* team?" asked Williams.

Emerson had been wondering the same thing. So had all of Babydoll. He broadened scan again. There they were, only thirty-two of them, just crossing back over *Triumphant* in pursuit of the *Bolivar* fighters. They must have overshot *Triumphant* in an attempt to get *Bolivar*'s forces to follow them to its far side for some reason—probably some little trap *Triumphant*'s commander was waiting to spring—and then been surprised when *Bolivar*'s ships pulled up short. Caught unawares, it had taken them this long to shed velocity and angle back. They were going to be too late. Babydoll was in the meat-grinder.

By now the rest of Babydoll had figured that out too. "Well, the cat's *really* out of the bag now." That was Davenport from *Dirtbag* on all-channels.

"You said it, Dav," replied Varick. "Okay, everybody, listen up. If we are ever going to make it back to base we have to make it through to our people. We can shotgun it, try a tight formation, or split to subwings. Any preferences?"

Emerson was shocked. No wing leader, especially Varick, would ask for advice on a call like that unless he had given up—or was treating it as a courtesy, akin to a last request.

"I call shotgun. Every man for himself." Davenport again.

"Shotgun," was the terse reply from Deitrick in *Leaping Eyegouger*, another sub-wing leader.

Except for Varick, that left Emerson. "Splitting to sub-wings'll give us our best chance. But you guys do what you want. Van Derventer and I have to stay with Jackson even if you call shotgun."

"I agree with *Banshee*," said Varick, "and I'll make my vote count twice, so we go with the split. Tight pattern'd just get us enveloped. Man for man'd get us picked off piecemeal. We go in Big D, tight diamond, right down their throats. On the mark, we starburst left, right, over, and under. *Eyegouger*? Trade rear guard with *Banshee III*. That'll give *Bad Mac* the most cover 'til the split."

"Good," said Deitrick. "I want a front-row seat for this anyway."

They were already in Big D formation and on course.

As they closed, Varick gave the call to fire at will. Babydoll opened up, and so did the Feds. *Fireball*, the ship to Varick's left, lived up to its name and came apart in shards, but it had been flying slightly above the pattern, so they were spared any chain reaction from that. *Long Arm* was not so lucky. Davenport's *Dirtbag* took a snake right in front of it, and the two collided. But Babydoll was taking its toll of Feds as well. Instead of firing dead ahead, they had first fired on the enemy's flanks, left and right, and caught a few napping. Then they turned their attention to the center.

When they were so close they could have read the markings on the Fed ships, Varick called, "Mark!" And the split was on.

The Feds had learned their lesson for the day about flying close formations so they had spread out, wide and deep, giving Babydoll a horrible gauntlet of fire to thread.

As rear guard on the split, it was *Banshee III*'s job to break low and under the enemy formation, but it was so deeply spread that she was still threading through them as she angled down, fighting to break out below.

They were taking hits as often as they were avoiding them. Boards were smoking and flashing red. Secondaries began to wink out. The *Bad Mac* overshot them on a climb back up through the thick of the enemy pack. *The Valkyrie* was still on her tail.

Williams, who couldn't look any more panicked as he frantically manned his failing forward armament, did. And Emerson was already angling back up toward her as he hit the ship-to-ship. "Jackson! What's going on?" The Feds had their EM jams going, so it took him several tries to reach her.

Finally, her static-filled reply came back, weakened with more than the jams, "Lost something, *Banshee*. Can't dive or go left. Have to— Oops! Almost caught one. Have to climb. Nelson's dead. Tell Kees to join up with you. Tell Mark . . . I love him."

Williams was firing like a man possessed, every shot counting, ripping his way through the Feds. Tears streamed down his cheeks, but he kept his focus locked desperately upon the screen. Emerson heard his moaned "No-o-o-o-o-o-o-o!" rise to a maddened scream.

"Stay with her, Kees," Emerson called. "We're on our way."

Emerson flew like Williams fired: possessed. He slammed in full power and shot so fast down a corridor between two Feds that they couldn't train on him, but Williams raked them. Then he hit the attitude jets and angled up, actually clipping the antenna on another Fed as he flashed by.

Valkyrie had moved up and was riding just above *Bad Mac* by the time *Banshee III* came in below her, taking a hit that would have been hers.

"*Banshee*, you idiot!" It was Varick, off to the left and above them, still with the remaining two ships of his sub-wing. They had broken out above the main body of the enemy pack, and Emerson's sub-wing was not too far from doing the same. From Varick's point of view, it looked as though Emerson had chosen their course, taking the crippled *Bad Mac* through the grinder with him. "Send her up to me!" Varick called. And then on all-channels, "Jackson, leave that fool and make your way to us. We'll cover you."

"Stay put!" Emerson called.

"*Banshee*, I gave an order!"

Just then Kees and *The Valkyrie* fireballed and were gone. *Banshee III* moved up in front of *Bad Mac*, but their course, while taking them up, was angling away from Varick.

"*Banshee*, execute that order!"

"Do it!" yelled Williams, and he spared one hand from the firing controls to slam back at Emerson for emphasis. Before he could get it back to the board a missile snaked past, just missing them. But it blew *Bad Mac* to atoms.

Williams sat frozen. Emerson slapped control of forward-screen arms to Prock and yelled for him to take over. They were almost out and could see their reinforcements streaking in behind the few Fed fighters still in their way, but in that maze of fire it was too late. Numbing concussion rocked *Banshee III*, and she spun away into the darkness.

When Emerson came to, the ship was in a slow tumble and had been holed in too many places for them to patch. Miraculously, no one was seriously hurt, and their suits had held, but the bad news made them wish they hadn't.

The main boards were out. Most secondaries had failed. Some battery power was left, but its duration was suspect. A cobbled-together secondary nav computer told them that they had been out a long time. The battle had been long ago and far, far away, along with anyone who might have been looking for them, assuming anyone on their side had survived to make the attempt. They had traveled from just outside Ganymede's gravity well to near Europa's orbit and were picking up considerable velocity from Jupiter's pull.

Major propulsion systems were fritzed, so there was no way to shed velocity. They were on a one-way ride to Jupiter, the hard way.

Communications were a problem. Their tumble kept placing their ship between the antennae and what they were aiming at, until Prock jury-rigged a couple of attitude jets and smoothed it out. Even then their failing batteries could barely cut through the chatter of the magnetosphere, but a chance encounter with a passing Jovian weather satellite enabled them to boost signal and patch through briefly to Yoshitsune station on Europa.

The news, while it lasted, was still bad. If they could hold orbit around Jupiter for a while at Europa's distance out, Europa would swing around enough for a Northern Hemisphere tanker, currently groundside at the station, to launch, slingshot around Europa, and attempt to pick them up. Other than that they were in the wrong place, at the wrong time, at the wrong speed. No one else, civilian or military, would be able to reach them before they spiraled in toward temperatures of fifty thousand degrees Fahrenheit and pressures of over three million atmospheres.

Just before communications had faded, Emerson had told Yoshitsune to launch that tanker and come get them. Thompson had just shaken his head and said sadly, "It's not going to work, Emerson. We have enough reserve air to last that long, but we'll be well past Europa's orbit by the time they show up. We've got no power. We're fried."

It was the most anyone had said to him since they had come to. Williams was not speaking to him at all, and mostly had sat in silent gloom while he and the others had mechanically gone about trying to rectify their situation. Now it looked as though the other two were ready to join him, sit down and wait for oblivion. Emerson was just about out of patience with the lot of them.

"We've got meth, don't we?" he asked.

Prock looked up. "Yeah, the fight didn't last that long. We still have a couple of full tanks of methane."

"And a lot of good they are, too," reminded Thompson. "The propulsion secondaries are out and no way to fix them. I tried."

"That's true," Emerson said, brightening with an idea, "but maybe if we—"

"Can it, Emerson!" Williams shouted, breaking his long silence. "Give it a rest. Your boy-scout optimism is making me sick. You're not the den leader here anymore. Death has a way of evening out rank, and I don't expect to be having to answer to command after today, so I'll be hanged if I'm going to die listening to puke from you about how we're still going to make it." He glanced around at Thompson and Prock for support. "We are going to die, Emerson. And it's your fault. You got Jackson killed and now us, too."

Emerson was stunned. "Jackson killed? I was trying to save her. Risked all our necks to do it."

"Then why didn't you acknowledge Varick and send her to him when you had the chance?"

"Simple. Varick had been up from us but to the left. Jackson couldn't go left. And besides, things were happening pretty fast. While Varick was calling us, most of the Fed ships between us and our reinforcements were rising to engage Varick's sub-wing, leaving us what I hoped would be a comparatively free corridor of movement. Even if I could have taken her Varick's way, it would have been into heavier fire."

Williams seemed to crumble as he relived those final moments, but he was unrelenting. "You could have acknowledged and executed the order as best you could. Varick would have moved right to cover us."

Emerson was mystified. "That is just what I *did*, stayed with Jackson, climbing up and right."

Williams's fury with him was unabated. "No it wasn't!" he screamed. "You never acknowledged the order!"

Emerson was confused. Had he acknowledged the order? Maybe not. Things had been happening so fast that there had been no time for long explanations. But he couldn't imagine why such a minor detail should matter. Then he saw it the way Williams must be seeing it.

Williams had been frantic to save Jackson. Varick had offered help. Varick was the best wing leader, and Williams's friend. Williams wanted that help, but couldn't deal directly with Varick to get it because the "new meat" kid was sitting in the pilot seat that should have gone to Williams. All Williams could do was keep firing, keep the Feds at bay, and listen. He'd kept waiting for the acknowledgment from Emerson that would bring Varick in on the problem, but it never came. In frustration, he had moved his hand from his controls to hit Emerson.

If he had kept both hands on the boards could he have intercepted that missile, or maybe kept the ship that fired it busy until they were past? There was no knowing, but the thought was a torture to Williams. He blamed himself for not blocking the shot that took Jackson out, but he blamed Emerson for making him miss that one all-important target and for all that had followed after that.

Emerson looked at Thompson and Prock. They would

not meet his gaze. They might not blame him as Williams did, but sides had been drawn and it was obvious that their loyalties would not be with him.

As he clung to the hull of *Banshee III*, Emerson put the finishing touches to his handiwork. They were now inside the orbit of Europa but not, he prayed, too far in for this to work. If his calculations were right, he should still be within his window of opportunity, but it would be close. It had taken him more time than he would have liked.

Thompson and Prock had finally listened to his plan and, more to pass the time than anything else, agreed to help him. Williams had lapsed back into silence and would not be budged.

Emerson hated what had happened. He would have given a lot to settle their differences. After so many years of constantly being the odd man out, it was all he really wanted. In all honesty, he did not feel at fault for what had happened. But there had been that one small error, one tiny omission of duty. And now Williams would never forget or forgive.

So what he thought didn't matter. It was done, and he had failed. Failed, as a person, to win their respect. Perhaps even failed his duty.

If he sat back and did nothing, that would be how it would end for him, in failure at every level. That prospect was growing more and more imminent as Jupiter pulled them faster with each passing second. And more and more hateful to him. He could face death. Compared to his loneliness, oblivion might even be a welcome release. But not like this. Not as a failure after a lifetime of struggle to rise from being a miner's kid in the boonies to ace pilot in the top fighter wing in the Jovian system. Not while there was a single card left for him to play.

Emerson figured he had at least that one card. It might not be much, but at this point they all didn't have a thing to lose by trying it. It wouldn't salvage things between him and the crew, but his personal life had been a failure as far back as he could remember, and he was used to that. His duty was something else. He had never before failed in that.

Williams might not acknowledge it but Emerson was still pilot, still responsible for the lives of his crew, and he would do what he could to bring them home safe and sound. If he could manage only that much, it would be enough.

They didn't think much of his plan, but he knew it would work. To get back to Europa's orbit and be in place to meet the tanker, they needed to accelerate. They couldn't use their fuel the standard way, but he calculated that the force of an explosion of their remaining tanks would give the command cabin, if separated sufficiently from the rest of the ship, adequate boost to make it. The computer had agreed.

It helped that the rear of the cabin had been designed with shielding to protect the crew from the explosion of their fuel supply, should it take a hit in battle. All that remained was to separate the command module enough from the ship that it would easily tear loose, use the attitude jets again to get it properly aligned, re-rig a detonator from one of the shells, rig that to the methane tanks, and figure how to set the thing off. The latter had proved to be more of a problem than any of them had counted on, but time was running out, so Emerson had insisted on leaving them to puzzle out a solution while he got the mechanics in place.

Everything was ready now. He floated in place, still holding a plate from the hull which he had had to remove to set the detonator against the fuel tanks. He took a last look at Jupiter and sailed the plate out toward it. An offering, part of *his* ship, his command: all that he had left. Let Jupiter be satisfied with that if it was hungry. He had other plans for the *Banshee* and crew, and this time he would not fail. He'd get the job done right, come hell or high water.

He switched on com. "Everybody strapped in in there?"

"Yeah," Prock's voice crackled in his ear, "but we still haven't figured any way to set off the detonator.

Come up with any bright ideas yourself? We're cutting
it close on time."

Emerson smiled to himself. What's the matter, boys?
Starting to think this might work? "As a matter of
fact," he said, "I have. Hang on. I'll be right in and
show you."

"Leave it to the boy scout," grumbled Williams.

Emerson sighed and thumbed a remote he had
brought with him. He looked down at the detonator.
The thing had been designed to be armed by a signal
in the ship's firing sequence, but no signal would deto-
nate it. That had been their problem in using it. It
required impact.

"What's going on out there?" Williams called. "The
forward cannon just cycled over. What are you doing?"

"Nothing much, Williams. Just my job. You guys sit
back and relax. I'll be right in." He raised a wrench
over the detonator. "Williams? I . . . never mind."

They blacked out from G-force as the blast sent
them hurtling back up the gravity well to an orbit
somewhere near Europa.

The Panamanian Exiles

The occupation of Panama in 1993 by the United
States began a twenty-year era of Yankee domination
of that small country. The occupation began as a reaction to the rise of right-wing death squads after the
assassination of President Argenta. When these quasi-
military units began intimidating and then killing United
States citizens, the RDF was dispatched to occupy
Panama City. The landing of the 82nd Airborne along
the coastal plains meant the virtual destruction of the
local "defense force." In a matter of weeks the U.S.
had completely overwhelmed the country, and radicalized all of the other Central American nations in the

process. The Panamanian occupation and the annexation of Northern Mexico were two of the greatest factors that brought about the formation of the Confederation.

Once the United States had occupied Panama, it was left with the problem of what to do with the country. The current administration had run on the Free Enterprise ticket. As a result the entire country was leased to the Tirner Corporation. It was the ultimate step in corporate government, the leasing of a conquered nation to a private corporation.

In order to administrate Panama thousands of administrators were imported from the States. Soon the corporate headquarters of the Tirner Corporation was moved to Panama City, bringing a further influx of almost ten thousand former residents of Atlanta. The reaction of the Panamanians was to be expected. A war of liberation, complete with arms supplied by their neighbors, gained momentum. The response was also as expected, a growing sense of alienation and a concurrent increase in violent repression.

After over a decade, the managers formed a separate society within that of Panama. Dwelling in separate enclaves, the Tirner managers and their families had virtually no contact with the residents of the country they controlled. Soon they developed their own culture, consciously modelled upon that of the antebellum South. Soon hundreds of persons whose parents had never been within thousands of miles of the Old South were enjoying mint juleps.

In 2008 the election of the People's Party resulted in the revocation of the occupation contract. Not surprisingly, the executives of the Tirner Corporation refused to relinquish control. Unwilling to repeat its earlier assault, the United States placed an embargo on the country and refused to negotiate with their former citizens. This increasing isolation enhanced the cultural shift by the managers, until they had nearly succeeded in recreating most of the forms of the antebellum South, substituting economic for legal slavery. Considering the similarity of the situations, their system proved quite successful.

When the Confederation finally achieved enough strength to mandate an end to the situation, the Panamanian managers had been in place for a generation. Further, their skills and expertise were too valuable to be simply destroyed. Equally important was the fact that massive wealth was still controlled by the Tirner managers. Still, the Confederation could not allow a continuation of the situation. Nor could the members of the unpopular culture of the Tirner executives safely remain once they had lost their control of the population.

The Confederation's solution was both inspired and amazingly effective. The former Tirner executives, as a group were assisted in a mass immigration to Ganymede. The result was a complete success. The Tirner "Southerners" were able to transplant and maintain their already isolated culture into an area where their expertise and initiative would be of the most benefit. The Confederation turned a problem into an asset. When war with the United Nations became inevitable, there was no question as to where the transported Southerners' loyalties would lie. Their pilots formed some of the most highly decorated units in the Confederation Interstellar Aviation Corps.

THE GLORY OF WAR

by Brynne Stephens

The ships were coming in too fast, too many at a time. Fleet Captain Callista Nakashima leaned forward in her command chair, knuckles white on the armrests, eyes on the forward screen as she spat out orders, oblivious to the blood running down from her temple to pool in the collar of her tunic. Maneuvering a starcruiser this huge was slow at best; with one engine out they had almost no chance of surviving, but she'd blow herself out the aft airlock before she'd surrender. "Hard port! Fire the retros! Tac-scan, status now!"

Another explosion rocked the bridge, nearly throwing her out of the chair. The last hit had wrecked the command console—her auto 'straints were shot. She had no choice but to try to hold on.

"Incoming message, sir, TacCom."

"Let's hope it's reinforcements, troops. Nakashima here, TacCom. What's the word?"

"The word, you little meep, is that if you're not home in less than one nanosecond, the Colonel's gonna kill you."

Callie checked the little skimmer's chrono and swore.

"Sorry, I'm on my way." This was the third time in a week that she'd been late coming home from class because she'd detoured through the Zone, skimming over the cold blast craters, weaving among the twisted wreckage and half-buried debris of the crashed fighters. The war had passed this moon, exacting its toll of death and sorrow, taking lives and homes and fortunes and moving on. Callie had been too young to care when the war had started, and her father often said that it would still be raging when she died.

Not that it made any difference to Callie—the closest she'd ever gotten to combat was the Deserted Zone, site of one of the first dogfights over Ganymede. Callie's mother hated for her to detour through this place, but she'd understood, and hadn't told the Colonel, her father. He'd find out though, if she was late and he scanned for her beacon.

As if reading her thoughts, the directional scanner—DircScan in Callie's private tech-talk—came on in a twinkling rash of green lights spreading across the panel. Her heart seemed to stutter, but the signal beeped twice, telling Callie that it was her mother's home beacon that had spotted her. She switched to auto, annoyed as well as relieved. Callie knew she flew the skimmer well enough to be able to guide it into the docking bay, but her mother still wouldn't let her try.

Her oldest brother, Taylor, piloted the skimmer by remote while she sat and fumed. He and her other three brothers had all been allowed to dock by themselves since they were younger than she was now, and it just wasn't fair.

The little skimmer slid easily through the rocky tunnel that led to the bay and into the house. Since the war almost everybody lived underground. There hadn't been more than a handful of bombings in the last five years, but people were still scared. All of the grownups, including Callie's parents, who had lived through that first raid were paranoid about its happening again. The newer settlers called them "moles" and built their own dwellings defiantly above ground in domed clusters like the one that held Callie's school.

The skimmer bumped gently against the strip of rubber padding that ran around the bay wall at bumper height, and settled to the ground, the hiss of depressurization echoing through the small cave. The guide lights reflected off of the dull silver finish of the skimmer, highlighting the Southern Federation Air Force insignia that Taylor and Hal had added at her last birthday, just under the civilian reg numbers near the tail fins, on the nose, and on both smooth sides above the fuel tanks.

Callie waited until the small airlock tube was in place, locked to the ring around the skimmer's canopy in a tight mechanical kiss, then tabbed open the skimmer's crawl-through and pulled off her helmet. Taylor was waiting for her on the other side of the tube, a wet facecloth, towel, dress, and shoes in his hands and a lopsided grin on his face. Taylor was a full ten years older than Callie, but they were best friends. He looked so handsome in his dress uniform! Next year he'd be up for a Special Forces commission, piloting one of the fast little prototype one-man fighters they called SkyBabies. Callie was almost as proud of him as she was jealous.

Callie struggled out of her shipsuit, skinning it down over her legs as Taylor threw the dress over her head. Once her arms were in the long, puffy sleeves, Taylor rubbed the wet cloth over her face and hands, then bent and yanked her boots and socks off. She struggled her feet into her dress pumps as she fastened the tiny pearl buttons that ran diagonally across her small chest. At fifteen Callie was still flat-chested, and she was glad. Her shipsuit was tight already, and fuel for the skimmer took all of her allowance. If she grew too much too soon, she'd be grounded by lack of funds. Taylor pulled the elastic out of her long braid, unraveled it, and dragged a comb through Callie's hair as she struggled with the last three buttons. She'd wanted a military cut like Taylor's, but her mother refused even to consider it. Southern ladies don't cut their hair, period.

Callie had pointed out that Southern ladies don't generally live in caves either, and had her allowance denied her for two excruciatingly long weeks.

Dressed and combed, Callie smoothed her long skirt down over her thighs and took Taylor's arm just as the inner door opened to reveal Hal, the butler, coming to bring them to table. His name was really Carl Halliburton, but Taylor had started calling him "Hal" after seeing an old videodisc with a malevolent computer by that name. Hal had seen it too, and when the children were younger he had played his role with deadpan sincerity, scaring and delighting them at the same time. "Lieutenant Nakashima, Miss Callista. Dinner is served." He took Callie's shipsuit, the cloth and towels, and her backpack full of books and stood aside to let Callie and her brother pass, resisting the urge to steady her as she teetered by in her hated dress pumps.

A butler isn't the most valuable member of a moon colony if all he does is announce meals. Even though Callie's father was rich enough to afford to bring (and support) a pure butler on settlement, Hal was much more. He helped run Colonel Nakashima's mining empire while serving as the household computer expert. He was an excellent bodyguard, a skilled (if unlicensed) med-tech, and had been well enough educated to occasionally tutor one or another of the children when needed. He was Callie's second-best friend, and her childish determination to marry him had mellowed out to a gentle crush, slowly growing, just beyond her notice.

The Colonel and Callie's three brothers all stood as she and Taylor entered the room—nowhere were Southern manners so appreciated as at Colonel Nakashima's.

Brett, Dale, and Alexander—twenty-three, eighteen, and thirteen years old respectively—were smaller copies of Taylor in their gray-blue uniforms. Alexander had just started pre-flight school; all of the Nakashima men were outstanding pilots. All of the Nakashima *children*, Callie thought bitterly, but Southern ladies don't go to war. Southern *women* do—Callie's classmate Lydia was going to military school next term, but her parents did what they liked, bound only by those traditions they agreed with, ignoring the rest.

Of course, even if Callie got around her mother's magnolia strength, there was the Colonel to worry about, with all of his own centuries of tradition. Southern women don't fight, and neither do female Nihonjin.

Taylor held her chair for her and Callie sat carefully—twice last month she'd balanced wrong on her medievally uncomfortable high heels and had fallen, once missing the chair completely and once taking the entire tablecloth with her. She understood how birds must feel—the only time Callie felt graceful or beautiful or *whole* was when she was flying.

As soon as she was seated, Hal poured water into her wine glass and added a bit of Burgundy—another Nakashima family tradition. Taylor, Brett, and Dale no longer had theirs watered, one more point of jealousy for Callie—her mother's wine was nearly as diluted as her own.

Sarah Nakashima smiled as her eldest son removed her napkin from its silver ring and laid it gently in her lap. Looking at her perfect peaches-and-cream skin, blond hair upswept, slim shoulders straight and soft, it was easy to see why the Colonel had broken hundreds of years of custom to marry her; a gajin in Nippon Ganymede, an artist, privately funded by a family fortune beyond counting—not that the Colonel had accepted her dowry. He hadn't needed to, already being one of the richest men on luna. Marrying Sarah was the first, last, and only time he had ever flaunted tradition, either his people's or his wife's.

"Are you packed yet, Taylor?" Sarah's voice was soft and cultured, the accent pure Terran Georgia— magnolia blossoms and mint juleps, hoop skirts and velvet-clad iron strength, passed from mother to daughter through centuries of time and the darkness of space. How had they kept the softness of those rounded syllables alive in the cramped, sharp cold of the colony ships?

Callie looked up, dropping her napkin ring. "Packed fo' ah-what, Tay-lah?" Callie had gotten so skillful at her mother's accent that only Taylor knew she was mocking Sarah. Not out of meanness or dislike—like her brothers' freedom, Sarah's beauty, refinement, and poise were also out of Callie's reach and always would be.

Colonel Nakashima answered, the soft light from the gas candles reflecting from the rows of medals over his heart. "We're expecting trouble near Europa, my dear."

And you needn't trouble your pretty little head about it. Never said, but always implied.

From his place near the kitchen door, a few feet behind Callie, Hal saw her shoulders tighten, the sharp bones like tiny wings visible where the formal dress left her bare. He too had heard the unsaid condescension, and he smiled. The colonel and his lady had their hands full with that one, and it would get worse as time went on. Exactly twice Callie's age, Hal was becoming aware that his feelings for her went beyond those of his station. He was content for her to make the first move, though, as he knew she eventually would. They had plenty of time.

The com unit attached to his belt beeped discreetly and Hal slipped into the kitchen to answer it.

Callie looked over her shoulder as Hal left the room, and frowned. Looking back at Taylor, she saw his fist tighten on the stem of his wine glass. "Is this it?" Callie asked, excited.

Brett answered, breaking a corner from his flour biscuit, buttering it carefully. "It's probably a problem at Zephyr Mine. The night foreman's sick, and his replacement is hooked on crys—"

"Now Brett, I am certain that Callista is not interested in mining. I'm sure she'd rather hear about young Ashley Beauregard?"

Callie sighed. Sarah was determined to have her betrothed at sixteen, and every time one of her brothers produced a friend who had even *heard* of Georgia, Sarah started drawing wedding invitations on her MacManners Plus. Ashley Beauregard was born on Ganymede, and his parents were Terran French-Canadian, but that was, apparently, close enough.

Callie half-listened to Brett go on about his newest eligible friend, making discreet faces at Alexander, who choked on his jambalaya.

A sudden silence fell, and Callie turned to see that Hal had stepped quietly into the room. Taylor's knuckles were white where he held his glass, but his face gave away nothing.

Hal avoided the family's eyes as he bent to murmur

in the Colonel's ear. The Colonel nodded, and replaced his glass on the table, spilling a little of the dark red wine onto the snowy linen. Callie watched in fascination as the stain spread. "It's time to go, son. Europa's under siege, and you've been called."

He made it sound holy; Taylor had been *called*. Callie wanted more than anything to be able to go in his place, but she didn't get to voice her thought because at that moment Taylor's wine glass snapped at the stem, the fine crystal shattering as it hit Taylor's silver finger bowl, red wine mixing with lemon-scented water, staining the tablecloth and dripping into his lap, slow pink tears raining onto the floor.

Four days later, once again at dinner, Hal's belt com beeped. This time, he beckoned the Colonel into the kitchen, and there was the sound of breaking glass, the crash of antique copper pots.

Colonel Nakashima made his way to the head of the table and looked at Callie, unable to face his wife or his other sons. "Taylor will not be coming home," he said.

There was no need to say more.

Callie paced her room, unable to stop the tears that had been falling for hours. Her mother had fainted, and the boys were tending to her while the Colonel and Hal tried to find out exactly what had happened. To Callie, the details didn't matter. The UN bastards had killed her brother, her best friend, and she wanted blood back.

She stumbled on the hem of her formal dress and cursed, pulling off her pumps and hurling them at the wall. She had to duck as one bounced back at her, so Callie picked it up and threw it again, as hard as she could, wrenching the muscles in her back and shoulder. The hard heel-tip bounced off of her mirror, leaving a small star that radiated cracks, fragmenting her reflection into a hundred tiny points of light.

Behind her the door chimed softly and then whispered open, and Callie turned to see Hal. "Can I get you anything, Miss Callista?"

Callie shook her head, and then fell to her knees and began to sob. Hal crossed the room and took her in his arms, holding her tightly, rocking her, stroking her hair with a white-gloved hand, whispering soft, meaningless words until she fell asleep.

Callie woke suddenly, in the middle of the night, disoriented. She was under a blanket on her bed, her long skirt tangled around her legs. The nightlights glowed softly, showing a silent figure sleeping in a chair by the side of her bed. She felt a surge of joy, and flung herself into his arms—but it was Hal.

He held her by the shoulders as he stretched his cramped back muscles. "Callie. Do you want a sedative?"

"No."

"You should rest."

"How can I sleep? I have to—" What?

He sighed, releasing her. "There isn't anything you can do. Let me give you something to help you."

She backed away from him, tripping on her damned skirts, an idea forming. "No; thank you, Hal. I need to check on Alexander, and then I'll try to sleep, I promise."

She tried to move past him to the door, but Hal stepped forward and blocked her way. He knew every nuance of expression that had crossed her face since she'd been a baby, and he knew that she was up to something now. But the grief in her eyes was too deep to penetrate without crossing the boundary they were not yet ready to break, so he simply nodded and stepped aside.

Callie stopped long enough to touch his cheek, then gathered her skirts and swept past him and out the door.

"Callista . . ."

She looked back over her shoulder and smiled softly, the moment imprinting on his heart. Callie: rippling golden hair, childish body, long legs, and slender bones like tiny wings; then she was gone.

*   *   *

Callie slipped into Alexander's room and hesitated, her resolve weakening when she saw him. He was curled up on the bed, the covers pulled up over his ear, one corner of the comforter in his mouth, like he used to sleep as a baby. She kissed his forehead, and then gathered up the discarded uniform he'd laid out on his chair, militarily precise even in his grief.

They were about the same size, though Callie had longer legs, so the uniform fit well enough. She stuffed her dress into the cubbyhole beneath his bed.

The Swiss Army Knife, its design virtually unchanged for decades, was on his dresser. Unable to see in his darkened mirror, Callie did the best she could with the tiny scissors, dropping the long strands of silken gold into the waste bin beneath Alexander's sink.

She kissed him again and then tiptoed down to the dock, pulling on her shipsuit and helmet before crawling through the tube and into the bay.

Callie had never been allowed to fly at night, but the little skimmer had so many fail-safes and backups that she wasn't afraid. The methane-oxygen mix they used for fuel was in standard-sized canisters—even hampered as she was by the tight shipsuit, it was only a few minutes work to transfer a couple from Dale's skimmer to hers, giving her a full load. Her skimmer wasn't meant for long distances, but she was familiar enough with orbital mechanics to know that Europa was as close as it was going to get, for now. By the time it swung around again, in about ten days, the family already would have grounded her.

Callie climbed into her skimmer and sealed the canopy, then engaged the engines, slowly filling the cabin with air. It wasn't fuel she'd have to worry about, but oxygen. She simply wasn't equipped for a long flight. Still, she was certain she could get to Europa. They wouldn't dare turn down one of Colonel Nakashima's sons wanting to enlist. By the time they figured out she wasn't Alexander, she'd have avenged her brother's death—many times over, she hoped.

*   *   *

Carlo swore as the tandem fighter's starboard railgun burst into fleeting sparks, a large part of the fin spiraling away from the ship and into the dark, sending them into a roll. Behind him Perry screamed, a long, gurgling sound followed by a thump and the flash of the instrument panel short-circuiting. The tiny cockpit filled with smoke and the stench of burning hair. Carlo slammed on the autopilot—not that it would do much good the way they were rolling—and turned in his seat. He put out the small electrical fire caused by Perry's sparking the com unit wires he was trying to repair. The shielding on the old tandem fighter panels had always been faulty—every U.N. pilot Carlo knew hated the damn ships, Carlo included.

He had just fired the aft thrusters, both top and bottom, and had switched them off just as the Fed boy had appeared and managed the lucky shot that had blasted away the railgun and sent Carlo and Perry into a roll. Once the fire was out and the autopilot off, it took all of Carlo's skill to keep the tandem fighter from losing control.

The current situation simply fueled Carlo's impatience with the tandem fighters, the U.N. Air Force, and the war. He hadn't wanted to enlist, but draftees don't get to be pilots, and his family desperately needed the money he'd bring in as a commissioned officer. If he survived he'd test-fly for real money, maybe keep his sisters and brothers from carrying on the dubious family traditions.

Carlos slipped into the rhythm of the roll and waited until the guns were realigned with his target, then blew the Fed boy back to hell. He reengaged the thrusters, but it was too late to straighten out the roll with the ones on starboard gone. The g-force pressed him back against the pilot couch, and he relaxed into it, not fighting it as so many rocket jocks did. Carlo's greatest strength as a flyboy was his willingness to be a part of his ship, to work with it. He'd learned a long time ago that there are a lot of things that simply can't be fought, some battles that can't be won.

They'd been poor all of Carlo's life; his father was

hooked on crystals and his mother didn't believe in birth control. Some of the rich-kid pilots had trouble adjusting to barracks life, but six children in a three-room rent-unit had stripped Carlo of any need for privacy. The other pilots sensed Carlo's quiet, open assurance, and he'd made a lot of friends. Everybody's big brother, and that was fine with him.

The field looked clear, so Carlo tried to head back for Europa—and found that his fuel and oxygen were dangerously low. There must be a leak somewhere, but his board showed green except for the gone railgun.

"Hawk leader, this is Falcon two, come in. Hawk leader, do you read, come in?" All of Carlo's wing was named for Terran birds, since some general's wife had decided that colors and simple numbers weren't "inspirational" enough. The Air Force, goddamn.

Apparently Perry hadn't been able to fix the comlink before biting it. Carlo could hear the static-ridden calls of other pilots from far away, but a few more tries and it was obvious that no one could hear him. Well, they'd find him soon enough; his beacon was still working. And there was a full repair kit in the back—if he could straighten out the roll and find a place to set down, he could patch up the railgun fin and get back to base.

Too bad he couldn't patch up Perry.

They'd only been assigned to each other for a few weeks before this run, so Carlo wasn't all that attached to his partner. He imagined that there was probably a mother and father, maybe a wife and some kids who would grieve, but that was war. You shoot at people, they tend to shoot back. It's a job.

Checking navigation, Carlo saw that he was actually closer to Ganymede than anywhere else. It would be night where he was, handy if one had to set down behind enemy lines. A quick scan as he dropped closer to the surface a while later showed him a deserted area full of wrecked fighters, both U.N. and Southern. A good place to hide until he could limp home. Shifting in his seat, the skinsuit binding uncomfortably, Carlo set course for the middle of the Zone.

*   *   *

Callie set course for the Zone, getting used to night-flying before she tried to get to Europa. Still unable to stop crying, the inside of her helmet was fogging up as she struggled to calm herself. Aware of her limited oxygen, she took deep, slow breaths, letting her anger take over.

Taylor was dead.

No way around it; she couldn't talk him back to life, crying wouldn't soften Death's heart, all of her allowance for a year wouldn't buy him back.

Callie had never felt so helpless, so not-in-control, so young. She hated the U.N. forces more than she thought it was possible for one person to hate anything.

And why Taylor, when she gladly would have gone in his place? He'd never wanted to go to war, hadn't wanted to be a pilot, but as Colonel Nakashima's first son Taylor had never had a choice.

He had never had a chance.

Well, Callie would see that he was avenged. She'd studied the war with an intensity that had impressed her brothers, worried Sarah, embarrassed the Colonel, and made her a good target for the other girls' teasing. She knew how dogfights worked, regardless of what the videodiscs showed, and was a damn good pilot. She wasn't afraid. A few more deep breaths and Callie was calm, letting her anger balance her grief.

Skimming low over the Zone, she had almost zero visibility, so she switched on the little skimmer's headlamps . . . and almost crashed as a big, bright *something* blurred across her path, headlamps nearly blinding her. She caught a glimpse of retros firing and the bristle of railguns and then it was gone. Heart pounding, Callie reached up and activated her doppler scan. She hadn't expected to find anyone out here; other kids took joyrides in the Zone, but not at night.

So who was it?

Callie fired the port rockets aft and turned, craning in the cockpit to find where the strange ship had gone. Nothing.

*   *   *

Carlo swore as he registered the near-collision with the unidentified craft. He switched off his headlamps and tried to steady the fighter, which was still rolling. He managed to get one of the larger wrecks between himself and whoever-it-was, hoping to confound their dopscan while he switched on his own, but since he couldn't hover there he had only a few seconds before being picked up again. In a desperate bid to straighten out the ship so he could *think* Carlo fired the port thrusters straight downward, and sent off a burst from the top railguns. It was wobbly, but it worked. The rolling stopped, and Carlo fired both aft thrusters and the port sides so that he could make his way back to where he'd last seen the little craft.

Who probably knew he was coming.

Callie felt a burst of fear lift the newly shortened hair at the back of her neck as her doppler scan registered the kinetic-kill projectiles bursting out from behind the wrecked troop-carrier to her left. Aware that too much maneuvering would deplete her fuel enough to keep her from getting to Europa, she put the skimmer into a turn and headed straight for the wreck.

Carl Halliburton sat in the center of the small observation dome that Colonel Nakashima had built for Sarah on their twenty-fifth wedding anniversary, the portable comlink on a lacquered table in front of him. The rest of the family was asleep; except for the panicky sound of his heartbeat, the silence was absolute. He scanned the dark horizon, trying desperately to see with more than his eyes.

Somewhere out in all that darkness was Callie, alone.

Callie fired the front thrusters, a chill wave of excitement washing through her. The doppler scan showed a blip right straight ahead of her, moving on a wobbly course. She killed the headlamps, hoping to sneak up on whoever it was. If it was a Southern fighter, she'd claim to be Alexander and ask for an escort.

And if it wasn't . . .

Carlo smacked the dopscan readout, more in frustration than because it would help any. It must have been damaged, or maybe something had wiggled loose during the roll. He switched on the headlamps and stared at the tiny craft approaching him, its own headlamps off, which was good—he'd have been blinded otherwise. With the computer-enhanced vidsense, Carlo could just make out Southern insignia on the nose, along with some numbers. The craft was smaller and lighter than any of the Southern fighters he'd either fought or studied. And it had no visible weapons.

A chill crawled up Carlo's spine as he realized what it must be.

A *SkyBaby*.

The Southern AF's newest prototype, little more than a rumor back at base. They were supposedly faster and more maneuverable than any fighter yet built. Basically a big fuel tank with state-of-the-art reaction-control systems, once one got on your tail you couldn't shake it, outrun it, or be certain of hitting it with kinetic-kill stuff. They were supposed to bring in-space dogfights practically up to the level of what you saw on the old vid-discs. Bloody hell forever—he didn't know they were using them yet!

Well, this one wasn't on his tail, it was coming straight at him.

Carlo lined up the forward railguns and fired.

Just as Callie registered the fact that she was actually facing a U.N. fighter, her com beeped. Startled, she reached for it but the oncoming headlamps blinded her and she hit the aft port retros, sending the ship into a sudden sideways dive. Frantically trying not to crash, Callie wrestled the joystick, straightening out barely in time. Something exploded behind her, kicking her little skimmer forward. Her head snapped back and then forward, her nose impacting against her face-plate, breaking, sending blood down her throat and in rivulets into her mouth. The side of the skimmer caved in but held, keeping Callie safe from the unforgiving vacuum she flew in. Something inside of her broke, and blood bubbled up from her lungs, merging with the tears she could not shed, although it hurt; it hurt so much. . . .

Carlo watched in disbelief as the SkyBaby swerved at the *exact* moment he fired the railguns. What the holy hell kind of sensors did they have?

He fired the forward thrusters, but not fast enough. Debris from the kinetic-kill projectiles striking a derelict flew straight at him, taking out what was left of the starboard weaponry and smashing the headlamps. His board sparked and sputtered, and when the smoke cleared Carlo found that he was without dopscan as well.

What the *hell* was he up against?

". . . Nakashima Seven, come in. Do you read? Nakashima Seven, come in. . . ."

Callie shook her head, wishing she could reach her throbbing nose. She turned on the headlamps with a shaking hand. It hurt to breathe and every time she exhaled, blood spattered across the inside of her faceplate. The bastard had *fired* on her! A *civilian*! She finally registered the fact that Hal was calling her, but ignored him. If the U.N. asshole wanted to play rough, she'd show him how. Heedless of the fuel expenditure she turned the skimmer, fired the aft rockets, and switched off the headlamps.

Carlo watched in disbelief as the crippled SkyBaby turned and began chasing him. The smaller, lighter ship overtook him quickly, but passed him without firing. Without his headlamps and dopscan, the second the little fighter had passed him it was simply gone.

". . . Nakashima Seven, please. Callie!" Hal let his head fall into his hands, defeated—and then he heard her.

*   *   *

"Nakashima Base, this is Seven. I am engaging the enemy at sector four-two-six-six, one on one. Tell Taylor I'm on my way."

Callie turned the ship again and started her run.

Her father's people had a lot of traditions.

Carlo's head jerked up at the voice coming in over his comlink—it was a boy, a child! He searched the landscape ahead of him but could see nothing, not even the derelicts he knew were there.

And then Jupiter crested the horizon. With no atmosphere to diffuse the light, the huge red planet was simply, suddenly *there*, throwing red and orange fire over the twisted wreckage, outlining the small shape hurtling straight for him.

"Callie, no! You little bitch, I love you, *no!*"

Carlo stared at the comlink. Oh dear god, a girl—not a boy, a young girl, like his sisters! He fired the port retros but it was too late.

By the time he saw her, a spark of silver light, flash of face-plate, blur of speed—it was too late.

Carl Halliburton could not hear the explosion through the open comlink, never heard her cry out Taylor's name. Standing in the center of the observation dome, he saw the flash of orange sparks, dying from the lack of air, but he did not feel the impact as the ships came together, then fell away, he did not feel the ground shake when they crashed.

But he could still feel her fingers on his cheek, could still hear her sobs and all the years of her laughter. Staring into the glowing dark, he could still see her as she turned and smiled—rippling golden hair, childish body, long legs, and slender bones like tiny wings; flightless.

Supply Lines

One of the most important features in the Jupiter War was the immense expense involved in supplying virtually everything necessary to fight such a distant war. The men who fought this war were themselves a very costly commodity. The Jupiter War was fought by the most highly trained personnel of both navies. These were men who, if peace had prevailed, would have been the leaders and scientists of their society. Nor were the weapons they used any less expensive. One of the space fighters required several hundred thousand man-hours to produce. A cruiser or carrier took over a million man-hours of labor to produce.

The cost of supplying anything but military necessities from Earth was almost prohibitive. To transport a single hundred-kilogram missile had the same dollar cost as was needed to construct ten similar missiles back on the Earth. A partial solution to the supply problem had been the explosive growth of manufacturing in the asteroid belt. Another was the establishment and expansion of similar facilities on the Jovian moons. Even so, throughout the Jupiter War most of the armaments and supplies still had to make the several-month journey from Earth. One effect of this was that at their maximum number, neither side was able to field more than a few hundred warships of all classes at any one time.

The off-Earth manufacturing facilities were incapable of producing anything as sophisticated as a combat ship in substantial numbers. Nor in the near-Earth orbital factories was either side able to rapidly construct any of the ships used in the war. As a general rule a fighter took ten weeks to produce, a carrier almost a year.

Another irony of supply during the Jupiter War was that munitions that had taken months to arrive were fired off in a few seconds of frenzied combat. Ships as well rarely survived for as long as they took to build, much less transport, in the high-speed battles in the Jovian system. The rapid lethality of modern space warfare meant that in this war attrition soon became the determining factor for victory. Each side dealt with this problem in many ways. One solution tried by the U.N. was to levy commercial ships from civilian sources and convert them into combat vessels. Generally the results were spectacularly unsuccessful. Most converted merchants had neither the structural stability nor the agility to survive in modern space combat. But a few of these converted merchants did have other advantages, some of which came as an unpleasant surprise to those who met them.

WILLIE LAWSON GOES TO WAR

by William C. Dietz

The conference room, like everything else on the Al-
tar Corporation's near-earth orbit space station, was
heavily used, and in need of refurbishment.

The friction caused by countless arms, printouts,
and coffee cups had worn away large sections of the
table's phony wood grain and revealed the white plastic underneath. The two men eyed each other over this
empty surface like boxers in a ring. The oldest spoke
first.

"I don't like it."

Rawlings ran fingers through thinning hair and did
his best to look sympathetic.

"Frankly, Willie, neither do I, but we have no choice.
When the front office says 'Jump,' my boss asks 'How
high?' "

Willie Lawson scowled. His hair was cut so short
that it looked like a cap of solid white fuzz. It made a
dramatic contrast to his dark brown skin. His face was
lean, with squint lines around the eyes, and a good
solid chin. "Your boss is full of shit."

Rawlings sighed. Why him? Why did *he* have to
deal with the crotchety old bastard? Because his boss
was afraid too, that's why.

"Look Willie, I know how you feel about the *Alice
B.*, but try to look at it from the company's point of
view. The *Alice* is sixty years old—"

"Sixty-one years old," Willie put in, "the same age
as I am."

"Right," Rawlings said patiently, "the *Alice B.* is
sixty-one years old, and therefore the most expendable
ship in our fleet. The U.N. is short of ships, they're

77

going to take one of ours, and it would be stupid to give them a newer hull."

"It isn't right," Willie said stubbornly. "The *Alice* wasn't designed for war. She's a freighter, for God's sake. She won't stand a chance against the Feds."

Rawlings took off his old-fashioned wire-rimmed glasses and held them up to the light. He saw a smear and rubbed at it with his tie. It was a trick he used to buy time. Willie was right of course, the *Alice wouldn't* last very long, but he couldn't say that. He couldn't say that the ship, like Willie himself, had lost its usefulness. Rawlings replaced his glasses and cleared his throat. "I think you're overstating the negatives, Willie. I admit the *Alice* wasn't designed as a war ship but she's a tough old bird, and a Q ship isn't a destroyer. All the *Alice* has to do is *look* vulnerable, lure 'em in close, and whammo! Fried Feds."

"So the decision is final?"

"I'm afraid so."

"Then I'm going with her."

Rawlings shook his head. "Willie, that's impossible. The navy's going to gut her, install weapons systems, and provide their own crew."

Willie stood. He was tall and whipcord thin. His dark blue shipsuit was old but clean. "Bullshit. The company's got pull, so use it. Remind 'em that I've got a commission in the naval reserve, twenty-one percent of their common stock, and a bad attitude. Which would they rather have? A happy camper? Or a nasty fight at the next shareowners' meeting?"

Rawlings didn't have to ask. He knew the answer. Willie Lawson was going to war.

Lieutenant Peter Perko kept his face absolutely blank as he strode down the corridors of the U.N. battle station *Winston Churchill*. His uniform fit as if it had been tailored just for him, which it had. He anticipated each salute before it came, returned it with the same perfection that characterized everything else he did, and marched down the hall as if on parade.

The fax, complete with the admiralty seal and the

words ORDERS-CLASSIFIED, EYES ONLY, rested safely inside a zipped inner pocket. He could feel it there, heavy with potential, waiting to be opened.

What would it be? A position of considerable responsibility certainly, something appropriate for an officer ranked number two in his class at the Academy, and number one in the Advanced Tactics School he had just completed.

Yes, the number-three position on a cruiser wasn't too much to hope for, or even number two on a tin can, or—his heart skipped a beat at the very thought— his own command. Something small but dashing, like one of the new S-class Assault Boats, or a Tac Ship.

But whatever the fate which awaited him, Perko would enjoy or suffer it alone. By now his peers had already ripped their orders open and headed for the O Club to celebrate their good fortune or share their despair.

Perko hated such occasions and avoided them whenever possible. Much better to celebrate one's victories alone, hugging them close to be enjoyed over and over, than to throw them out like pearls before swine.

And defeats . . . well, those were certainly to be endured in isolation, suffered through until the pain was little more than a dull throb. Then with back straight, and face blank, you ventured out to try again.

Perko arrived in front of his compartment, punched in his access code, and waited for the hatch to hiss open. The room was tiny, barely large enough for a bunk, storage underneath, and a small desk with built-in computer.

Perko stepped inside, heard the hatch close behind him, and sat on the folding chair. He undid two brass buttons, reached inside his jacket, and withdrew his orders. For a moment he let them rest in the palm of his hand, savoring the suspense, looking forward to what he would find.

Then he ripped them open, scanned for the appropriate line, and read his fate: "To travel with all possible speed to Asteroid P-5678, there to join an undesignated ship-type freighter, accepting the duties

of executive officer, and discharging the same in ac-
cordance with the rules, regulations, and traditions
known to you."

For a moment Lieutenant Peter Perko stared at the
orders in complete and utter shock. A freighter! A
goddamned freighter! Surely there was some sort of
mistake, a glitch in the BuPers computer, a screwup
by some incompetent clerk.

He spent the next hour making com calls, one of
which was relayed all the way to Earth and would cost
him a full month's pay. All to no avail. Everyone
agreed. There was no mistake, no glitch, no screwup.
Peter Perko was about to become the XO on some
clapped-out freighter.

Shame rolled over Perko in a warm wave. Tears ran
down his cheeks. How would he explain this to his
father?

Lieutenant Junior Grade Julie Christoferson held on
as her Skipper, Lieutenant Tom Bowers, put the ship
into a tight right-hand turn. Suddenly there were holes
over her head where none had been before. Bowers
jerked inside his harness and a gout of red mush rode
the ship's atmosphere out into the coldness of space.

Momentarily safe inside her space armor, Christoferson
swore as red lights came to life all across her control
board. Her one remaining computer assessed the damage and delivered the news. It wasn't good.

Christoferson rolled the Tac Ship left, hoping to
throw the Feds off. Europa appeared and disappeared
under her. A dirty white slushball, covered with a
crust of frozen water, and cross-hatched with ridges of
ice.

At least the tankers were clear, their hulls full of
precious water, already headed in towards the U.N.
space stations that orbited earth.

Now Christoferson's job, and the job of the other
Tac Ships, was to buy the freighters some time. Even
if it meant dying to do it.

The hull shook as the ship took a hit from a mini-missile. More red lights came on. Christoferson chinned the intercom. "Perez? Tembo? Do you read me?"

Silence.

Christoferson gritted her teeth. Dead. Both dead. Time to punch out. Sometimes the S & R people got you home in time for dinner . . . and sometimes they never showed up. It was up to the luck of the draw and your own personal karma.

In order to reduce the chances of an accidental separation there were two separate operations for her to perform. Christoferson lifted a protective cover, armed the system, and pushed a button.

Bolts exploded, vapor out-gassed, and the command module tumbled away from the rest of the ship, its radios bleating for help.

Suddenly there was silence. Complete and utter silence, as another piece of debris fell into orbit around Europa. The delta-shaped command module tumbled end-over-end and had already started the long but inexorable fall towards the moons surface.

It was then that Christoferson glanced toward Bowers and saw that his helmet, head included, was floating a foot over his body.

She screamed and screamed and screamed, before the insistent bonging of the intercom brought her up and sweating from tangled sheets. A glimmer of sunlight outlined the fully drawn shade.

The voice belonged to Porter, one of the Trauma Center's orderlies, and more than a little smitten with Christoferson's good looks.

"Sorry to bother you, Lieutenant . . . but you said to call if your orders came in. Well, guess what, I peeked, and you're second on some freighter! Neat deal, huh? Should be a piece of cake after what you've been through."

Christoferson thanked Porter and killed the intercom. Reaching over to her nightstand she grabbed a pack of illegal stim sticks and lit one. They were sending her back into combat again. She tried to feel something, anything, but couldn't.

*　　*　　*

Ironically it was a crisp, cold day, full of sun, and brisk with the promise of winter. The kind of day best used for raking leaves or tossing a football.

But there were no leaves in the military cemetery, or trees to shed them, only endless rows of stark white crosses that marched away to top a low rise.

As the last notes of taps died away, Chief Warrant Officer "Guns" Naisbit stood at rigid attention. A squad of marines fired the traditional salute while some civilians lowered his only son into the ground.

Under normal circumstances marines would've done that, but it was wartime and marines were in short supply.

Not bodies, though. No, there was lots of those, and more on the way. They kept 'em frozen until they had enough to justify a run. Then they brought 'em home stacked like cord wood in the hold of some ship. So many, buried so often, that the media didn't come anymore.

By the virtue of some good or bad luck, Naisbit wasn't sure which, he'd been dirtside when Tony was killed. The official records called it "a major ship-to-ship action in defense of critical supply vectors," but Naisbit had been in the navy for a long time and had sources of his own. Sources who informed him that Tony's squadron had been jumped by a superior force, had called for help and been ignored by an admiral who didn't want any part of an action he might lose. So Tony, along with five hundred and sixty-three other men and women, had died.

Naisbit remembered his son's graduation from OCS, how proud he'd been, how much Tony looked like his mother.

She'd looked good too, standing there by her second husband, clapping with delight when her son's name was read and he accepted the insignia of his new rank.

Second Lieutenant Tony Naisbit, USMC. It had a ring to it, a meaning, a significance.

But that was gone now, nothing more than a series

of on and off impulses in some giant computer, a debit in the game of war.

The strange part was that Tony had died defending something that earth had so much of, water, the same substance he'd loved to sail on.

But there had been no sailing off Callisto, no joyful rush of wind and wave, only the giving and taking of death. A process as old as man himself.

Naisbit bit back tears as the black staff sergeant handed him the flag that had draped Tony's coffin and give him a salute. Naisbit returned it, handed the flag to his ex-wife, and made himself a promise.

The Feds were going to pay. Nothing comes free. Not even blood.

The orders had been sitting in Lieutenant Commander Nathan Shimmura's electronic in-box for more than a week before he got around to reading them. Paperwork, reports, and the other fine points of administration were not Shimmura's strong suit.

Shimmura was a technoid pure and simple, a being who lived on a plane where all things were expressed in terms of stress ratings, algorithms, gear ratios, atomic structures, and power loads. Things he could depend on, manipulate, and control.

For the last two weeks Shimmura had been totally consumed by the job of fitting new drives into the battle cruiser *Lincoln*. A touchy job even in a fully equipped dockyard and almost unheard of anywhere else, especially in the asteroids, at a Level III maintenance facility.

The *Lincoln*'s commanding officer, a woman named McIntyre, was well aware of Shimmura's orders and, being no fool, did nothing to bring them to his attention. Shimmura was her only hope, and she'd be damned if they'd get him till the drives were in.

But McIntyre was fair if nothing else, and once the drives were installed she arranged to have the orders brought to the engineer's attention and ordered a scout to get Shimmura to his next duty station on time.

Although why an officer of Shimmura's rank and

abilities had been assigned to some rust-bucket of a freighter McIntyre couldn't fathom. But so what? Everyone knew admirals were crazy and this proved it.

As for Shimmura himself, or just plain "Shim" as he preferred to be called, once aboard the two-person scout he found any number of problems that required his attention and began to fix them.

Shimmura hummed as he worked, hands caressing tools, mind probing ahead. It made little difference where he was headed or what waited at the other end. He had problems to solve and the means to solve them. What more could he ask?

Willie Lawson fired the sled's braking jets, checked to make sure the locator beacons were on, and examined his ship. There was a scratch across the front of his face-plate and it caused things to ripple when he turned his head.

The *Alice B.* was the only one of many ships being refitted for wartime duty. She hung there like a desperately ill patient, countless tubes and cables running in and out of her durasteel body, dependent on others for her every need.

Her already powerful drives had been taken apart and completely rebuilt. The holds that had once hauled tons of supplies from earth to the roids had been subdivided, filled with weapons systems, and reinforced. A new tac comp lived deep in her hull; its fiber-optic circulatory system pumped information out to every part of the ship, and brought more back as sensors came on-line.

Yes, in a few days, a week at most, the *Alice B.* would be ready for war. Or as ready as she'd ever be.

The funny part was that she'd look exactly the same, the big, vaguely delta-shaped hull, with none of the aerodynamic grace common to atmospheric craft. Not a warship, not a liner, just a beat-up old freighter.

And that was the idea behind Q ships. Hoping to capture the freighter intact, Federal raiders would come in close, weapons suddenly would be revealed, and presto—victim becomes predator.

That was the plan anyway, and Willie hoped it would work.

Willie took a moment to look around.

This was the U.N.'s only base in the asteroids. It was protected by a number of heavily fortified rocks and ran round the clock. The heart of the complex was a large planetoid some four hundred miles in diameter called "Big Red," after the reddish color of its outer surface.

Heavily mined years before, Big Red was nearly hollow and crammed full of factories, offices, living quarters, storage facilities and more.

With Big Red as a backdrop Willie watched as tugs pushed smaller asteroids toward the huge, free-floating processors, where they would give up their precious manganese, platinum, cadmium, chromium, molybdenum, tellurium, vanadium, and tungsten. These minerals and many more were required in order to fight a protracted war.

The problem was that these were third- and fourth-rate rocks, asteroids too light in valuable minerals to justify attention during peacetime, and barely worth-while now. That along with the fact that you can't eat and drink metals.

The multitude of colonies that now swam in near-earth orbits needed a steady flow of organic matter and liquids in order to balance their biospheres. The asteroids were a source but a damned poor one, since very few were rich in light elements such as hydrogen, oxygen, carbon, and nitrogen.

Still, a whole generation of rockrats had eked out a dangerous living pushing asteroids in toward earth, risking their lives in ships that were little more than pressurized tin cans.

Willie knew. He'd been one of the few to strike it really rich, to find a "melon" as the rockrats called them, and to turn that find into something more than a three-month drunk.

Willie had started the company now known as "Atar, Inc." and sold most of it before getting in over his head. Willie Lawson wasn't qualified to run a multi-million-dollar corporation, and knew it.

What he *was* qualified to do was run supplies out to the rockrats, load up on refined metals from small processors out in the belt, and haul the stuff back. That's what Willie and the *Alice B.* had been doing for a lot of years now, and between that and his company stock it was plenty.

But the bad old days were over, the belt was close to picked clean, and the good stuff was on Jupiter—well, not Jupiter herself, but on her moons, especially Europa, Ganymede, and Callisto. Huge iceballs that could provide near-Earth-orbit habitats with life-giving water. Water that was a lot cheaper to obtain than lifting it from earth. Water worth fighting and dying for.

So the idiots who ran earth started a war. A nasty affair, which pitted the Southern Hemisphere and its orbital holdings against the North, and its holdings, leaving Willie in the middle.

The truth was that Willie didn't care *who* won as long he and the *Alice B.* made it through. The *Alice* was more than a ship, she was a symbol of an opportunity lost, and he'd stand by her to the end.

Willie heard a woman's voice in his headset. "Commander Lawson . . . this is Red Area Control. Please report to compartment one-niner-four, level six, grid coordinates twenty-one seventy-six at sixteen hundred hours standard, over."

Lawson swore under his breath. Another damned meeting. If meetings were battles the U.N. would win hands down. During the last couple of weeks he'd been to meetings on logistics, strategy, physical hygiene, tactics, intelligence, morale, and god knows what else. He'd slept through most of them.

"That's a roger, area control, one-niner-four, level six, grid twenty-one seventy-six at sixteen hundred hours standard, over."

Willie fired the sled's jets, put the skeletal vehicle into a tight turn, and scooted toward the huge illuminated 4. It was one of Red's six launch bays, each one handling a different kind of traffic, and filled with activity.

Even from a distance Willie could see the flare of braking jets, green and red navigation lights moving across the blackness of space, the blue wink of welding torches, and the white stutter of alignment beams as a ship slid into dock.

A few moments later Willie added his lights to all the rest as he entered Bay 4 and grounded the sled.

It was a huge, cavernous place full of space-suited figures, automated machinery, stacks of cargo modules, and blue-green light.

Enlisted personnel saluted the flashes welded to each shoulder of Willie's space suit and he felt silly repeating the motion.

Willie had long regarded his commission in the naval reserve as something to put up with rather than work at. It was law. A hassle imposed on anyone with a master's certificate and a certain amount of experience. And once you had the commission, rank came with the passage of time. Willie supposed that if he lived long enough he'd become an admiral! The thought made him laugh.

An hour later Willie had taken a quick shower—there wasn't any other kind on Big Red—and donned a new uniform. It at least met Willie's standards for usefulness and simplicity. It was space-black, equipped with a multitude of velcroed pockets, and baggy enough to be comfortable. '

The corridors were heavily traveled and it took a while to reach the point where corridors 21 and 76 came together. Willie looked around, and sure enough, there was compartment 194. The hatch was open and he stepped inside.

The compartment was small as meeting rooms go, with an oval table, and seating for six. Only one person was present, however, a large man in a captain's uniform, with white hair and a spade-shaped beard. He had piercing blue eyes.

The man stood and held out his hand. "Commander Lawson . . . I'm Dr. Forbush . . . oh damn. I've done it again. Sorry about that. *Captain* Forbush now . . . not that it makes much difference. Thank you for coming. Pick a seat, any seat, it's just the two of us."

Willie selected a chair and sat down. "Just the two of us, sir? I'm surprised. I've been to a hundred meetings during the last few weeks and they were always packed to the overhead with attendees."

Forbush chuckled. "I know what you mean. In this case however you are the *only* commanding officer present by virtue of the fact that the Q-25 is the *only* ship of her kind."

"Q-25?"

"Q-ship number twenty-five," Forbush answered patiently. "If all goes well the U.N. will commission twenty-five vessels, starting with number twenty-five, and working backwards."

Willie shook his head in amazement. "Don't tell me, let me guess. The designation 'Q-25' sounds better than 'Q-1.' "

Forbush grinned agreeably. "See? You're already thinking like an admiral. Now let's get down to business. I understand you're something less than pleased with the Q-ship concept, and fond of asking, 'Who the hell thought of this anyway?' "

Willie started to say something in reply but Forbush held up a hand.

"Don't bother to deny it—I know it's true. The answer, by the way, is 'me.' I'm the one who suggested the use of Q-ships. I'm a military historian, but more than that, a military historian with good political connections. Good enought that when I suggested Q-ships some important people were willing to listen."

Once again Willie tried to speak and Forbush held up a hand. "And before you launch off into a diatribe against my blatant use of political influence, let's talk about *you*. A rather wealthy captain who used his political influence to get assigned to his own ship."

There was a long moment of silence while the two men stared at each other before both broke into laughter. It went on for some time.

Finally Forbush reached under the table and brought

up a half-empty container of Scotch and a couple of plastic glasses. "How 'bout a drink?"

Willie agreed, and found the historian's whiskey to be very smooth. "So, we're both rotten, now what?"

Forbush swirled his whiskey. He held it up the light and examined it with a critical eye. "Now we help win the war."

Forbush talked nonstop for the next two hours. He started with the Trojan Horse, worked his way up through the early privateers, and ended up talking about the Q-ships of World War II. He did it with such conviction and passion that by the time he was finished Willie believed in them, too. Not that he wanted to command one especially, but believed in them and their capacity to hurt the Feds.

According to Forbush the U.N. had a temporary advantage. After early successes by the Feds things had finally shifted. The U.N. had a slight advantage. They were getting more supplies to the people who needed them than the Feds were.

As a result the Feds were doing everything they could to capture U.N. freighters intact, thereby gaining both a ship *and* its cargo. They had even converted some huge passenger liners like the *Kenya* and the *Argentina* to military use, turning them into commerce raiders. These ships were powerfully armed and carried extra personnel to function as prize crews.

That allayed one of Willie's worst fears, that the *Alice* would be blasted on sight and never have a chance to fight back.

So given the fact that the *Alice B.* would be the first of her kind, and would have the advantage of surprise, Willie tended to agree. And by the time the meeting was over he was even slightly enthusiastic. Or was it the whiskey? Well, whatever it was it felt good, and he stumbled off to bed.

One of the few good things about the *Alice B's* conversion to a Q-ship was the fact that it made her roomy by comparison with other warships.

Even after the installation of weapons and additional armor the space previously taken up by her holds translated into a few extra square feet of room for each compartment, including the wardroom.

Like the interior of most warships the wardroom had a rough, functional look, with lots of exposed conduit, junction boxes, and air ducts. A long rectangular table dominated the center of the room, its surface covered with coffee containers, food, empty glasses, and printouts. All of the officers, plus the ship's senior ratings, were seated at the table, an arrangement that Willie liked and Perko didn't.

Perko had argued against including the ratings, indicating that such familiarity ". . . would break down the necessary distance between leaders and subordinates."

Willie had countered by saying that "these 'subordinates,' as you call them, will decide whether our rank-heavy asses live or die. It would be nice if they knew what was going on."

His face bleak, Perko sat on Willie's right. He was a handsome man, like a recruiting holo come to life, with even features and a square jaw.

Willie was still getting to know his XO but some things were already apparent. Perko was extremely intelligent, competent, and unhappy. Having read Perko's file, Willie thought he knew why. Perko came from a military family—his father was a general, no less—and was as they say, "career-motivated." His kind would see the war as an opportunity for advancement, the kind of advancement that comes on a tin can or cruiser, not an experiment like the Q-25.

Then there was Christoferson. She wore her black hair military-short, sported a nose stud, and chain-smoked non-reg stim sticks.

Everyone liked her, and Willie was no exception. She was beautiful but didn't use it, and extremely competent.

There was a haunted look in Christoferson's eyes though, the same look marines refer to as "the thousand-yard stare," and Willie wondered how long she'd be able to keep it together. Her file said she was okay, cured of post-combat stress syndrome, but Willie had his doubts. She'd bear watching.

Willie shifted his gaze further down the table to where Naisbit sat, or "Guns" as everyone called him. Here at least was a true professional. Naisbit had sixteen years in, had risen through the ranks, and knew every weapons system the navy had. Neither his file nor his behavior hinted at problems of any kind. A solid asset.

And speaking of assets, seated at the far end of the table was Lieutenant Commander Nathan Shimmura, black hair hanging down into his face as he used a pocket tool kit to work on a component Guns had brought to his attention, blissfully unaware of his surroundings.

Here was absolute proof that one could rise on ability alone, because Willie felt sure that Shimmura had never had a political thought in his whole life, and never would. He never ordered his techs to do something he wouldn't do himself, and had a hard time keeping his hands off the tools. The *Alice B.* was in good hands.

Also present were Petty Officer First Class "Doc" Tresner, a cheerful woman of intermediate age with medical responsibility for the entire crew, and Petty Officer Third Class "Sparks" Yetter, Doc's best friend and the ship's leading com tech.

The rest of the crew was not present but probably listening in via jury-rigged mikes. Some COs spent a lot of time sweeping for bugs but Willie didn't bother. The truth was that if the wardroom had been a little larger he would've invited all of them in.

Willie cleared his throat. "All right . . . let's get down to business. By now all of you realize that Q-25 is something of an experiment. Nobody's done this before . . . not since World War Two anyway . . . and conditions were a bit different to say the least. That means there's no rule book, no manual, no set of instructions telling us what to do.

"We *do* have an adviser however, a Captain Forbush, who among other things is a well-known professor of military history. You might also be interested to know that Captain Forbush played a role in choosing some of you for your present assignment."

Perko frowned, Christoferson looked mildly interested, and Shimmura tightened a screw.

"As Captain Forbush likes to point out, our main defense is deception, and that will require a certain amount of acting. By now you have noticed that while the *Alice B.*—excuse me, the Q-25—has undergone extensive modification, her outward appearance remains essentially unchanged. She still looks like the beat-up freighter she once was.

"That's important, if we have any hope of luring Federation war ships in close enough for Guns to put them away. But that's just the beginning. In order to convince the enemy that we *are* what we appear to be, we must act the part at *all* times. We may even allow ourselves to be boarded.

"At the conclusion of this meeting each of you will surrender your uniforms, plus all personal items of military issue, and anything else that might suggest your actual identity. You will receive civilian clothes plus any other items you may need."

"Excuse me, sir," Perko put in, "but doesn't that qualify us as spies, and entitle the enemy to execute us if we're captured?"

Willie smiled grimly. "Number One is quite correct. That's why all of you are entitled to withdraw at this time. You will be kept on Big Red for the duration of hostilities, or until the end of the Q-ship program, whichever comes first."

Perko considered Lawson's words. It was an approach-avoidance situation. What good was escape if he ended up stuck on Big Red? No, it was better to stay on the Q-25 and see what happened.

Willie looked around the room. "No takers? Okay, there's more. In order to make sure we don't screw up when the chips are down, you will no longer use military rank when addressing each other. In addition, do your best to avoid the use of military jargon."

Willie smiled. "I demand sloppiness aboard this ship, and I'll tolerate nothing less."

Christoferson put a boot on the edge of the table and pushed her chair back. "You can count on me, skipper. This is *my* kind of ship."

Willie nodded approvingly. "Excellent. Our second officer shows a real aptitude for civilian sloppiness. Now, for a review of operations . . ."

The meeting lasted another three hours. When it was over everyone retreated to their quarters, where a selection of civilian shipsuits and other gear had been laid out on their bunks.

One by one Perko folded his uniforms and placed them in the duffle provided for that purpose. It didn't seem fair. He'd worked so hard to earn the uniform, and the rank that went with it. Now, when he should be wearing it with pride, they were taking it away.

As Perko placed the last uniform in the bag, light glinted off of something and caught his eye. It was a holo cube. It showed Perko in dress blacks, his father at his side, and the Academy in the background.

Graduation day. It was a picture of how things were supposed to be. Perko shoved it toward the back of a drawer. Maybe it would bring some good luck.

With the exception of a last-minute visit from Captain Forbush, who toured the ship shaking hands with everyone and wishing them luck, the Q-25 slipped away with little or no fanfare.

No one knew the full extent of Fed intelligence operations but they assumed that Big Red harbored at least a couple of spies, and it seemed wise to draw as little attention as possible.

Thanks to Forbush, all the base records still listed the *Alice* as a freighter, and substantially understated the vessel's defensive as well as offensive capabilities.

Their orders were simple. Find technical problems and solve them, give the crew a chance to practice their jobs, and defeat any Feds who took the bait.

Willie hoped the Feds *wouldn't* take the bait and stayed within U.N.-dominated space as much as possible. The ship's sensors brought them to battle stations frequently over the next couple of weeks, but with the exception of some signals too weak to identify all the traffic they encountered was friendly.

Thanks to her new drives the *Alice B.* could give a destroyer escort a run for its money, but it wouldn't do to have a beat-up freighter making that kind of speed, so Perko and Christoferson had orders to keep it down. As a result it took them the better part of twelve standard days to reach Battle Station *Gorbachev.*

Heavily fortified, and protected by a carrier task force, the habitat was a refueling station and a logical stop for an itinerant freighter. Forbush had insisted that the *Alice B.* maintain the appearance of being on a schedule in case she were followed.

So the days passed one at a time, full of mind-dulling vigilance and unending drills. Most of the crew looked forward to the drills, because something was better than nothing.

There were all kinds. Weapons drills, in which Guns launched an unmanned drone and they tried to destroy it; damage control drills, in which Shim announced a pressure leak and people rushed to plug it; and medical emergencies, in which everyone took turns as both medic and patient. Then there were boarding drills, in which the crew practiced being boarded, evac drills, in which they pretended to punch out, and "ship in peril" drills, in which they simulated a tow.

This is where Perko excelled, driving the crew harder than Willie would've dared and getting better results. Recognizing the other man's superiority, Willie stayed out of the way. When push came to shove and the chips were down, the drills would save lives.

Was the balance between his personality and Perko's a matter of good luck? Or the result of careful planning by Captain Forbush? Willie suspected the latter.

Time passed, and slowly but surely response times grew shorter and shorter, until even Perko had a hard time finding fault. Praise still tended to come from Willie, but the combination of personalities seemed to work and the crew became a team.

As a result Willie was in a good mood when the *Gorbachev* filled the center of the viewscreen. From his command chair above and behind Christoferson and Perko, the battle station looked like an old-fashioned top, with a bulbous hull and a pair of spindly antenna towers pointing up and down.

Like all habitats its size, the *Gorbachev* had been constructed in space. So, with no need to negotiate planetary atmospheres, the battle station's designers had been free to cover its surface with solar panels, heat-exchangers, weapons blisters, observatories, antenna arrays, access ports and other less identifiable installations.

Long before the *Alice* got within torpedo range of the habitat they were challenged, recognized, and provided with an escort. Willie was under no illusions about the escort. It was there for the *Gorbachev*'s protection, not his. One wrong move and the freighter would be so much free metal.

The escort consisted of two S-class assault boats, speedy little ships bristling with weapons and fast enough to run circles around a destroyer.

Perko didn't say anything, but Willie noticed the way he glowered at the screens and snapped at the Assault Boat pilots when they ventured too close. Much to his own surprise Willie found himself feeling sorry for Perko. Maybe Forbush would give him a transfer somewhere down the line.

It took about four hours to dock, complete the usual raft of formalities, and clear the crew for liberty. It was, and would be, one of their few opportunities for some R&R, so Willie turned everyone loose.

Given the strength of the *Gorbachev* itself, and the carrier task force that guarded it, there was little danger of being caught with their pants down.

One by one the crew finished their duties and, still swathed in civilian clothes, made their way through the pressurized umbilical and into the battle station proper. Once there they were quickly caught up in the unending flow of foot traffic that filled the *Gorbachev*'s corridors, and were carried along.

Although run by the military and used to guard an important sector, the battle station was much more than an orbital fortress. It was a center for trade as well and, because of that, boasted quite a few amenities, including restaurants, stores, nightclubs and more.

Still, a military base is a military base, and Perko felt naked without his uniform and the rank that went with it. There were other civilians here and there, *real* freighter crews for the most part, mixed with a sprinkling of scientists and technicians. Having no desire to try to explain his way into one of the station's officer clubs, Perko followed the path of least resistance and wandered into a civilian-style bar. The service was quick, the drinks were strong, and one hour later Perko felt pretty good.

He was just about to order dinner when a couple of tech types entered the area arm-in-arm with a tipsy Jake Laferty. The same Jake Laferty who'd been the bane of Perko's existence during his time at the Academy, and still rated only just above the rank of maggot in the naval officer's personal hierarchy of life-forms.

Laferty was short, with a body that would turn to fat in middle age, and a beet-red face. As he entered, Laferty's beady little eyes scanned the bar, looking for someone to put down or suck up to.

Perko turned and tried to fade into the background. The last thing he needed was a dose of Laferty's noxious personality. It was a wasted effort.

"Hey! Wait a minute, guys! There's Prick-head Perko! Hey, Prick-head! How're they hangin'?"

Perko groaned. It was like his worst nightmare come true. Within seconds Laferty was there, friends in tow, a big grin on his meaty face.

"Well? Aren't ya gonna ask us to sit down?"

Perko got to his feet. "Sure, go ahead and sit down, I was leaving."

"Leaving? Leaving? What the hell you mean, 'leaving?' Me 'n' the boys just arrived. We gotta have a drink with 'ol Prick-head."

Laferty swayed slightly, leaned forward, and tried to read the patch over Perko's pocket through bleary eyes. As he did so Perko saw the silver pips on Laferty's shoulder-boards. The sonovabitch had already ass-kissed his way up to Lieutenant Commander!

Laferty laughed. "The *Alice B.*? What the hell is an *Alice B.*, anyway?"

Laferty's eyes widened in sudden understanding. "A freighter? Ol Prick-head's serving on a freighter? Oh, that's rich, that is! Wait till everyone hears this!"

Laferty broke into drunken laughter and the technoids looked bored.

As Laferty's laughter rang in his ears something snapped deep inside Perko. Something that had started at the Academy and built up over the years. A combination of resentment, frustration, and rage.

The blow started low and came up fast. It hit Laferty on the point of his chin and rocked him backward. Stepping into this newly vacated space, Perko followed up with a series of quick body blows. They felt good.

Laferty never had a chance. Caught by surprise, his reactions slowed by alcohol, the Academy's part-time boxing champ and full-time bully slumped to the floor.

Perko looked at the tech types and they backed away.

Perko looked down, saw how stupid Laferty looked, and laughed. He was still laughing when the military police came to haul him away.

By chance Willie and Christoferson left the ship at the same time, entered the flow of foot traffic, and were swept along together. Neither had a destination, so it seemed natural to drift along and talk. Or so it seemed.

But as they walked along Willie noticed heads turn and suddenly realized why. Christoferson was strikingly beautiful. She had a heart-shaped face, a long athletic body, and moved with an arrogant grace that managed to be both intimidating and sexy at the same time.

Willie gave an internal sigh. There had been a time when women, some anyway, *liked* to be around him.

The dashing young rockrat, risking his life to supply earth-orbit habitats, his face on the news vids for weeks at a time.

But not anymore. These days beautiful young women used him as a shield against younger men. Shit. Willie forced a smile and gestured toward a restaurant that proclaimed GOOD FOOD in foot-high yellow letters. "How 'bout it? My treat."

Christoferson smiled. "That sounds like the best offer I've had in about twelve days. You're on."

They entered the restaurant, a cheerfully plastic place full of unusual color combinations, and chose a booth. The booth sensed their presence and a menu appeared in the table top.

The menu offered a wide selection of choices, but the knowledge that most of them came straight out of the habitat's recycling vats, and were processed to taste different, made the whole thing seem a little silly.

Willie speared his choices with a stubby finger and they lit up brighter than the rest. Christoferson did the same and their drinks arrived a few minutes later.

Willie held up his drink in a toast. "To us, the crew, and the ship we sail on."

Christoferson raised her glass as well. "I'll drink to that."

A minute passed while both took a sip of their drinks. Christoferson broke the silence.

"Speaking of the ship, skipper . . . what makes her so special? Or am I speaking out of turn?"

Suddenly Willie was back there, conning a thirty-two-year-old ship into the belt, following the tone. It was a steady, mind-numbing sound that grated on his nerves.

But what could they do? You don't ignore a distress signal out in the roids, not if you want someone to come when it's *your* ass on the line, a day that will almost certainly come.

So bit by bit Willie had taken the ship inward, past tumbling rocks of all sizes and shapes, toward Interstellar Metal's proccessor 46.

Back in those days Willie had been both captain and pilot, unable to afford a larger crew, and unwilling to surrender control. Looking to the right he'd seen Alice, beads of sweat covering the broad expanse of her forehead, eyes narrowed in concentration, delicate white teeth biting the fullness of her lower lip. God, she was beautiful.

The tone grew louder and Willie forced his attention back to the task at hand. They were getting close. Real close, there up ahead, a slowly spinning roid and a glint of reflected sunlight. Suddenly a burst of garbled sound.

"All ships . . . all ships . . . buzz . . . crackle . . . pop . . . since 0815 standard. We have shut off all air to that portion of the plant in hopes . . . pop . . . pop . . . pop . . . crackle . . . All ships . . . all ships . . ."

Alice turned the volume down. "It sounds like a fire, Willie. Put her down a safe distance from the plant and I'll go in."

They argued the entire time it took to match speeds with the asteroid and set the ship down. As usual Alice won, and as usual she did it through sheer force of logic. Alice was already struggling into her space armor when she delivered the telling argument.

"Listen, Willie, and listen good. You've got a six-person crew, remember? And you're the only one good enough to get the ship out of here. You die and we all buy the farm. Got it? Good. Now give me a kiss and check my seals."

Willie kissed her, checked her seals, and watched her bound over the asteroid's rocky surface to a domed-shape processing plant. She would find the survivors and guide them back.

Except she didn't, because there were no survivors beyond the garbled tape, and because the fire reached a stash of explosives while she was still inside.

Willie had seen it with his own eyes. Seen the surface of the dome sucked inward, seen it push out again as it blossomed red and orange, suddenly gone with the oxygen that had fueled it.

No one ever figured out what went wrong at processor 46, or why Alice Brown had to die, and now some twenty-nine years later no one cared. Except Willie that is, and he was old enough to know it didn't make any difference. Dead is dead.

Willie looked up and realized that he'd been talking, letting the words pour out, baring his soul to a near stranger.

A tear trickled down Christoferson's cheek. She reached out to hold Willie's hand. "I'm sorry, skipper. Life sucks, sometimes."

Willie nodded, and the food came, saving him from the necessity of a reply.

They talked about other things after that, brighter, happier things. The food was awful, but it was the best meal Willie had eaten in a long, long time.

Guns waved the weapons techs forward. It had taken all four of them to lift the heavy case and carry it through the umbilical and into the battle station. He would've preferred moving it through a cargo area but beggars can't be choosers.

"Come on, you airheads! We haven't got all day! The captain wants this stuff moved, so move it!" Guns winked to show he didn't mean it.

The weapons techs, Skupa, Tarbox, Puente, and Orlander, smirked at each other. The whole thing was a lark as far as they were concerned, just one more episode in the never-ending annals of military theft.

Guns was what the navy called a "cum shaw artist," an expert in the necessary skill of unauthorized acquisition. It was a time-honored process through which excess is traded for shortage and everyone comes out happy. Far from legal, but winked at by commanding officers desperate to balance their supply inventories or hoping to stockpile critical spares.

Tarbox, a young woman with red hair and lots of freckles, helped Puente, a dark-haired youth with black, sparkling eyes, to set up the cart. Moments later it was ready, and with the crate strapped in place they set off down the corridor. One wheel had an incessant squeak and was getting on the warrant officer's nerves.

Naisbit led the way, the perpetual frown of a testy officer firmly in place, scattering pedestrians right and left. It was an old trick. If you're *not* supposed to be doing something *look* like you are.

A pair of strolling military policemen appeared from around the curve of the habitat's hull. They walked like beat cops everywhere, swaggering along, secure in the strength of their armor and the weight of their batons.

Guns drew himself up straighter, turned a stern eye on his troops, and picked up the pace. Maybe they could bull on by without a challenge.

No such luck. One of the military police saw them, tilted his visor up, and pointed his white baton in their direction. His voice was artificially amplified and simultaneously fed via radio to the battle station's security center. "Hey, you! Yeah, the bozos with the crate, hold it right there!"

Guns made his face blank and held up a hand to his troops. Confident but not obnoxious. That's the way to go. Give an MP a ration and they'll give it back. Multiplied.

"Yes, corporal?"

The corporal looked Guns over. He didn't like civilians. His lip curled upward. "We've got rules about transporting cargo through pedestrian walkways."

Guns nodded sympathetically. "That's what I told the old man, but would he listen? Hell, no. Said he wasn't about to pay docking fees on the cargo ring for one friggin' crate. Said to hump it through the halls. Asshole."

The argument was calculated to appeal to that part of all enlisted people that hates officers. Unlike most officers, Naisbit had been an enlisted person himself and knew how it felt. The corporal nodded understandingly.

"All right then, but don't do it again. Take the next access lane left, drop two levels, and go where you please. It's all cargo down there."

Guns gave him a grin. "You're all right, corporal. We're out of here."

The corporal gave them a nod, rejoined his partner, and continued up the corridor.

Guns let out a sigh of relief. Thank God. One look inside the crate and he'd do hard time pumping hazardous waste into used roids. That's because the navy objects to the distribution of drugs, especially addictive ones, within its own ranks.

In this case the drug was "Orbit," so called because that's where it put you, and Naisbit had enough to keep a hundred users high for a year.

Basically it was a form of amphetamine, similar to the mild stimulant sometimes issued during prolonged combat, but much more powerful. It had taken every cent of Naisbit's life savings to purchase the drugs on Big Red.

Now Guns would use the drugs to trade up, to buy something that would avenge Tony's death, that would give it meaning. A club, a big club, which he'd use to smash the Feds.

Naisbit turned around and smiled. "Come on! Get your butts in gear! Let's deliver this baby and pick up those spares. After that the drinks are on me!"

The weapons techs laughed and followed Guns down the hall.

As usual Shimmura was a little surprised to find himself on liberty. Work was his fun and he didn't know what to do without it. But the skipper had practically forced him to leave the ship, proclaiming "it would do him good," so here he was.

Shim drifted down the hall, his mind seeing the ways the habitat was put together, and imagining workable alternatives. He thought of the battle station's hull. Why a globe, when wheels were so much more elegant?

Shim had just started to answer his own question when someone touched his arm. "Hey sailor, how 'bout buying me a drink?"

Turning, Shimmura found himself looking down at a woman even smaller than he was. She wore a skimmery body suit that hugged every curve of her lithe little body, an artificial flower in her long black hair, and a big smile. The woman delivered the line with such insouciance, with such good humor, that Shimmura's stereotypes failed him. The automatic "no" that he'd given to a hundred hookers before her froze on Shim's lips and became a "yes."

Moments later he found himself deep in a darkened room, almost floating on a cloud of her perfume, sipping a drink he didn't want.

It didn't matter. She said her name was Susie and she didn't normally work in bars, but was forced to because she'd been fired from a regular job and didn't have enough money to get home.

Shimmura didn't believe a word of it, but loved the sound of her voice, and the fact that she didn't expect him to talk. Previous women always wanted him to say things, to talk about them, or things he didn't care about. This was bliss.

Susie touched his arm and turned his skin warm. Shimmura didn't know it, but he was in love.

When the *Alice B.* left the protection of the *Gorbachev* it was for real. No more cruising in friendly sectors, no more snuggling up to orbital battle stations. For better or worse, they were on their own.

Willie wasn't sure how liberty had affected his crew, but with the possible exception of Perko he thought it had done them good. Christoferson seemed more relaxed, Naisbit walked around looking smug, Shimmura seemed more human, and Perko was, if not happy, changed.

When security had called to tell Willie about Perko, he hadn't believed them, and forced them to describe the man in question. When the description matched, Willie had reluctantly made his way to the security center, still certain there was some mistake. But there was no mistaking the man himself, his confession, or the holo vid of some guy named Laferty lying unconscious on the floor.

As Willie signed a form accepting responsibility for

Perko's punishment the fuzzy-cheeked duty officer asked what it would be.

Willie shook his head sadly. "A few days on the surface of the hull should do it. The radiation zips through your suit, cooks your brain, and makes you real peaceful from then on."

The ensign's mouth was still hanging open when the two men left the center.

"Come on," Willie said, "I'll buy you a drink."

Perko agreed and thanked Willie for bailing him out, but didn't explain the fight. And Willie, being Willie, didn't ask.

In any case Perko seemed more relaxed now, as though the fight, and the mark on his otherwise pristine record, had relieved some sort of pressure. Or as Christoferson put it, "He's still obnoxious, but less so."

Willie scanned the screens for the thousandth time that watch. It made no difference that the sensors would pick up another ship long before it showed up on visuals, and it wasn't even his job, but looking was something to do. Nothing, as usual.

The bridge was dark and quiet. Rows of indicator lights glowed steadily red, amber, and green. Buttons glowed waiting to be pressed, computer screens scrolled through lines of data, and the crew spoke to each other in quiet voices.

Willie turned back and forth inside his space armor, trying to alleviate the pain. With the exception of a shower taken every second day they were living in the their space armor now, helmets at hand, conscious of the fact that they could come under attack at any moment.

Especially on this course, a long, gentle curve that would take them in toward Jupiter. That, plus the starboard drive that Shim had programmed to cut out every now and then, should result in enemy contact. After all, what warship could resist a fat old freighter with a bad drive?

That's what Willie was thinking when he drifted off to sleep. He did that a lot now, catching catnaps in the command chair rather than retiring to his cabin. It drove Perko, Christoferson, and the rest of the bridge crew crazy, but they understood. If something threatened his ship Willie would be there to deal with it.

That's why Willie came almost instantly awake when the alarms went off. Com tech Joy Yeter was the first to speak. "We've got a hot one, skipper . . . three-by-three."

Willie knew that "three-by-three" meant that the target had been confirmed with radar, infrared, and radio direction-finders.

Sparks pressed her earpiece into her ear. "Just a sec . . . yeah . . . there goes a coded burst. A squirt transmission of some sort."

Willie felt his heart begin to beat faster. The sensor alarms had already brought the crew to their battle stations—no problem there. The squirt transmission would be something along the lines of "Fat target in sight, will engage." A routine signal to let Fed HQ know what the ship was about to do.

His task, and the crew's, was to make sure that it was the last transmission the raider sent out. The success of the entire Q-ship program depended on maintaining the element of surprise for as long as possible.

"Incoming transmission," Sparks intoned. "I'll put it on the com screen."

An overhead vid screen swirled to life. A woman appeared. She had prematurely gray hair and a hard expression. Like Willie and his crew she wore space armor.

"Unidentified freighter, this is the Confederation ship *Southern Cross*. Cut power to all drives and weapons. We will board in approximately thirty minutes. Any attempt to disobey my orders will result in the destruction of your ship."

Willie nodded towards Sparks. Now for a little acting. "Put me on."

A black box whirred down out of a recess in the overhead. A red light came on. Willie did his best to look flustered and scared. "Don't fire! We're cutting power now!"

Christoferson touched a button and the drives cut off. The Confederation officer nodded. "Excellent. If you continue to obey my orders you will survive." Then the screen cut to black and she was gone.

The next twenty minutes were the hardest of Willie's life. Each minute lasted an eternity and made its own sweaty contribution to the already fetid atmosphere in the control room.

Things were better for Guns and his people, who could pass the time by checking their weapons, and for Shimmura and his power techs, who had the entire ship to worry about.

Then the waiting was over and things happened in quick succession. First came visual contact with the raider, along with detailed sensor readings. Sparks droned it out.

"We have visual contact, with three-by-three sensor confirmation, a hundred miles and closing. We have computer verification of a Santiago class destroyer escort, assumed to be nuke-capable, and armed with radar-seeking, heat-seeking, and remote-guided HE missiles. Secondary armament consists of two gatling-type auto-cannons mounted port and starboard, a pilot-operated bow cannon, and the capacity to launch two fighters. I have no, repeat no, return on the fighters."

Willie nodded, keeping his voice absolutely emotionless. He chinned the shipwide intercom and gave thanks for the special shielding that had been installed to keep the enemy from listening in.

"Okay people, this is it, remember our strategy. We let 'em get real close, where our heavy-duty secondary armament can do the most damage. Then, just before they board, we let 'em have it. Guns, remember to target their communications, and watch out for message torps. It wouldn't kill us this time, but it might the next."

Guns, located fifty yards away in the heavily armored fire control center, had heard this strategy only about a thousand times, but still managed a cheerful, "Gotcha, skipper."

After all, a good subordinate knows better than to take offense at repetition, because chances are that some dumb shit needs to hear it again.

Besides, this was pay-back time, and Guns was in a good mood. He licked his lips in anticipation. The only question was, should he hit 'em with his big club, or wait for a more significant target? He'd only have one chance, so he didn't want to waste it. Time would tell.

Christoferson flexed her fingers. In seconds, minutes at the most, they would summon full power from the ship's drives, and position *Alice* for the kill.

Could she do it? Already Christoferson could feel the fear bubbling up from deep inside, not about death, but about her ability to function.

What if the fear took over? What if the shrinks were wrong about her, and everyone died because she went into mental and emotional lock-up, screaming mindlessly as the ship blew up around her?

Sweat trickled down from her hairline and slid down her temple. She reached to wipe it away and hit her helmet instead.

In the drive room, and in communication with power techs, in the two backup control positions located elsewhere in the ship, Shimmura hummed softly. His position was like an electronic cocoon, a heavily armored globe which, like Naisbit's, was designed to separate from the rest of the ship in an emergency. The inside surface of the globe was covered with screens, readouts, and control panels. Their combined light cast an eerie glow over the interior.

Part of Shim's mind was there, caressing the ship's systems, making sure that everything was green. But another part was thousands of miles away, deep in a fantasy about Susie, and the life they could have together. Her likeness was taped to an equipment rack over his head.

Shimmura heard Willie say, "Stand by to engage the

enemy," and reached up to touch her picture with a gloved hand.

As the two ships came together the freighter was bathed in waves of electronic activity. Radar bounced off the hull, laser-based range-finders stabbed here and there, and a wide variety of sophisticated sensors sampled heat, radio transmissions, radiation levels, and more.

As the signals came in they were sorted, measured, and analyzed by the on-board tactical computer. Based on that analysis a full-spectrum electronic countermeasure strategy was created, tested through simulation, and readied for use.

So as the Confederation DE pulled up close, and ordered the freighter to open a lock prior to boarding, everything was ready to go. What followed was quick and lethal.

Willie gave the orders. "Power up, activate ECM, engage the enemy."

Confederation officers looked at each other in surprise as a heavy blanket of electronic interference blinded every one of their sensors. Their computers would sort it out, but that would take precious seconds.

None saw the huge hatches open along the freighter's port side, or the silent sparkle of the mini-guns, or the sequenced launch of sixteen heat-seeking missiles.

But they felt them as the high-explosive cannon shells detonated along the length of the DE's armored hull and the missiles exploded, some finding their way inside.

Screams filled the intercom and were abruptly cut off as suits lost pressure and their occupants died. Primaries were destroyed, secondaries came on-line, and computers fired weapons based on where the enemy should be if they hadn't changed course or speed.

The Confederation captain keyed her com tech. "Get a message off to Sector Three HQ: 'Engaged enemy. Revise former estimate to U.N. destroyer, or destroyer escort, disguised as a freighter. Out.' "

The com tech tapped some keys. A series of red lights came on. "Sorry, Captain, our primary, secondary, and tertiary antenna arrays were all destroyed during the first five seconds of battle."

The captain felt something cold drop into her stomach. So this was something more than a disguised raider, it was a carefully designed and executed trap. A Q-ship. There was nothing to do but fight her way out. Time to improve the odds. She chinned her intercom. "Launch fighters."

Willie felt the entire ship shudder as Guns launched another flight of missiles. Some were picked off by counter missiles but others made it through. They looked pretty as they blossomed and disappeared.

"I have two new bogies," Sparks said tonelessly, "and computer confirmation of two Brazilian-made Spector fighters, both armed with dual cannon and ship-to-ship missiles."

Willie fought to keep his voice calm. "Evasive action and engage."

Christoferson chose the second of three computer-generated maneuvers. The first was more aggressive but more dangerous as well. The ship rolled left, fell, and came back up on the far side of the DE. This had the effect of shielding the *Alice* from one fighter while giving Guns a crack at the other.

He fired a single ship-to-ship torpedo. It was larger than a regular missile, carried a huge warhead, and came equipped with a sophisticated artificial intelligence. The AI might or might not prove a match for the Fed pilot, but it would keep the sonovabitch busy for a while, and that would be plenty. Guns smiled as the torpedo locked on and the fighter maneuvered to evade it.

"Here comes number two," Sparks warned, but Christoferson didn't need the reminder, she could see the fighter in her heads-up display. A red delta coming her way, spitting metal death, trying to kill her.

Fear rolled over Christoferson like a wave, crushing her under its weight, turning her mind to mush. She tried to think, tried to connect thought with action, but nothing happened.

A voice came from a long way off, Willie's voice,

deep and calm. "Don't worry, Sparks, number two's been here before."

Christoferson remembered the way it was off Europa, shells hammering the length of the ship's hull, slicing through Bowers like a knife through butter. Well goddammit, they wouldn't do it again!

The fingers of Christoferson's left hand danced over the buttons in the armrest of her chair while her right hand moved the small joystick.

All over the ship the crew felt G's pile on, as *Alice* pulled up and curved right.

The fighter followed. It fired missiles.

Guns fired decoys. They blossomed orange as the missiles found them.

Christoferson put the ship into a left-hand turn. Guns fired every weapon on the port side. It was like a curtain of high-explosive death. The fighter ran into it and exploded.

Christoferson continued the turn, heading back toward the *Southern Cross*. "Nice shootin', Guns."

"You pick 'em and we'll pop 'em," Naisbit answered nonchalantly.

Christoferson scanned her HUD. It was empty of targets. "Hey, skipper, where's the other fighter? And the DE?"

"Destroyed," Willie said calmly. "The DE blew about thirty seconds after you engaged fighter number two, and fighter number one blew up a minute after that."

It took a moment for the news to sink in. Christoferson couldn't believe it. "You mean we won?"

"Yup," Willie said levelly. "We won."

With Willie in command, and Christoferson at the controls, Perko had been little more than a spectator during the battle. A cheer flooded the intercom and Perko chinned it off. He slumped back in his chair and let the tension drain from his body.

He'd survived, and done so without disgracing himself. Without peeing in his pants, throwing up, or turning into a screaming lunatic. All reasonable things to do, but frowned on by the navy. Good. Now he was blooded, a true warrior, a member of the elite group who'd seen the elephant.

And the funny part was that it didn't mean jack shit. There was no glory, no sense of accomplishment, no meaning. Just fear, death, and survival. It presented a problem. What the hell would he believe in now?

Days turned into weeks and the *Alice B*. took three more ships. Another DE, an assault boat, and a fool-hardy tug that detected their intermittent drive and tried to take them with a single auto-cannon and dual missile-launchers.

Reluctant to fight such a mismatched duel, Willie called upon the tug to surrender, but her commanding officer refused to listen and committed suicide by trying to ram. The tug had vanished in a flower of flame, so completely destroyed that the pieces didn't even register on the Q-ship's sensors.

By now the *Alice* was low on fuel, critically short of ordnance, and in need of maintenance. Though not critically damaged, the ship had taken quite a beating from her four opponents, and Shimmura needed dock-yard facilities in order to make repairs.

To the best of Willie's knowledge, none of the Con-federation ships encountered thus far had managed to get off a message that identified *Alice* as a Q-ship. So Willie was careful to maintain the appearance of a freighter on its rounds, and headed for a U.N. re-search station known as *Tito Two*. *Tito Two* was quite a way off the normal prewar trade routes, and because of that had escaped attack. Efforts were now under way to arm the habitat and turn it into a training base for commando operations. In the meantime it served as a Class IV maintenance facility and refueling stop for the Q-25 and a variety of other black-bag operations.

Even though Willie knew that *Tito Two* wouldn't have much to offer in the way of entertainment, he was looking forward to an opportunity to relax and escape the pressures of combat. As a result he had already started to slip, to let up on his constant vigilance, as they neared the habitat's location.

The radio call jerked him back to reality. It was preceded by a long blast of static.

"This is U.N. base *Tito Two*, repeat, *Tito Two*, calling all friendly forces. We are under attack, repeat, under attack by elements of a carrier task force. Estimate two cruisers, four destroyers, with carrier-based fighters as support. This is—"

"It's a recording," Sparks said. "The Feds are trying to jam but the station's communications computer is jumping from freq to freq on a random basis. They landed on one of the fourteen bands we're monitoring."

Willie grunted an acknowledgment. He pulled a keyboard over to his lap, tapped some keys, and watched output from the ship's navcomp flood the screen located next to his command chair.

The display showed a stylized sun, the planets, and a blinking light that represented *Alice*.

Willie tapped some more keys. A grid appeared showing the relative positions of *Alice* and *Tito Two* along with three approach vectors and numbers representing speed and distance.

If they chose approach vector one, and charged in at full speed, it would still take two hours to get there. And two hours was a long time. Too long in an age when major battles were fought in minutes or even seconds.

Willie shook his head sadly. "Sparks, boost and relay their message in case we have some friendly heavies lurking around the neighborhood. After that encode and squirt it to HQ. It won't help the poor bastards on *Tito Two*, but command needs to know."

Naisbit came on line. He sounded anxious. " 'Won't help the poor bastards?' What're you sayin', Skipper? We're goin' in, ain't we?"

Willie's throat felt dry. For the first time since leaving Big Red he regretted his open-intercom policy. The entire crew would be party to everything he said.

"No, Guns, I'm afraid we aren't. Even at full power it would take us two hours to get there. Add to that the fact that we'd be outnumbered, low on ammo, fuel, and everything else, and it becomes a suicide run. On top of that the very presence of a freighter armed as heavily as this one is would compromise the entire Q-ship program. Sorry, Guns, but that's the way things are."

Naisbit knew his voice was shaking, tried to control it, and failed. It was Tony all over again, men and women dying, abandoned by those they trusted.

"Sorry? Sorry? Listen, you chickenshit sonovabitch! Men and women are dying on that station! What is it with you, Lawson? Is it this ship? Is that what it is? You care more about this ship than the people on *Tito Two*?"

Christoferson said, "Now wait just a minute . . ." but Naisbit ignored her.

"How about you, Perko? Have you still got some balls? Or did you leave 'em on Big Red?"

Perko swiveled his chair around and looked at Willie. He found his commanding officer's face completely blank, as if to say, *make your decision—him or me.*

A host of thoughts swirled through Perko's mind. He thought about how tradition, and to some extent his training, called for a valiant effort in the face of overwhelming odds.

He thought about the undeniable fact that Willie was right, that a valiant effort would mean certain death, and do nothing to help the men and women of *Tito Two*.

And last but not least, he thought about the fact that he'd changed, and didn't give a shit about guts and glory anymore.

When Perko spoke his voice was cold as ice. "That's enough, Naisbit. Your comments have crossed the line into insubordination and are teetering on the edge of mutiny. One more word and I'll order you confined to quarters."

There was a long, hard silence, followed by a brittle *"Yes sir!"* from Naisbit, and click as he went off-com.

Perko locked eyes with Willie. He gave a slight shake of his head as if to say, *Ignore Naisbit, it doesn't mean a thing.*

Willie sighed, nodded an acknowledgment, and gave

Christoferson a new course. Then Willie got up, grabbed his helmet, and headed for his cabin.

Once there he lay down and tried to sleep. But tired as he was sleep wouldn't come. He tossed and turned, wondering if Naisbit had been right. Could they have saved *Tito Two?* Had he been too conservative? Too worried about his ship? Hours passed before sleep finally came.

The stars were a vast backdrop behind the tanker. The vessel was two miles long and consisted of a command module, four interconnected silver globes, and a set of drive units located at the stern. The side-thrusters mounted at regular intervals along the tubular side-rails were used for close-in maneuvers.

High-capacity hoses snaked between the tanker and the *Alice B.* as the freighter took on fuel. She had already loaded ammo and food from a small supply ship that was already on its way somewhere else.

Further out, dashing back and forth like a hunting dog searching for scent, a U.N. destroyer kept watch. The same destroyer that had brought Captain Forbush all the way from Big Red.

At the moment Forbush was something less than comfortable, floating in zero G inside the Q-ship's wardroom and trying to look as though he enjoyed it. Zero-G conditions were SOP for fueling, since any amount of spin would tangle the tanker's hoses.

Willie had been dealing with weightlessness for more than thirty years, but not so Forbush, who felt more than a little queasy. He tightened his grip on a handhold and used his other hand to wave off a bulb of coffee.

"No thanks, Willie, I had some before I came over." Forbush made a production of looking at his wrist comp. "Which reminds me, I'm due aboard the tin can in about fifteen minutes."

Willie managed to keep a straight face as he nodded. Christoferson was right, Forbush *did* look like "a flying whale."

Forbush cleared his throat and tried to ignore his

nausea long enough to force a smile. "Well, that pretty much wraps it up. You should feel very good. The mission has been a tremendous success, the Q-ship program is up and running, and the Feds still don't realize what we're up to."

"Yeah," Willie said dryly, "we're a real success all right. Tell that to the survivors of *Tito Two*. If you can find any."

Forbush felt himself drift slightly, and wished he'd accepted Willie's invitation to strap himself into a chair. The university might have been boring, but at least there was no danger of drifting around the faculty lounge.

"You've got to stop that nonsense, Willie. You made the right decision, and it will say so in my report to the Admiralty. There was nothing you or your ship could've done to save *Tito Two*. Sad but true. Are you sure you want to keep Naisbit aboard? I could take him with me and assign him to the base garbage scow."

Willie shook his head. "No, Guns deserves one more chance. If he blows that I'll strap his ass to a torpedo and send him in your direction."

Forbush laughed. "Well, have it your way. Help me find my way out of here and I'll leave you to it."

Pausing to let Forbush find handholds and maneuver his way around obstacles, the two men pulled themselves to the lock. The destroyer's gig waited on the other side.

Careful to grab a handhold with his left hand, Forbush held out his right. "We couldn't have a better Q-ship commander, Willie. Good luck, and good hunting."

Willie shook the other man's hand and let go as the hatch started to cycle closed. He liked Forbush, and meant it when he said, "Thank you, sir, have a good trip, and save me some of that Scotch! By the time this is over I'll need a drink!"

The closing hatch cut off Forbush's final words, but there was no mistaking the cheery wave or the fact that he forgot to hang, and hit the overhead with the top of his head.

* * *

The next eleven days seemed to drag by. Except for a couple of false alarms there was nothing to break the monotony of each watch. Just the never-ending hum-drum of shipboard life.

As time passed and the crew continued to live in their suits the air became fetid, the food tasted strange, and tempers grew short. Arguments started over inconsequential things, personal quirks began to wear, and conversation became little more than ritualized grunts.

So when the alarms went off Willie heaved a sigh of relief. Finally, something to do besides smell his own sweat. Unfortunately, the feeling was short-lived.

"We got trouble," Sparks said calmly. "*Big* trouble." She didn't have to say more. The pictures flooding the command module's screens were worth a thousand words. It was a ship, a *big* ship, six times the size of *Alice* and bristling with weapons. She was miles long and covered with a maze of weapons blisters, heat-exchangers, launch tubes, solar arrays, and more.

"What the hell *is* that?" Christoferson asked in amazement.

"And how the hell did it get so close without us knowing?" Willie added.

Perko looked up from a small screen. The ship's tac comp had compared the video to known hulls and come up with a match. "Well, I can answer the first question. *That* is the liner *Argentina*, now known as Confederation Commerce Raider AB-78."

"And *I* can answer the second question," Sparks added, "or I *think* I can. Their detectors are better than ours. *Much* better. They saw us before we saw them, positioned themselves along our projected course, and turned everything off. Drives, radios, everything."

"And not knowing they were around we walked straight into the trap," Willie finished. "Smart. Real smart."

"They're on the horn," Sparks said. "It's the usual 'kill power and prepare to be boarded' routine."

Willie's mind raced. This was the very situation he'd always feared. Trapped by a powerful opponent and unable to run. Should they fight, hoping to get lucky? Or pretend innocence and try to bullshit their way through?

Willie decided on the latter. He chinned the intercom. "Okay, now hear this. Secure the drives, seal the weapons sections, and prepare for company. We'll use boarding routines 'B' for bravo, I repeat, 'B' for bravo."

Boarding routine 'B' involved trying to pass *Alice* off as a tramp freighter of Panamanian registry by using a whole set of carefully prepared phony documents, computer records, and personal identities. But no matter how carefully prepared the backup materials were, their story was still paper-thin. What were they doing in that section of space? Where were they headed? Why? Willie would need answers to those questions and more.

It was a desperation-only option but Willie was desperate enough to use it, and didn't like the thought of surrender. Especially when all of them could be shot as spies.

All over the ship people raced to get out fake documents, activate phony logs, and dump incriminating evidence. Everywhere that is except the Fire Control Center, where Naisbit shook his head disapprovingly, released his harness, and headed for the weapons compartment number twelve. That's where he kept his club, his secret weapon, his equalizer.

Now was the time to get it out. It was too bad about Lawson, but the man was paralyzed by fear, and completely useless. Like the admiral who let Tony die. But that's what professionals are for, to step in when the chips are down and make the right decisions. And even more important, to avenge Tony's death.

Perko turned to Willie. He smiled wryly. "The Big Bad Wolf's at the door. Shall I let him in?"

Willie nodded. The raider had wasted little time launching a shuttle, chock-full of troops no doubt, which was now alongside. He gathered his faculties, plastered what he hoped was a silly smile on his face, and headed for the main lock.

The lock had already opened by the time Willie got

there. A squad of heavily armed marines spilled out
and threw him against the wall. They pushed him
around a little, frisked him for weapons, and fanned
out to search the rest of the ship.

Willie was still turning around when a Confederation officer appeared. She'd waited just inside the lock
until receiving an "all clear" from the marines.

The officer was short, middle-aged, and hard as
rock. Her eyes were like twin ferrets, darting here and
there looking for prey. She wore armor and a com set.
She spoke with a staccato bark, asking questions faster
than he could possibly answer them.

"What ship is this? Are you the commanding officer? Where are you headed?"

Willie forced himself to stay calm. He smiled ingra-
tiatingly. He answered her questions one at a time.

The ship was the *Maria*, registered in Panama. Yes,
he was the captain, and an underpaid one at that. As
for a destination, well that was in the hands of God,
and the commanding officer of Confederation Star
Base 73. He'd been ordered to go there and pick up a
cargo. Whatever it was, Willie hoped it wouldn't be
dangerous like the last time.

When he was all done the officer looked him in the
eye, lifted a well-plucked eyebrow, and said, "Captain, you are one lying sonovabitch. Let's see the rest
of your so-called freighter."

Naisbit swore as the case caught on the edge of the
hatch. Like all of the ship's four maintenance locks it
was too damn small. How the hell did the designers
expect someone to get tools or large parts out onto the
surface of the hull, anyway? Stupid, that's what it was.

Naisbit managed free the case and drag it clear.
Alice and the shuttle snuggled up alongside of her
were still spinning, so there was sufficient gravity to
walk around.

The naval officer checked to make sure the hatch
had sealed behind him and took a look at his target.

The *Argentina* was shaped like a huge cigar, long

and cylindrical, sunlight sliding over her surface as she rotated. Naisbit grinned. What a target!

It took him about three minutes to run a diagnostic routine on the power pack that was attached to his space suit, blast free of the light gravity surrounding *Alice*, and start the two-mile journey. In spite of its contents the case was light as a feather.

Perko gritted his teeth as the Confederation marines trashed his cabin. He sat next to his desk and watched as they ripped open his storage compartments, threw the contents on his bunk, and made jokes about whatever they found.

A corporal with the name MENDEZ stenciled on his breast-plate grunted something unintelligible, pointed to the drawers under Perko's bunk, and said something in Spanish.

A private pulled the first drawer out and emptied it onto the bunk.

Mendez plunged his hands into Perko's underwear, felt around, and withdrew a holo cube. He looked at the cube, looked at Perko, and shook his head sadly as if the XO had disappointed him somehow. There was nothing wrong with his English.

"Well, well. Since when do tramp freighters of Panamanian registry carry U.N. naval officers?"

Naisbit almost blew it. It takes practice to use a power pack effectively, and outside of the two mandatory drills a year he didn't get much. As a result the weapons officer came close to overshooting his target and heading for the sun. Fortunately he managed to kill power and get his feet down where they were supposed to be just in time.

Naisbit hit hard, absorbed most of the shock with bent knees, and looked for a place to hide. He didn't think the *Argentina*'s sensors would pick him up, but there was no way to be sure, and they might send marines out to look for him.

*   *   *

Perko did the only thing he could. He reached under his desk, broke the .9-mm automatic free of its magnet, and fired twice in quick succession. The first shot was a clean kill, hitting Mendez right between the eyes, but the second hit the private's shoulder, throwing him backward but failing to penetrate his armor.

The private hit the bulkhead, bounced off, and yelled obscenities as he brought the machine pistol upward.

Willie saw the Confederation officer's eyes widen as she heard something via her com set. Turning, she went for the handgun holstered under her left arm.

Not knowing what she'd heard, but fairly certain it was bad, Willie threw his arms around her and hugged. It wasn't very fancy but it did prevent the woman from pulling her gun.

The officer lunged upward, trying to hit Willie's chin with the top of her head. She was too short to make it work. Then the officer's head jerked sideways as Sparks shot her through the left ear.

Willie heard a buzzer go off as she slumped in his arms.

Naisbit swore softly as a pair of Confederation marines stalked by the entrance to his metal cave. The bastards *had* detected his arrival and sent some grunts to check it out. Oh well, if they were like most marines they'd assume the whole thing was a wild goose chase and call it off after ten or fifteen minutes.

The weapons officer looked around. His hiding place had been formed where a section of armored duct curved up and over the edge of a solar panel. It was as good a place as any. He opened the case and started the arming procedure.

There were two marines standing outside Shimmura's position when the "repel boarders" buzzer went off. He couldn't reach the weapon hidden just beyond the marines, so the engineering officer did the next best thing and triggered the armored hatch that sealed him inside his control cocoon during combat.

Fast though the hatch was, it wasn't fast enough. A marine fired. Her armor-piercing bullet went through Shimmura's space suit, through his shoulder, through a rack of electronics, and flattened itself against the hull metal beyond.

The impact of the bullet threw the engineer back into his seat. It felt wet inside his suit. Shim saw the picture of Susie that he'd taped above his controls and wondered if he'd ever see her again.

Perko and the Confederation marine squeezed their triggers at the same moment. The private's bullets hit the steel deck and ricocheted around the compartment like lead banshees. One creased the side of Perko's face as he squeezed the trigger and kept squeezing. The marine's face turned to red mush.

Willie straightened from laying the officer's body on the deck. There were two more dead marines as well, one killed by Christoferson and the other by Sparks. Willie turned to Christoferson, who had returned to her controls. "Status?"

"Perko had a close call but survived. He and some others are guarding the lock to prevent them from sending more marines through. Shimmura is wounded but managed to seal himself inside his control-escape module. There are two marines trapped in the drive room but the rest are dead."

Willie nodded as he strapped himself into the command chair. "Good. It could be worse. Send those marines a message by pumping the air out of the drive room. The can surrender now or later when their tanks run dry, whichever they prefer. After that let the shuttle roll up between us and the *Argentina*, blow the lock, and get us the hell out of here."

Christoferson's fingers were a blur of motion as they flew over the keys. Then she watched the screens, waited until the shuttle was in perfect position, and blew up the main lock.

The charges had been placed there as a last-ditch defense against boarders, but did a bang-up job of separating *Alice* from the shuttle as well. The smaller ship was literally hurled at the *Argentina*, sheltering *Alice* for a few precious seconds and giving them a better chance.

Willie scanned the screens as he activated the intercom. "Guns, give me full ECM, hot chaff, and anything else that might throw them off. Find something soft, everybody! Number Two, give me full military power. Let's get the hell out of here!"

Willie was pushed down into his seat as *Alice* took off and Naisbit's voice came over the radio. "Sorry I can't be there to follow those orders, Lawson, but you're good at running, so I'm sure you'll find a way. You'd better hurry up, though, cause the marines are hunting me down and they're getting damned close. I've got a backpack nuke here, and when this baby goes off, blammo! Everybody gets reamed. See you in hell, Lawson." And with that Naisbit pushed a button.

For a moment, seconds only, a brand-new sun graced the heavens, and the *Argentina* disappeared.

All the talking, all the reports were over, and there was nothing left to say. Willie looked at Forbush and hoisted a glass of the historian's whiskey.

Out there, beyond the rock and steel of Big Red, the *Alice* still lived. Not the woman who had died so many years ago, but the ship, and most of those who crewed her. Thanks to Christoferson she'd cleared the nuclear explosion and lived to fight another day.

Willie still felt sentimental about the *Alice B.* and hoped that she'd make it through the war, but if she didn't, well those were the breaks.

Perko was gone now, commanding another beat-up freighter called the Q-24, and on his way to the Admiralty only knew where. Meanwhile Christoferson had moved up to XO and seemed to be enjoying it. And Shimmura . . . well, his shoulder would recover but not his heart, for Susie had disappeared. At the moment the engineer was taking refuge in his work, dealing with things more predictable than emotions, and ignoring everything else.

So, Willie thought to himself, that leaves Forbush, myself, and the other twenty-seven billion people of earth, all making the same stupid mistakes our ancestors did, and surviving in spite of it.

Willie smiled across the table. "To us!" And both men downed their drinks.

Midgame

Having had three decades to build its military strength in the Jovian system, the United Nations was able to dominate the war for its first months. This advantage was reversed by the arrival of four Confederation carriers early in 2055. The Feds were quick to take advantage of their superior numbers and launched and declared a blockade of all U.N. traffic within the Jovian system. Taken as a whole, the U.N. colonies and research stations were capable of producing everything needed for minimum survival. Being at the far end of a four-month supply line, they had little choice. Unfortunately, no one produced everything it needed, or was capable of surviving for more than a few months in isolation.

As supplies dwindled, the U.N. commanders realized they would soon be forced to fight, flee to the asteroids, or be starved into submission. Not unexpectedly, they chose to fight. The result was called the Battle of the Three Orbits. The name was created by the propaganda department of the U.N., who scored their greatest success of the battle by announcing their "victory" eleven minutes before any of the Confederation Broadcast Networks did. Those who actually fought in the battle rarely knew the names of any of the actions they were in. When they did, they normally referred to them as "the one where Sam bought it" or "that godawful mess off Europa." Most wouldn't know what you were talking about if asked about the battle using that name. They certainly wouldn't know which of the thousands of orbits that were assumed by the hundreds of ships that fought each other over that three-day period you meant.

By whatever name, the battle proved that the destructive power of their weapons meant few ships would escape damage or destruction in any but the most lopsided combat. The Confederation theoretically won, having forced the U.N. survivors back to their bases. The fed ships themselves were, without exception, too badly damaged to allow them to use this temporary advantage.

The strategic result of the Battle of the Three Orbits was that both sides were left with so few functional combat ships that the blockade was effectively broken. In this way the battle was a U.N. victory. The attrition among the two fleet's experienced spacemen was even greater and had an even more significant effect. It took two years to train a pilot capable of fighting the U.N. Hawk or Fed Aguila fighters. For the first time since the Battle of Britain, the men became again more important than the machines they flew.

It was well over a year before reinforcements could be manufactured and hurried out to each side's asteroid bases for staging to the Jovian colonies. It was during this time that the converted merchant ships were to play their short role. Driven by frustration and necessity, a number of other unusual measures were attempted.

LOSS OF INNOCENCE

by Carol Castle

The U.N. Space Command Corvette smelled new, of oil and signal-absorber and hot protective coatings. The rush repairs were going well, thought Captain Garrison Cheevers, as he continued his inspection amid the noise of machinery and workmen torturing material with the sustained energy only possible in light gravity.

The shirt-sleeve walkway between fusion drive and bridge had been struck full-on, damaging but not putting out of action more vital areas. This new hardened walkway lacked the internal panels that had squared off the old, and reminded him of the burrow of a wild animal. Appropriate perhaps, since the U.N. had been on the run and looking for places to hide when the *Gallipoli* was forced to withdraw to the dockyards on Mars three months before.

Cheevers felt a visceral connection here that he hadn't been able to find on leave in Australia. Within days of being released from hospital in Sydney, the slow-moving, self-indulgent, civilian way of life had galled him, had led to quarrels and harsh words that couldn't be withdrawn. The only solution had been to leave.

He regretted causing his wife pain, but Meredy seemed like a wraith from a quieter, gentler age. Real life was only found in the Jupiter war zone.

There was much to avenge. When the surrender under a white flag of the Fed ship *Diablo* proved to be a ruse, he had lost good mates. Bushy Treadwell, whose inspired piloting had pulled the *Gallipoli* out of many a tight spot, he missed most of all.

Living on supplies looted from wrecked vessels, the *Diablo* called herself "corsair" but "pirate" was more to the point, he thought with bitterness. Cheevers's mouth hardened as he renewed his vow to keep a special lookout for the *Diablo*.

"Captain Cheevers, sir," called a young, spit-and-polish rating.

"Yes, and who might you be?" he answered loudly, over the din.

"Courier, sir. An official signal arrived from Admiral Snowden's office. I have a copy of your new orders."

"Already? The repairs are not yet completed."

"The Admiral is aware of that, sir, and instructed that key workmen should embark with the ship to complete repairs en route."

The courier handed Cheevers a sturdy, sealed envelope.

Cheevers suddenly appeared older than his thirty-five years. Once he had looked forward to having his own command, but the responsibility thrust on him when Captain Bengal had been killed on the bridge, along with Bushy and the navigator, had literally been a trial by fire. Limping back, with oxy and water down to critical levels, by the time the tender took the survivors aboard Cheevers's black hair was streaked with white, and deep crevices were carved into either side of his mouth. He wanted to get back, knew how badly the *Gallipoli* was needed, but still had strong and conflicting emotions.

He scrawled his signature in the courier's book and went to the privacy and quiet of the bridge to examine his orders. He slit the envelope and inserted the enclosed chip into the control center, which unscrambled the message and displayed it. He noted the usual U.N. Space Command logo, but was surprised to find a self-destroying message.

He read quickly, before each line vanished:

Dear Gary,
   I thought it best to add a note. These are strange and trying times, and in this drawn-out conflict I sup-

pose we must resort to new strategies. Even so, I warn you that you'll be surprised by the pilots assigned to the *Gallipoli*. They are civilians and must be assigned to quarters of their own (which should be completed soon if not already). Since they are not in the service they are not required to attend the Officer's Mess or participate in ship's activities, such as training, conditioning, etc. This does not bar them if they desire to take part. Do not let their young age, eighteen, deceive you. They have been training for this purpose more than ten years. For all our sakes, keep in mind the desperate shortage of trained pilots.

Your friend, Sam.

Cheevers wished that his old captain, now vice-admiral, had been less cryptic. What the bloody hell was Space Command doing to him? The message implied that the new pilots, whoever they were, would be virtually free agents. If SpacCom had planned to undermine the authority of a new captain, they couldn't have done a better job. He tried to restrain his anger as he scanned the official orders that now filled the screen:

Captain Garrison Cheevers of the *UNSS Gallipoli*:

On the 21st of August, 2056, you are instructed to embark at best speed on a mission of great importance. You are to proceed, using evasive maneuvers of your own design, to the vicinity of Callisto, Moon of Jupiter, and there to assist in the protection of vital United Nations mining colonies. At the appropriate time, the *Gallipoli* will guard a convoy of freighters on its return voyage.

Your crew will be replaced to the revised minimum strength of sixty-five. During the aproximately two-month journey out, training in the use of improved Extra-Vehicular Mobility Equipment and weapons should continue.

Among the crew are six pilots, two for each shift. You are instructed to keep detailed confidential records of every aspect of their activities that impinges on their fitness for their duties, for later evaluation.

Vice-Admiral Samuel H. Pennington., UNSC.

Cheevers was puzzled and dismayed. He did not fancy conducting an experiment during battle conditions, even if the admiral had dashed off a personal note. Who or what were these new pilots who were supposed to replace Bushy?

No time for speculation—now that it was official, time was at a premium. Cheevers went to work feverishly to prepare to get under way within twenty-four hours. He was all too aware that a favorite time for sneak attack by the Feds was an occasion like this, a time of confusion when a ship was being remanned and resupplied. And a neutral zone was no guarantee.

Without ceremony, the bridge bulkhead door opened and a girl stepped through. Cheevers opened his mouth to protest about proper procedure, but the words died unborn. The girl wore regulation navy-blue pull-ons, but on her they were provocative. Her blond hair was cut short yet only served to emphasize her femininity. She wore no makeup, but didn't need it to add to the rosiness of her upward-curving mouth, the lesser pink of her cheeks and earlobes, and the perfection of her lightly tanned complexion. Her eyes were deep-set and the lightest blue, and radiated innocence and good nature.

Cheevers's heart sank. This was a girl to confound men's minds, a girl men would put themselves at risk to protect, and end up fighting over. Whatever her role, she would be a disruptive influence.

But there was more. She stepped aside, and following her was another young woman cast from the same mold, and following her, yet another. Cheevers was aware that his mouth was still open, yet couldn't summon the presence of mind to regain his dignity. For the three were alike. Not just alike, but models off the same assembly line—identical.

Another figure entered. This was the male equivalent of the same model—compact build, moved well, entirely regulation—and impossible. Behind him another figure followed, and yet another, till six were lined up in front of him.

Now that all six were crowding his bridge, Cheevers

could see that the men were taller and heavier, and there were small differences between them all in height, even weight, millimeters difference in nose, in eyebrows, yet so little that the overall impression was one of sameness. Surprising too that in their features he found a haunting familiarity.

"Will somebody tell me what's what's going on here?" Cheevers demanded.

"We're your pilots, sir, for this voyage anyway, civilians attached to the Space Service," answered one of the girls.

"Civilians, that's all I need. What else are you, clones?"

"No!" she shot back, offended. "Not clones. Only brothers and sisters. Simple enough. It happens all the time."

"That's enough impertinence. It doesn't happen by sixes, not on this ship anyway. Who are you?"

"I'm Aurora, that's Venus and Star, and the boys are Sky, here, Sunny, and Mercury."

"None of the names is familiar. Why do I feel I've seen you somewhere before?"

"Our father was Wainright Caine."

"Caine, the explorer? Discovered the caverns under Olympus Mons, didn't he? Of course. His face was in the news for years. Whatever happened to him? I heard he'd been invalided out—mental troubles. . . . Sorry, I didn't mean to be insensitive. It's just that you, the six of you, are beyond my experience. I suppose I'm trying to fit you in somewhere."

"Not necessary, Captain. You'll find we do our job better than any singletons. We've been raised together and trained, you see, to act in concert."

"I'm not sure I like this."

"The war has been going on a long time. If you think you can find another half-dozen pilots at short notice, go ahead."

"Am I in your way?" asked Cheevers with sarcasm.

"We should settle in, if you want to leave today. Sky, you take first shift with me."

The tallest of the young men shrugged, slid into the

well-padded swivel chair, and began to examine the control helmet.

"Am I not to be consulted?"

"I don't mean to be disrespectful, Captain, but leave the piloting to us. We've been training for this for ten years and we're anxious to get at it."

"Don't any of the rest of you speak?"

"Of course we do," said Star, who was a little rounder and with a broader smile, "but generally we let Aurora be our spokesman. She does it so well." She giggled like any teenager. "At least she thinks she does."

"I don't mind telling you that I'm going to have a word with Space Command about this . . . situation."

"If you wish, Captain. Until then . . ." said Aurora as she settled into the command pilot's chair before the batteries of instruments surrounding the screens.

Cheevers had to settle for sending a message. Without incident, loading was completed and the *Gallipoli* was launched and under way. In space they were under rule-of-silence, and no communication, except for the most dire emergency, could be sent either way. However, as the days went by, piloting tasks appeared to be adequately handled.

Cheevers noted that the women dominated the men, and he was uneasy about the consequences. He consulted the ship's library and found a disk with a subheading on multiple births. He read that identical twins were always the same sex. This left his pilots as fraternal, or perhaps a double set of triplets?

Continuing on, he read that when twins were not separated at least part of the time, the girls often bossed the boys since they tended to develop earlier. Scanning quickly, he also found that multiple births became common with the advent of fertility drugs and egg implants. Since a portion of humanity had left the protection of Earth's ozone layer for space and was now subjected to radiation that damaged reproductive abilities, techniques for isolating eggs and sperm for later implanting, after selective fertilization, had been developed.

He squirmed uncomfortably. Meredy had wanted to

try just that, but he had refused. In his opinion, fighting a brushfire war that threatened to become a full-blown conflagration was no time to think of starting a family.

The disk explained a few things. Among the crew, though, there was grumbling and speculation that could lead to trouble. It was not totally without grounds. Crew and troopers alike lived near the outer hull, sleeping in bunks three-high and eating together in the common mess, separated only by sex. In contrast, the quarters designated for use by the pilots were in the center of the ship, the safest section, and were relatively spacious and comfortable. And coed. But Cheevers had his orders; it couldn't be helped.

He tried to think of a way to defuse the situation. At the same time he felt it right that the twins—properly sextuplets—were isolated from the others, not only because of their youth, but because of their innocence of any outside their circle. They seemed to live for each other and for their work. There was no denying they enjoyed piloting, and the more intricate the maneuvers the better they liked it. From shift to shift there was no disharmony, no lost data recorded where another would not think to look. They were efficient, no doubt of that.

Still, Cheevers felt uneasy, as if this were the calm before the storm. Sooner or later, trouble would come. Would it be from the enemy or from within the ship itself?

At the same time the sextuplets' energy, enthusiasm, and physical attractiveness made them appealing, especially Aurora. He had no trouble telling her apart, though he had to admit that having the roster handy helped with the rest. Aurora was more outward-looking—and she was not above flirting. He was used to being sought out by females aboard ship, and in the past having a traditional wife at home had helped avoid sexual entanglements. Now Meredy and Earth were very far away in both a physical and emotional sense and Aurora was near, oftener than could be accounted for by accident.

Cheevers caught as many of the training sessions as he could, and never missed conditioning. Neither did Aurora, though her brothers and sisters showed up only sporadically. As he watched Aurora's firm young body move gracefully through the exercises, always close by, he sometimes lost track of his own rhythm. Her interest in him was transparent, but she was so young, so innocent of the possible consequence of an affair with a man much older than herself that he didn't take it seriously.

EVA training went on daily. Though it was neither practical nor safe to stop the ship's rotation to go walk about in space, the troopers had practiced "outback" off Mars. The DI, a small man with an amazingly big voice, kept them sharp by having them go over EVA procedures and race into the cumbersome "suits" that would transform them into mini-ships when the need arose.

Eight days out, Cheevers found time to join in. Before beginning, the DI took him aside. Grinning broadly he boomed, "These new suits are apples, Captain! They've been redesigned, see, with improved insulation and heat-emission spreaders."

"They're already radar nonreflective. That sounds good."

"Too right. The insulation is biological, the manual don't say what kind, and it don't bear thinking about. Anyway, infrared isn't supposed to be able to pick 'em up, but some of the blokes think they're too hot."

"Bloody hell, another experiment," said Cheevers in exasperation, then, realizing they were being watched, went on more calmly, "I've read about developments in bio-equipment amalgams, and I'm sure we wouldn't have been sent EVA equipment unless it had been well tested, Sergeant."

"Yes, sir!" said the noncom with a booming certainty Cheevers felt was for the troopers' benefit. It certainly didn't do his ears any good. However, the drill went well.

It did not escape Cheevers's attention that Aurora had managed to find a suit small enough to join in too.

The captain was expected to attend the once-weekly dance in the cramped space created when mess tables were folded away and a movable wall opened up to include the training area. Cheevers usually looked forward to it, aware that trips beyond the twenty-eight-day barrier created stresses that had to be eased, even among the most experienced of crews. Besides, any physical activity in the close confines of the ship was welcome.

Tonight, "Wires," the electrician's mate, was playing an electronic flute, piping tunes that were disquieting for Cheevers, evoking as they did club evenings at home in Medam Valley. The officers had pooled the daily tot of rum allotted to every service member and made a punch out of it that climbed the walls of the bowl in the center of the table.

Cheevers only became aware of Aurora when she leaned enticingly over the table and murmured, "Ladies choice."

"How could I refuse?" Only after he took her in his arms did he realize, "This is new. I've never danced to this one before."

"No worries. Hold on tight and do what I do."

And it wasn't difficult, a matter of releasing himself to the spell cast by the beat. When he pulled her tighter she did not protest. *She's too young*, he thought again, then realized he had been the same age when he first met Meredy. *Not unreasonable*, he conceded.

The combination of music and Aurora was intoxicating, and he couldn't remember enjoying an evening more. Certainty not for a very long time. He could feel her heat entering his body, displacing bleak loneliness, grief, and hatred of the *Diablo* that had festered there so long. Her eyes were the color of a hazy summer sky, and her skin that of ripening wheat. He became aware of his maleness and felt emotions he'd thought he'd a left million klicks behind.

Almost against his will, he heard himself saying it was too noisy for them to talk here, and would she like to come to his cabin for a "euphemistic" drink.

Her blue eyes opened wide, she smiled impishly and

declared, "My favorite drink. I've been wondering if you'd ever ask."

She was everything he'd hoped, her breasts full buds, yielding and fresh, and she filled his senses with an intensity of pleasure he'd all but forgotten. Afterward, as they lay contented in each other's arms, he asked about her life before she came to the *Gallipolo*.

"Not a lot to tell, really," she answered, cuddling close in the single bunk. "We led rather a sheltered life. We were a test-tube pregnancy, you probably guessed that. Not unusual among Space Service families, with radiation and such. Mom and Dad decided they didn't want to go through all that nonsense again, so when they learned it would be a multiple birth, they were happy. Mom decided to forget about numbers and let whatever would be, be."

"She was a brave lady," he said, stroking the smooth, silky skin of her back.

"I guess. I wish I'd known her. She didn't live long. After Mom died, Dad stayed home. He had us to raise. His old mates in Space Command talked him into training us as pilots. He knew they would be desperately needed and he would have given a lot to be one himself, but his health wasn't the best, mental or otherwise. He never was the same after coming out of those caves on Mars, you know.

"Anyway, Space Command set up special classes for us, starting when we were eight. It wasn't bad—better than regular school—and we went home weekends, except when Dad was in hospital.

"Space Command has the idea that we're perfectly compatible, the ideal piloting team. If they only knew." She chuckled ruefully.

"But you are the perfect team. Pilots we've had before were always in each other's way. Bushy had a hell of a job trying to keep the team in line. You always seem to know what the other is going to do."

"Well . . . it may seem that way. But how can that be true when half the time even I don't know what I'm going to do next?" She smiled and began to stroke his chest in small circles, till she found the patch of newly healed skin, now mostly covered by growing hair.

"Ooh, I don't like scars. You're dead good-looking but for that."

"I didn't like being wounded much myself, and I'd rather be lucky than good-looking."

"Too right. Sorry, about the scar. It's just that I have a thing about sickness. I guess it's because Dad was sick so much."

"Well, I'm fine, and even I can predict what you're going to be doing for the next little while," he told her, and pressed his mouth against hers again.

At 0800 hours, an enemy scout ship was detected by the *Gallipoli*. The auto-cannon homed in and boomed in response, without measurable success. Cheevers ordered the *Gallipoli* to pursue, but the smaller, faster ship ducked back into the asteroid belt where it was easy to hide and impossible to catch. Cheevers cursed in frustration. The tension level increased now that the ship's company knew they were a target on an unfriendly screen somewhere.

Aurora came to his cabin that night. Never having been in battle, she was innocent of the possible consequences of being sighted and he did not talk about it, or anything much, just accepted the joy she brought.

After she left to go on duty, he ran holos of Meredy for the first time since he'd left Earth. With her shiny, long black hair and slim figure, she was still a good-looking woman. He wondered if she'd found a new bloke yet and felt a stab of jealousy he recognized as irrational.

He knew he'd let her down, leaving suddenly as he had. He just couldn't take the ignorant questions of civilians who didn't even know what quadrant the most important battle in space had taken place in. Or what the casualties had been. And didn't care to know. All anyone wanted to say was that Australia shouldn't be fighting way out here, despite the shortage of raw materials.

The crisis had come at the ranch, a few days after he'd been released from hospital. While he was trying to read between the lines of the latest propaganda about the war, Meredy was rattling on about the low price of wool. Didn't she realize their neighbors and friends were out here fighting for their lives? The quarrel that followed had come so close to violence that he'd requested immediate reassignment. It had been granted.

With a rush of guilt he wondered what she was doing now at the ranch, but try as he would he couldn't make her seem real. The Jupiter War—and Aurora— were the reality here.

As days went by, he tried not to be too obvious in watching Aurora on the bridge. Her distant manner toward him did not seem to have changed. Towards Sky, her usual copilot, she was as straightforward and natural as usual.

Some of the speculation by the crew was vicious. He was informed that graffiti with jokes about "sex-tuplets" had been scrawled on their cabin door more than once. It couldn't be true—not of Aurora. The other twins seemed to want to associate only with each other, not liking or trusting anyone outside their special bond— perhaps—but wondering about it was fruitless. He would have it out with Aurora the next time they were alone.

They were nearing the far boundary of the asteroid belt and attack would soon be an ever-present danger. Perversely, he welcomed the idea, hoping for the chance to engage the *Diablo*, now that they were in her favorite hunting grounds. He ordered training intensified, pushing hard, but the men no more than himself. If they did meet the so-called corsair, he was determined the outcome this time would be different.

The DI was pleased when he joined in EVA drill after several days' absence. His presence motivated the troopers, who were frankly bored by hundreds of repetitions. Feeling the competion, Cheevers buckled into the seventeen parts of his EVA suit in jig time, and was tested for seal by his dresser. A rap on his helmet told him the first seal had been good, and a single digit held up that he was first to do so. He swiveled the helmet around and saw a few more taps, indicating some of the troopers were not far behind. He was about to switch on his mike and blast the hindmost when the warning claxon sounded. Immediately after, an explosion ripped the hull open as if it had been made of foil.

Sudden decompression propelled him into space, and he narrowly missed tearing his suit on twisted shards of glowing metal. He must have lost consciousness for a time, but when he again became aware he was tumbling, head over heels. He felt nauseated and his head ached unmercifully. For a moment he panicked and, desperate to stop the vertigo, reached for maneuvering unit controls. Then his training clicked in. Instead, he picked a reference point and concentrated on it each time round to orient himself.

An advantage of this runaway somersaulting was a sphere of vision, and he was able to see his ship as it disappeared behind an asteroid. Good, the first strike had not been successful.

Next time round he saw the enemy ship, coming closer. He was almost in line with Jupiter—its size here was as almost as large as Sol, and the globe made a good reference point. Once he was able to concentrate on the glowing globe, and relegate all else to the peripheral, he felt less dizzy.

He became aware of other EVA suits not far away. Some were moving under power. Others obviously had never achieved seal, or their suits had been holed. Explosive decompression wasn't pretty; he noticed splashes on his suit and anger gave him renewed purpose.

As he tumbled closer, he caught a flash of red on the hull. It had been a red devil, he would bet his life on it. A fierce hunger for revenge seized him: for Bushy, for the little DI with the big voice who wouldn't have had a chance, and for all the others.

The headache was still there, but he pushed it to the back of his consciousness. He saw one of his troopers run his M18 through most of its clip before being blasted by the *Diablo*. Cheevers had to stifle his impulse to fire wildly too.

Another trooper turned on his jets in a desperate attempt to escape. The *Diablo* finished off the helpless man without mercy. Cheevers noted that suits obviously holed or not moving were not touched. The notion came to him unbidden that if he stayed still, maybe he would get out of this. He stifled it as inappropriate, but used the idea it brought him.

Moving imperceptibly, feigning death, he applied a small blast of nitrogen on the left side to swing him fractionally right, on course for the *Diablo*. He knew his suit was nonreflective for radar, and it was claimed that infrared sensors wouldn't pick it up. This wouldn't take long; he keyed the spreader.

Another suit moved, feebly and without threat, and was blasted. Any compunction Cheevers had about trying to spare the *Diablo*'s crew died with him.

He was now closing fast with the corsair. He knew it would be battle-hardened, but there were weak spots in any ship that could be exploited. The trick was to find one before he became a target himself. Cheevers's tumble was bringing him close to the mirrors that were the eyes of the battle system of the attacker. If the optics could be put out of action long enough . . . His hand moved in slow motion toward the controls of the built-in M18. To aim it would be the thing—even with laser aid it wouldn't be easy, with this damned tumble.

He suddenly felt he was going to throw up. This had to be close enough. He aimed, locked on the laser beam, and fired off the whole clip. The next tumble revealed the port mirror had been crazed. He could not restrain his exultation, and yelled in triumph. The *Diablo*, effectively blinded on one side and with radar and infrared ineffective, now maneuvered to "look" from the other side. As it swung, shooting wildly, he reloaded with one hand in less than five seconds, grateful for the first time that the DI had made him practice it a hundred times.

There was time to bring his attitude to level while the ship swung to find him. He aimed a stream of projectiles at the starboard mirror while the angle was still sharp, and whooped crazily when it disintegrated.

The only place they couldn't hit him was against their own hull and he jetted directly for the corsair. The airlock would be secured, but not for nothing was the N18 called "the can opener". Now he could see the red devil clearly above the name DIABLO. He fired a full clip at the seam.

The airlock door blasted outward in lethal shards. The debris included pieces of suits, spouting red crystals. Cheevers realized the *Diablo* had been about to release troopers; he'd been just in time. Choosing the angle carefully to avoid ricochet, he loosed another stream of fire. Within seconds, the inner hatch was breached.

There was a violent explosion of air followed by debris, fittings, and men. He reloaded while waiting for the pressure to reach equilibrium, then dove in the opening and loosed another stream of fire. Damage was not enough. He would settle for no less than total destruction.

He unclipped his only stick of grenades, pressed it to the inner bulkhead, magnetized and activated it, and set it for minimum time till detonation. He expected the ship would contain much of the high-energy blast, but there were only seconds to try to get out of range. At this point, that was less important than destroying the wrecker *Diablo*.

Cheevers hot-streamed it out of there, holding his jets wide open till the tank emptied, but flying debris caught him anyway.

When he again became aware blood was trickling from his ears, and his head felt as though he'd been fighting a title bout. Pieces of the corsair were still spreading out from the point of explosion, and would for hundreds of klicks. Never again would the *Diablo* prey on unsuspecting U.N. vessels. An old weight lifted from his shoulders never to return, whatever happened now.

Jupiter hung before him, swirling as it had for aeons, standing out against a lacework of stars. It seemed to pulse, one moment small and bright, the next swelling to an all-encompassing globe with an angry red oozing wound. Once Jupiter had been considered the supreme God; it had certainly influenced his life. Aurora's smooth face, the shade of rich cream, swam before him. Then the crude graffiti scrawled on her door became superimposed over her even features.

Bland female tones startled him. Coming from his speaker, the suit's voice announced. "Ninety minutes of breathable air remaining."

So little time? The voice replacing the warning beep was new. Was it an improvement, or did it add to the ultimate loneliness of space?

He tried to read the time, but his eyes wouldn't focus and he wished the voice would give more information.

He couldn't wait for it, no time to waste. The *Gallipoli* had to be signaled, and quickly—if it still existed. He forced stiff arms and legs to move and tried to recall procedure, his bruised brain resisting, R & R would come later, he promised himself.

The suit's communicator—he reached for the "on" button and pushed it, but instead of the buzz of voices and sputter of activity from Jupiter there was only silence. He pushed "off" then "on" several times without result. It was dead, and without outside help there was no way to repair it. He felt a moment of panic, but this only sharpened his wits and, with it, his determination to get through this.

Without emotion, the suit announced. "Eighty-five minutes left." He wished the voice could be more helpful. The beacon. There was still the beacon to signal his position. Over and over he tried to activate it but there was no green light, not even a red. Nothing. Flying debris must have finished it. What else had been damaged?

"Eighty minutes left." Was the damn machine enjoying this countdown? He felt unusually hot and it made his splitting head feel worse. It was difficult to concentrate but he had to think of something else to try. The fact that he was alive proved the inner suit had not been holed, but even the EVA suit's being nonreflective to radar was a liability now.

"Seventy-five minutes to critical. Take action to return to ship." He cursed the calm, unfeeling voice. Sweat began to drip into his eyes, and stung painfully. He withdrew a hand from its gauntlet to wipe the sweat away. Again he tried communicator and beacon, without success. In spite of the danger, thirst became all important. He reached for and found the spout and sucked water greedily. Even it was warm. Between his aching head and the heat, it was all but impossible to think clearly.

"Seventy minutes. Activate beacon for pickup."

"What do you think I've been trying to do? Useless bloody machine!"

Hot, much too hot. He wiped his eyes again and checked the interior temperature gauge. Both it and his helmet visor had fogged over, though it was not supposed to be possible. He wiped them off and was alarmed to see that, in the absolute zero of space, his internal suit temperature had reached red. While he tried, unsuccessfully, to read the dial, the needle moved further into the red.

"Sixty-five minutes. It is critical to take action to return to ship." He located the speaker and pounded the useless, nagging voice to silence. Then he remembered.

He turned off the infrared baffle. He watched a stream of moist, hot particles puff into space and was immediately cooler. His spirits rose and for the first time he knew hope.

When the *Gallipoli* picked him up, the breathable air gauge stood at zero. Rough hands tore open the EVA suit. In spite of the thirty-minute safety margin, his suit air smelled like the end of an exhaust pipe.

Oxygen through a face mask smelled sweet and rich. His first words were to ask about the condition of the ship and crew, but the female medical officer, chunky and competent, only answered, "Everything's in hand, Captain. You've done more than your job, now let us do ours." After a quick once-over she declared him dehydrated and concussed, and ordered him taken to sick bay for further tests. His protests were answered with a stinging injection.

Aurora awaited him in a too-bright cubicle that smelled of antiseptic. When they rolled him in on a gurney, bloody and soaked with sweat, she turned away.

"No worries," he tried to reassure her. "I just need to clean up and get some rest. In a few days, I'll be fit again."

When she turned to face him, he was surprised to see that she was angry. Her cheeks were two red spots in a paper-white face. "I was so afraid," she accused, "I realized I've never really known fear before." She wiped eyes suddenly wet. "I can't take any more of it. I'm glad you're all right, but it's over between us, from this moment."

"Wait a minute. You can't blame me for being mortal. So you discovered people can die, even people you love. You had to learn that," he slurred, becoming uncontrollably sleepy.

"I was paralyzed with fear. I had to leave my post and couldn't do anything but cry. I should have known better, they tried to tell me what it would be like to love a singleton. I guess I didn't really believe that anything could happen to the great Garrison Cheevers until these last few hours. I can't go through that again. I'm going back where I belong. Sky has been more than patient."

So what he suspected all along was true. He was assaulted by confused images of Aurora and Sky—always off duty at the same time—in each other's arms. "Nobody is immortal, he can die too," he said cruelly.

"Perhaps, but in that case, I'll still have two more lovers."

Whatever survived of Cheever's innocence bled away then, in the implacability of her clear blue eyes. None too soon the drug administered by the MO took full effect and consciousness darkened into troubled sleep.

*   *   *

Optimism aside, Cheevers spent an uncomfortable two weeks in sick bay. His misery was such that he did not complain when the MO insisted on bed rest and drugs to keep the persistent headaches at bay.

In lucid moments between bouts he tried to think of good times, and came to realize that those times were inexorably bound up with—home. And Meredy. Meredy, bent over their big gelding, riding like the wind. Meredy, washing her lustrous black hair. Meredy feeding a lost baby roo with a velvety coat. Meredy—waiting by his hospital bed in Sydney.

Unbidden came thoughts about Wainwright Caine, who'd had his brains scrambled in the caves under Olympus Mons. He had tried to do right by his kids, but between intervals in hospital and the Space Service's isolating them for their own purpose, he hadn't been able to. Even when SpaCom had realized it was going wrong, they hadn't drawn back. Neither was Cheevers proud of his part in the mess.

He decided that from now on things were going to be different. Civilians or not, he was captain of this ship. The sextuplets—he winced at the word—were going to be separated, and if and when they got back he'd do his damnedest to see they got the therapy they needed. The Space Service owed Wainwright Caine that much, at the least. And he owed Aurora the chance of a normal life.

On the fifteenth day of September Cheevers woke for the first time, fully conscious and free of pain. He looked at a watch that showed time and date in a half dozen places, and realized with a pang that it was springtime in Australia. The grass would be greening and the creek running—at home. Suddenly there was a lump in his throat and a pain in the pit of his stomach that had nothing to do with his injuries.

Surely it wasn't too late to start over. Perhaps if they had a baby—other Space Service couples had made use of medical science. No multiple births though. Definitely not.

He wondered whether Meredy could ever understand, much less forgive him. He had to find out if he had a marriage to go back to. And had Meredy been able to keep up the ranch? Eight hundred sheep weren't much compared with the big outfits, but it was a great deal of work and responsibility. When he began to wonder about the price of wool he knew that, even a half billion klicks out, he had come home at last.

They were in the war zone now; a relayed transmission burst would not give away positions the enemy already knew, and in any case Callisto Command must be notified of their arrival coordinates. It was time the captain was back at his post.

Without waiting for the MO, he dressed quickly in clothes that were roomier than before. Making good use of the walls, he went to his cabin and folded down the desk unit. He keyed open a drawer and took out a small box he had not opened since the *Gallipoli* had embarked for Callisto. Inside lay the gold pen Meredy had given him on his graduation from the U.N. Space Academy. He ran his fingertips slowly over the engraved message on the side. It read: "I'll love you always."

With trembling hands he began to write. Considering the double time delay, the answer arrived sooner than he'd hoped.

The words were the same as those on the pen.

Not Suited for Combat

The "combat space suit" was one of those strange terms, an *oxymoron*. This means it was a self-contradictory phrase, the most quoted example of this being the much maligned "military intelligence." Virtually everywhere, but on Earth itself in the Solar System itself, had a terminally hostile environment. Any space suit was a container, in which was maintained a complete artificial environment that closely simulated that of Earth. Given the number of factors this involved, such as fresh air, temperature, pressure, moisture, waste disposal, and the like, the space suit the was a complicated and sensitive mechanism. By way of contrast, combat during the Jupiter War was hard on everything involved: men and equipment. To wear a space suit in combat was the equivalent of counting on a paper bag to keep you dry while scuba-diving: there are going to be problems. There were just too many things that could be damaged or break, with fatal consequences.

Even when something didn't kill you, a space suit capable of extended use on any of the Jovian moons was cumbersome and uncomfortable. From a military viewpoint the space suit had all the disadvantages of a tank, but none of the advantages. Wearing a space suit limited peripheral vision. It also prevented sighting equipment from being placed too close to the operator's eye. A Jupiter War space suit also was an *active* machine. It had to constantly perform a number of functions. This means that every suit had an ever-present electronic and heat signature, and it was made of highly refined metal. All of these factors made any suit comparatively easy to detect. There was very little that could be done about it. The shielding needed to eliminate these signals would have made movement impossible. A space suit was also much too small to have built-in ECM. Finally, the weight of the oxygen and suit components was not small. Even in a low-gravity environment, fighting the inertia of two hundred kilos of suit was a strain. Hurrying in the cumbersome, stiff suits was so awkward as to appear almost comical. Even beyond its vulnerability to damage, and the almost always fatal consequences of suit failure, the space suit simply made it hard to fight. That the marines and special units from both sides were able to mount numerous "land" actions using suit-clad forces is a tribute to human ingenuity and perseverance.

The Mark Six, Interstel Combat Suit worn by U.N. marines was a marvel of miniaturization and dependability by that era's standards. However, not among the twenty-first century's accomplishments was the development of an air-purifier capable of removing body odors from a space suit during extended wear. It was also a myth that after a certain point the wearer ceased to be aware of the stink this created. Eventually most marines simply learned to tolerate it. Nor was there any modification possible in the basic design that could prevent the chafing that occurred under the arms and between the user's legs. Finally, being in a space suit for days at a time meant that those wastes exuded by the skin were trapped against that same skin. This inevitably multiplied the odor problem—and *itched*, a torment complicated by the wearer's total inability to scratch.

ON THIN ICE

by S. N. Lewitt

A whole detachment of Confederate marines destroyed by the closet monster. No way to put that in a report, no way to make it make sense. And we do like to make sense. History is a science, after all, and military history is the core of the discipline.

There are the stories, of course. The ghost ships and the shepherds over the English Channel during the World Wars, the bogeymen in the jungles and the ancient gods interfering in the wars of men. And everyone laughs. So how can you explain Io? Somehow, I don't think the Archives Command is going to accept nightmares. And that leaves me no choice but to commend Spec. 2 James Llewelyn Reed, the stupidest man ever to wear the uniform, for the Order of St. Michael. And that hurts.

History is going to judge us, in the end. And I intend to go down in it, if for nothing else than for proving that it takes more than logic and firepower to win a war. Vindication. McAllister's resignation would be nice, too, but that counts for less. It is worth the weeks, months sitting on the ice, waiting. Ready. Because it might have been luck before, or Jimmy's sheer stupidity, but the next time proves me out. Once could be ignored. But there isn't going to be any once about it, and that's where my brilliance shines.

McAllister is wrong. A woman is perfectly capable of strategy. He has forgotten Jean d'Arc and Isabelle D'Este and Caterina Sforza, just to name a few. And he had forgotten the praying mantis and the spider. But he isn't going to forget me, ever. And that will be a perfect and fitting revenge.

The Confederates did everything exactly right. Selected a site next to the ice field, but under the cover and on solid footing. Set up perimeter according to Berante's outline before they erected the camp. Food and battery packs stored well to center, heavy equipment facing outward and around, good defense. Classic. Perfect. Any instructor on the general staff of either side would have given their commanding officer (had to be some green lieutenant) an A. Except in my class.

Of course, being Confederate, no chance he or she ever took my course. Not that it was popular, at least not with the higher-ups, who managed to remove it from the curriculum and me from the faculty. So far as they were concerned I taught ancient history, since bypassed by the wonders of technological improvements on firepower. I should have been teaching what would have happened if there had been air support at Thermopopylae, I guess, or Sitting Bull's nuclear strategy. So they put me on ice. I'd heard that joke once too often, and this time it was unfortunately true.

How the Confederates ever heard of the dump here, out back of Io, I don't know. Most of our own Command hasn't heard of it and doesn't have the faintest idea of what we've got down here. Most of them probably don't even know that more than one bush-runner cached the goods here and then went on. Or got caught in a lava flow and disappeared under the crust. The dark side of Io (which isn't dark at all, just deprived of the prime view of Jupiter) isn't exactly your prime tourist spot.

Frankly, I was amazed that they set down decently at all. There are thin spots in the ice, places where the magma splits the surface and wells up smoking like a scene from Baptist Hell. The low flats, for example, are always breaking and reforming, crusting over with a brittle shell that has threatened me more than once.

Or maybe they didn't know it was here at all, which, given current policy, seems about as logical as anything else. They just settled down to steal a little ice—plenty of hydrogen going to waste out here and no one shooting at you like you were trying to net it up from old granddad Jupiter itself. Plenty of oxygen, too, and let's not forget the pure bravado of setting down on some patch of dirt the enemy owns, be it in name only.

Name, that is, and me and Jimmy Reed, my inventory clerk.

And we were sitting pretty. The cache had an underground fortified "living area" that mainly consisted of control panels, instant rations, and a chemical head. The converters managed to use the hydrogen and oxygen frozen on the surface to supply my needs without need for additional support, and the geothermal batteries were pumping more juice than three of me could need.

Besides which, they weren't looking for us. I could see that from the way they set their camp. A few quick jet-over patrols to make sure the terrain was suitable, maybe mark our earlier attempts, but nothing like a regular search mission, let alone a serious attack. No, those boys back home must have figured this to be virgin territory. Sort of like the old time cowboys did. Turnerism and the expansion of the West. My research didn't exactly agree with that point of view.

"What are we going to do, boss?" Jimmy asked. Jimmy didn't know squat about Turner or guerrilla warfare or even how to go interactive with the one radio cannon (small gauge) we hadn't cannibalized yet.

"Well," I told him, "I don't really know. Naturally I would prefer a friendly chat, some coffee cake, maybe a couple of hands of bridge, that kind of thing. Just like the faculty lounge at the Staff Training College. But I have the oddest suspicion that the present company might not be exactly neighborly, seeing as how they are all loaded with firepower and keep their blast-shields lowered. You know, it looks as if they think we're about to unload a few megatons out of pure boredom."

Jimmy blinked. "But we don't have a few megatons, boss. Want me to shoot out their jetpacks?"

And the history books say that we were the aggressors. Now I ask you, isn't it simple, when someone shows up on your doorstep and points a gun in your face you don't exactly feel like inviting them in and making them tea. Admittedly, invaders get a touch paranoid, but then perhaps they have every reason to. And even in what looks like virgin space, territory unmarked by human feet, there is always the sense that something is lurking. The closet monster has never really been defeated.

Which is to say, there were a whole lot of them and two of us. Pity they were so outmanned. I mean, if there had been a few more of us then we would have had a reasonable-sized camp that could be identified from a flyby. In that case the only options would have been pass or slug it out.

Slug it out with brute force, being the preferred strategy of rigid thinking, has always baffled me. The British wore red coats and marched in straight lines. They still teach recruits to march in straight lines. Even when it'll kill them. And it invariably does. So I watched as the young lieutenant set up guard shifts and perimeter patrols, lay out hot mines, and generally do all the correct and approved things. Pretty soon, I'd bet, they'll have the infrared scanners up. Not that I was worried. There's enough insulation in the bunker to convince a polar bear this was cold. And we were deep enough that against the background of the inner layers themselves we wouldn't show up at all. Even the geothermal batteries were passive, charging off the excesses of Io in formation.

The only real danger at the moment was that Jimmy would take those damned training tapes too seriously and go out and try to play hero. That was probably the worst part of the job. It's one thing to get me away from any career path, away from anyone who would listen to strategy that could pay off. But to stick me with a half-idiot like Jimmy was worse than loneliness. The boy was unteachable.

And I had tried. Believe me, I had done everything possible to instruct him in the finer points of military history, chess, even his own job. He was hopeless. He had been sent because it was the only place he couldn't do any damage, I suppose, but there was the added fillip that he infuriated me. Constantly. This time I sent him off to catalog our weapons store, which sounded like a real job and kept him out of my line of fire before I sent him into the enemy's.

Oh, I forgot to mention Jimmy's one redeeming quality. He could shoot anything at all. Deadeye, sharpshooter—an anachronism in modern warfare just like everything else. He enjoyed going out in a softsuit and shooting used heating trays from the ration tins across the flats. And he hit them dead on more often than not. Well, I had wondered how the stupid survived to reproduce and here was a prime example. The thing of it was, if Jimmy said he could shoot out the jetpacks I was perfectly prepared to believe that he could. And he'd enjoy doing it, too. Not that that would help in our current dilemma.

I wasn't exactly thrilled with the situation. I wouldn't be surprised if one of my old colleagues, one of the ones who sat in on the hearings when I was canned, had planted a leak to a double agent. Or let it out that there was nothing at all on the backside of Io, practically issuing a written invitation. I could easily believe that one of them had set me up. McAllister in particular, I suspected. McAllister never forgave me for flunking him, and went on to publish six papers disputing claims of guerrilla warfare against conventional tactics.

Of course, it's as easy to believe that the whole thing was simply the fault of stupidity, too. McAllister is just the type to say that there aren't any outposts on the backside of Io at some cocktail party because ignorance and martinis are an excellent match. Security sucks on the cocktail circuit.

However, McAllister or no, done was done and I was stuck. Much as I hated to admit it, there was a certain amount of time constraint. Not that my posting was due up anytime soon, but we were due to have another inspection run from the quartermaster general. Maybe this time someone could even use the ammunition stockpiled under the bunker, along with a carton of replacement II-M37 chips (now superseded by the II-RL1, which has twice the redundancy because it has twice the trouble), and thirty-seven tonnes of freeze-dried brussels sprouts. Not to mention the basic hydrogen and oxygen mined and ready for shipment, or the additional smart-seekers that lock navigation on to an enemy radar reading. Those might actually be of some use.

Still, the quartermaster general was due at the end of the week, the first interesting thing to happen since the volcano erupted and those geologists from Resource Planning came out on a boondoggle. Maybe I could let the inspection team get taken prisoner. Might serve them right, too, for being on McAllister's side when I got booted. But these probably weren't the same guys, and I could at least see their point. Guerrilla warfare does tend to rely heavily on what is at hand, and doesn't have a well-developed theory of supply.

I pulled the readout on my screens. The ice-field was calm, a perfect flat bed of pristine white between me and them. They were set up on solid rock three kilometers straight across the ice. Not dug in yet, and they wouldn't be for a while, not unless they had better tools and motivation than the smugglers who built this bunker had, and I seriously doubt that. Tools haven't changed all that much, and the bush-runners out here had more motivation than one lousy old strategist on their heels. No, they were going to be camped upside for a long time.

According to classical theory there were a lot of things I could do. First and most common was run. Only out on Io there isn't a whole lot to run to. Their cannon could vaporize our scout before we ever cleared the blackout horizon, and if I didn't think they'd have someone monitoring who'd spot my trail I was even more stupid than McAllister. There was Greenway Camp on the Jupiter side, but the idea of getting there without the scout was even crazier.

I could always go in and try to blow their main battery. In theory that was an excellent alternative. I even considered it. After all, I have nothing against classical theory, except when it's wrong.

One person alone could do it. Several primitive tribes prided themselves on their skill at sneaking in and out of camps unnoticed. A well-placed explosive maybe, for a diversion. Cut the perimeter line, jump in, and go for the battery. Not impossible. Only that left the full armed complement of some thirty troops or so (my estimates were a little lower than the computer's), who were fully alerted to an enemy presence and madder than a stung wolverine. I decided that was not fun.

No, there had to be some way to get rid of them and leave the supplies standing. And present them to the quartermaster on the next inspection round. That would be amusing. It might also get me off this godforsaken rock to somewhere where there was still some action, something I could do. Not exiled alone with Jimmy out in the backwater, further from mind than the lowest dungeon of France. I read *The Man in the Iron Mask* when I was a child and it scared me half to death. I thought that a French dungeon was the worst place a person could ever be sent. And then I got posted to Io.

I just had to remain flexible. The military's greatest problem is rigid thinking. On the one hand you want troops who will run at people who are shooting at them, which is counter-intuitive at best. You want people deconditioned, ready to obey orders without question, and creating that requires sacrificing a certain amount of critical thinking. Say a very large amount, when it comes to running at enemy fire. So you end up with some people wearing blinders, who aren't aware of the options outside the approved square.

That was what I'd been trying to teach, that creative, reactive thinking. Permitting the Tao, if you will, to flow. Even the Chinese have forgotten that one. Witness the kids up on the rise. They aren't aware of the environment out here. They aren't aware of me. But Sitting Bull would have known. He would have become one with the Earth, flown over with Eagle, been blessed by the Sun. Sitting Bull would have been aware of some anomaly in the current of Io. Would have recognized the closet monster for what it was, the projection of force, and not the childlike nonsense it appears.

For all I have studied of the old ways, the ways that have died, that have been crushed by numbers and firepower, I still don't have the control that the old masters did. I can feel the *Tao* but I can't merge with the force and let it take over, winning by doing nothing. It is the doing-ness that creates failure. All very well and good, but that doesn't solve my problem. Numbers. And firepower.

There were only two weapons available to me. Surprise, which is included in classical thinking, and creativity. A chance to prove that I was inadequate, as McAllister would no doubt tell me. I banished him from my mind. McAllister would get me killed faster than the thirty Confederate troops out across the ice. McAllister would make me angry, make me act out of emotion rather than out of reason. And that would kill me more surely than the ice itself.

So instead I abandoned my post in front of the screens and crossed the fifteen meters to my bunk. Narrow, metal, and made up with a scratchy wool blanket, it was the nearest to comfort I could get on Io. I sat on the covers, which would have gotten me seven punishment details at OCS, crossed my legs, and began to breathe very steadily. Long, deep breaths, and with each one I imagined my mind becoming clearer, cleaner. With each one anger and fear and ambition faded. There was only the puzzle, the question to be answered.

Every problem contains its solution. Every situation

holds the key to its opposite. There is always a way that no one has seen, that no one has followed. Cool and detached, not at all involved in the outcome, I studied the problem presented. I imagined the enemy camp as I had seen it depicted on the screens.

The Confederate soldiers were restricted to three domes. Otherwise they wore hardsuits, and while suits are utilitarian no one likes to wear them. They are also impregnable, or at least so the literature says. A very useful thing for battle, sealed into a personal shield. They are also terribly clumsy even for the most experienced wearer.

When I was first learning to use the suit it was all I could do to walk. Jetpack training took weeks, and I had to practice longer yet again when I reached Io. There was no way around it. The jet is attached to the back of the suit and the gloves are stiff and bulky. Once I thought that the jets should be part of the suit, with the controls inside the gloves, but I was told there was too much danger of setting them off by mistake. Later I realized that the real reason was that the jets were terribly expensive and every suit doesn't need one, nor did anyone need one all the time. So Supply could purchase fewer and pass them around. That reinforced my trust in the basic nature of man.

Wearing that stiff, unyielding suit and trying to control a jetpad in those gauntlets, I often thought of the knights in armor. Theirs wasn't so different from ours, pound for pound of protective mass. They didn't have environmental controls and additional oxygen, but they could take off the helm when not directly under attack. Thinking about knights and calling myself "Sir Eleanor" (I did debate proper usage) paled very quickly when I actually had to use the thing regularly.

The softsuits are protection enough as long as there is no danger of enemy fire. If the only adversaries are cold and vacuum then the softsuit is not only more comfortable, but more given to free movement. Come to think of it, all Jimmy's shooting was done in the softsuit. But I didn't think that the gang across the ice was going to go for it. Can't use a jet on a softsuit, can't mount it and can't land. And they were too hidebound, too rigid, to see that freedom of movement might make up for protection.

So I saw them in my mind's eye, two by two around the perimeter in hardsuits, three domes shining gently against the rise. One for supplies, innermost. The second living quarters, and the third for the battery and power lines. Their transport between the domes and the perimeter, an armored line of attack complete with cannon (low-charge; has to be, even with the link in to the battery) and drive. It probably functioned as the command center, too.

And between us, quivering, the ice. Perfectly innocent, even in the readings, it had been all I could do to train Jimmy not to walk out on that tempting flat. No matter what the geothermal readings, it couldn't be trusted. The magma of Io is too volatile and the ice on the field is far too shallow to withstand any serious change. Jimmy didn't understand any of that. All he knew was that his orders were to keep off the ice and that he got punishment details (cleaning out the galley, scrubbing the spotless floor) when he disobeyed.

So all I had to do was entice the entire marine column onto the flats. And since they hadn't landed there and had done only fly-over patrols, I had to assume they were at least aware of the possibility of danger.

"Look at what I got, boss." Jimmy interrupted my meditation. I wanted to strangle him. I had told him a million times not to bother me when I was thinking, but obviously, since he never thought, he couldn't tell when someone else was doing so.

He was holding out a pistol like it was a treasure. Another was strapped around his leg, something out of a collective fantasy. I shook my head.

"No, Jimmy. These aren't going to be effective. They're in hardsuits, and it takes more power to penetrate the shell. These are toys."

He looked terribly disappointed. "But boss," he pleaded. "I could take out the jetpack. That isn't hard. Or hit the control pad. That's harder, but at the right angle I could manage. The jetpack's easier, though."

But I didn't want to discourage him too badly. "Wouldn't you prefer a rifle for that?" I asked, carefully supportive. "Why don't we put the idea on hold until you find better equipment, and we can consider it from there."

Jimmy brightened noticeably and ran off. I hoped that finding a rifle would take longer than his interrupted inventory (how easily he gets sidetracked and forgets what he's supposed to be doing) while I worked on a diversion that would in fact bring all those Marines onto the ice.

One alone in a hardsuit wouldn't do it. But enough of them, enough . . . Enough to make me think of the Russians, who historically have let their terrain and climate defeat their enemies. Like my own ancestors, they had a respect, even a love for the land, that gave them an advantage that killed others.

The scout, maybe. That could be an answer. If we won I could simply use their transport to get out, and besides the inspection team was coming. They might not be thrilled to waste another scout on the backside of Io, but in return for an entire Confederate marine column I didn't think they would put up too much fuss. Booby-trap it, scoot it out onto the ice as if it had landed. And then when there were enough of them around, explode it. If not the weight then the impact of the explosion should shatter the ice field and swallow them.

And what if their lieutenant was cautious, the way they are taught to be? I wondered about that. I would have to get him to send enough grunts that at least the majority of them would be eliminated in the one single attack. So the trap had to be radio-controlled. I would have to pack it carefully and watch the screens. Let them send out one or two patrols to investigate. Maybe I could even hook up a readout that would look like a wounded pilot, alone. That would surely get them out.

And would save me from having them take out the scout at a distance with their transport cannon.

Even the greenest officer probably wouldn't waste a wounded pilot. Too much information to gain, and restrained by bad enough injuries the prisoner couldn't pose much threat. No, I congratulated myself on devising the perfect trap.

Now I just had to do the labor. Jimmy still hadn't returned from his hunt for the rifles, and I wasn't sure whether to get him to pack explosives while I wrote the emergency code or leave well enough alone. Since space was cramped and I craved the absence of idle (and boring) chatter, I opted to leave him down in stores while I did the job myself.

I grumbled a little, went out to inventory and pull the stocks I needed, when something caught my attention. Something not quite right. I had to look twice before I saw it. One of the softsuits was missing. The big one. Jimmy's.

I swore under my breath. That idiot was going to destroy my work, and all for nothing. He couldn't do a damned thing and there he was, out taking potshots and calling attention to our presence. A presence that I hoped very much to hide.

Stupid kid. I'd always known that he was useless, that all my lessons were wasted. Well, at least trying to teach him something useful had passed the time for me. But it had been no profit to him, none at all. And now he'd gone and disobeyed orders and was headed out to play hero and pick off enemy marines. A quartermaster's clerk.

As I struggled into my own hardsuit I cursed Jimmy all over again. The suit ideally needed a second person to check the mountings, which was one of his jobs. So he was running me out and making me take the risk of securing the suit alone. He would be lucky if the enemy blew his head off before I did. I doublechecked the seals and then clanked through the airlock and onto the surface of Io.

The surface here is impressive. More than any of

the other moons (none of which I've ever visited, but I've seen the pictures), more than the Mars concession cities or the Lunar Enclave. Io is brilliant, one of the brightest things in the system, its ice reflecting even the feeble thin sunlight that comes this far. Jupiter light on the other side is even dimmer and multi-colored, but I preferred the stark contrasts of the "dark." With so little atmosphere to muddy the view, every angle and shadow is crisply defined. It is surreal, disorienting in its absolutes.

I searched for Jimmy. In the white suit he was hard to find. He seemed to be keeping to the brights, just one more white in the glare. So good so far. And there were no footprints, none of the famous marks scuffed all over the surface of the Moon and Mars. No, Io is frozen hard. It would take more than a boot to mar that surface.

I studied the surroundings methodically, first studying the area nearest the bunker entrance and the surround. Nothing moved at all. I couldn't trust my eyes to make out a man-shape in the brilliance. Movement was the only thing that would give him away. My eyes scanned further, out onto the blank ice field.

But the field was no longer so blank. Steam rose from fissures as the magma rose, turning the whole thing into a white take on hell. Yellow-red molten core rose and dyed the crevasses pink and gold, shadows of the threat they represented. A singular figure strode through the steaming mist, shadowed in outline like a demon coming to claim the souls of the damned.

He walked upright and tall, not hiding his presence in the least. In fact, his whole walk across the ice was a challenge. His hands were at his sides and his power-rifle was slung casually across his back.

He was crazy. There was no other way to explain it. Those lines, when I studied them more carefully, were too regular and straight to be the work of nature. I'd seen enough of the vents to know that they generally never followed a set pattern, yet here one was. Artificial then. Jimmy must have done it, used up the full charge in the rifle. And now he was walking into an enemy encampment completely vulnerable.

They were standing at the perimeter staring at him. The two who had been assigned to patrol were joined by two more, and then by three others. The marines didn't unhook a single weapon. I suppose at first they were facing their own monsters, nightmares that were made of imagination and vapor and would laugh at them and never break the insubstantial stride. Fear coming for them, the past and legends all combined.

I know the South Americans, many of them, still practice *macumba*. They deny it, but it's there, just like the old magic of Africa and Asia. The Chinese, much as they are a logical and pragmatic race, have never completely abandoned their superstitions of the spirit world. Perhaps no people ever do. Even I saw what I had been taught to see before I saw what was really there.

And what was really there was nothing but Jimmy, too stupid to do anything but confront them head-on, and the natural ice of Io, doctored a little by the power rifle. All very simple and clear, even if it did look like something from a nightmare made flesh.

And then Jimmy stopped walking. He was maybe two thirds of the way across the ice, although the field is deceptive and distances are impossible to eyeball.

The patrol should have shot there and then. Maybe he really was out of range, but they should have tried. Not that they knew Io well enough, that it has the highest albedo in the solar system, that distance here cannot be perceived on any planet or shipbound basis. They should have shot. Even if it was hopeless they should have put up a show of arms, warnings, proof that they were serious. Jimmy was only in a softsuit, after all. A white softsuit that rose from the steam, yes, but penetrable by real bullets all the same.

Instead the two marines in their bulky hardsuits stood as if they had been frozen in place. Six more appeared, two descending by jetpack. Jimmy remained, eerie in the reddish glow of magma, visible heat surging to the surface. And then he took one step back.

That did nothing to reassure them. People should be easy to identify, friend or foe. This was nothing of the sort. It approached and retreated without any regard to Confederate proprieties. And they couldn't see the new fissure that was growing in the ice, the reason Jimmy had moved. He had to be on this side when it split or he might never get back. For all one can jump forever in the low gravity, it isn't advisable on the ice field. Flaws created by tensions between surface and mantle, between hot and cold, between fluid and rigid, were disguised under the level surface.

I wanted to ask him exactly what he was doing out on the ice. He wasn't smart enough to plan it, of that I was certain. He wasn't able to predict or control the surface as it tore raggedly, fighting and yielding to the molten core. I wanted to tell him that he had destroyed my plans (now that the ice field was both destroyed and exposed in a single action), made our situation hopeless.

I didn't dare. Opening communications would tip off the enemy now, and our only hope was that they were startled enough, shaken enough, that they wouldn't simply fire at the invader like decent perimeter guards and go on about their rounds. If they overheard our conversation, and there was every reason to believe they would, they would know that the apparition that seemed to float in the mist was simply a low-ranking inventory clerk in mega-shit.

They moved forward, eight awkward figures groping in the mist. They knew better, weapons at the ready, but they were still in the grip of primitive truth and so they held on to their rifles more like talismans than for assault. Where the hell were their officers, I wondered. Why wasn't anyone ordering them to break up, go in groups of two, shoot the invader, do any of the things that make sense.

But the human psyche is not based on sense, and the military mind is rigid. Once molded into shape it cannot adjust to the preposterous without breaking. Eight troops in hardsuits started to move onto the ice.

They were joined by three more, who set down in jetpacks and began to walk.

On the opposite edge near the perimeter the other six marines held a firm guard. Maybe there were more in the compound. I could check later, but I didn't think it likely.

Jimmy stepped back further, glancing over his shoulder at me. I couldn't see his face but I'd lay money he was smiling, proud of himself for making such a display. He gestured with his rifle, vaguely waving it in the direction of the marines still in the perimeter. Then he jerked his thumb up.

I wanted to shake my head vigorously, but in a hardsuit that is not only difficult to do but impossible to see. He wanted me to jet over and take out the troops waiting behind. Great. I would be exposed, a perfect target for any of them, and they must have had the long-range guns out. Not that I could see clearly, for the steam hazed everything over—which was perfect cover.

I still hesitated. Not out of fear, naturally, but because if the marines out on the ice caught the flash of a jetpack in action it might lure them back to reality. Back to the universe where enemies have flesh and blood and can be killed, where Io is an active geological entity and where conditions are irregular. To wake from their own demonic nightmare. No sudden moves. Nothing at all to disturb the illusion of hell.

And then the ice split. The small crack gave in to the forces below and opened beneath them. Maybe the weight of eight fully equipped marines in hardsuits and jetpacks had something to do with it.

As soon as the rift opened I moved. It was like I had been waiting all my life for that one second. The jetpad responded under my hard glove faster than I could credit and I came skimming across the ice.

The enemy never saw me. They were all running out over the smooth flats to where their comrades had disappeared under the ice. I had all the leisure in the world to cut them off one at a time. Too heavy, too clumsy to move quickly, there was little they could do when the energy rifle melted the thin crust under their feet. Io itself did the rest. Without a decent atmosphere the sound of cracking ice didn't travel at all. In the swirling steam they didn't see me, not when they had been concentrating on the ground.

Jimmy met me back in the airlock. He had come off the ice, stripped off the softsuit, and made a cup of coffee for me, hot and thick when I got in. The warmth radiated into the internal glow of having done something incredible, something amazing. The Order of St. George or St. Michael for sure. Or maybe both. McAllister would commit suicide at the very thought of it. Vindication in combat, where it matters.

"Well, we're going to have something to present to the quartermaster general at the next inspection," I said, praising Jimmy roundly. "Tomorrow we'll go in and take inventory of what they had. Excellent indeed. No doubt we'll both get merit ratings in our personnel files."

But Jimmy didn't seem entirely satisfied. "What if they come back?" he asked slowly.

"They won't," I reassured him.

"I mean to look for the others. If they don't hear from them they'll come looking," Jimmy refused stubbornly.

However, no matter how badly stated, he did have a point. There would be a search party coming, and they would be coming in heavily armed and ready for trouble. And the inspection team on the way at the same time. I didn't like it at all. Not at all.

But I refused to think about it, to let it disturb the pleasure in a job well done. I had that much right, so to celebrate I had Jimmy break out the Christmas rations and we each ate two portions of pudding, which was the best food we'd had since either of us had arrived. We went to bed on full stomachs, and warm with the knowledge that we were heroes.

And I had nightmares. All night I dreamed about demons, about Mephistopheles coming to claim Faust's soul, about the ghost warriors of the buffalo dance who it was predicted would return to the Plains. I

woke and slept and woke, but the dreams recurred.
There were the three witches of Macbeth and the
monster Grendel—all lived in my subconscious mind
and refused to submit to the rational truth. Another
truth, older and more dangerous because it was less
controlled, surfaced.

I felt like I had not slept at all in fact, as if the
visitations of the nightmares were a message from my
own mind, if I could only read it. But no matter how
little rest I'd had, I knew I was awake and there was
nothing at all I could do about it. So I got up, threw
some cold water over my face, and reheated the coffee
from the night before. I carried it over to my station in
front of the screens by habit, which was the only way I
could function at all.

There on the screen was the message. I read it
through twice before the full impact hit me. "Quartermaster general's inspection postponed due to emergency supply conditions. Will notify with resched."

They weren't coming. I drained the mug numbly,
my mind an irrational mess of demons and the quartermaster general and the whole of Io, too. And then I
saw it, perfect and pristine. I couldn't help smiling.

Jimmy, however, wasn't smiling when I ordered him
into a softsuit. "How come we got to haul half that
stuff out onto the ice?" he demanded. "It's just going
to sink and go to waste and we could use it. And
they're going to come back for it, too."

I don't like people who are afraid to work and I told
him so in brusque terms. He groused, but went because he had no choice. He would have the chance to
see it all.

Somewhere in that battery dome was a homer, emit-
ting a traceable frequency so that no group would be
completely lost. On a place like Io where there didn't
seem to be much danger of an attack that made good
sense. And that's what I had to move.

By midday (on our independent rotation schedule)
Jimmy was done. He would see. They would come,
more Confederates, to find out what had become of

their troops. And they would land at the site of the beacon, moved a mere hundred meters. Moved a hundred meters onto the ice. The cracks we had opened the day before had sealed with cold. Always the battle between the interior and the surface, now erasing all marks of violence. No trace of the Marines who had died beneath the surface remained. Perhaps their hardsuits held, and they were trapped forever in the magma of Io until their oxygen ran out, watching the red-hot floes of lava sheeting their visors. I hope they died quickly, but I feared the other was more likely.

So the camp was set, looking perfectly peaceful and assured out on a flat expanse. Innocent and deserted, it had the air of something left just for the moment. I set the homer off and walked away. I didn't want even the heat of my jetpack scorching a clue into that virgin trap.

Jimmy had pulled the shrimp scampi from the ration shelves for that night's dinner. Either he was in a very good mood or he didn't trust me at all. I wanted wine, but that wasn't permitted. (The French had lobbied hard to insist that it be exempted from the general ban on alcohol in all military installations and aboard ships, but they'd lost. It was the one incident in the entire history of the U.N. that made me question the level of civilization in the Western world.)

Searchers would come. I could feel it. And when they spotted the camp, set up exactly according to textbook case, they would have to come have a look. Set down a little ways away, perhaps, in case the camp was trapped. But by then it would already be too late. The heat of landing even a scout would weaken the ice, and the weight of it fully loaded would do the rest. Simple. And the marine outpost on Io would join the other ghosts of history, scoffed at and remembered for generations.

"So what do we do now?" Jimmy asked.

I smiled and silently thought of McAllister in a hardsuit, come to investigate. . . . "We wait."

Miles To Go

The most fuel-efficient orbit directly from the Earth/
Moon system to Jupiter took over two years to travel.
A ship that expended methane to accelerate, or decelerate the entire time could cover the distance in just
under four months. To accomplish this, a ship had to
dedicate about eighty-five percent of its initial mass to
fuel.

The length of the supply lines in the Jupiter War
predicated two developments. The first was the growth
of the asteroid settlements of both sides. The asteroids
were unofficially considered neutral ground by both
sides. Since there were literally millions of asteroids
neither side could claim sovereignty over even a small
percentage of them. While rich in minerals, the asteroids were also totally lacking in any other resources.

As the war continued the neutrality of the asteroids
was maintained, but the war zone moved closer to
them. Eventually any ship farther out than the bulk of
the belt was considered fair game. Had the war continued for an extended period, there was no question
that one side or the other would violate the asteroid
truce. Once one side was losing, the temptation to
interdict the enemy's supplies farther down the line
would become irresistible. After the asteroids, attacks
on the U.N. holdings on Mars, and then both antago-
nist's bases on the Moon, would soon follow. After
that, it could only be hoped that wisdom would prevail
before Armageddon.

War, if expensive in almost any currency you consider, does stimulate technology. The second development was an explosion in the research and development
of nearly every aspect of space travel. Necessity still
remained the mother of invention. This particularly
included experimentation on new forms of ship's drives.
After fifteen years of asking, scientific institutions found

themselves fully funded for even such esoteric and exotic programs as developing a faster-than-light drive.

Many of the facilities for this research had been located in the Jovian system. The purpose of this was to protect the Earth from accidents that were in some cases potentially earth-shattering. Many of these new technologies proved dead ends. The MAM—matter-antimatter drive—came too late to affect the outcome of the war. It did have an immediate effect on a few small actions, and laid the groundwork for the power sources so badly needed only a few years later. Like many scientific advances, MAM development was both hurried and nearly eliminated by the vicissitudes of war.

DASHER

by Todd Johnson

The office was well appointed but obviously Navy. Behind the huge mahogany desk was a plush chair whose back was just a little too straight; the bookcase had several carefully selected classics, including *Spock's World*, arrayed on the top shelf, but the lower shelves all contained books of naval tactics and regulations; the pictures on the wall were elegantly framed but all of great naval encounters. The walls were covered in dark-grained wood, bespeaking more money than mere naval pay. Incongruously, the desk sported a replica of the long-lost space shuttle *Challenger*, nose-up and ready for its last flight, and a detailed model of the first probe to leave the solar system, *Voyager*.

In the plush chair sat a gaunt, wiry naval captain. The naval captain was attired in dress uniform, declaring to every knowledgeable onlooker that here was an officer who spent more time in the staff room than on the bridge. In front of him, in front of a much less well-appointed chair, in fact a standard issue chair, stood a navy lieutenant at attention.

Captain Poindexter allowed himself one more intimidating minute of staring at the lieutenant, one eyebrow arched, before he growled: "At ease." As the lieutenant unbent, he added: "Be seated."

Trudeaux was not standard navy issue. For one, she was a woman. That was not terrible in itself but she was also a test pilot, an engineer, a physicist, and just about everything the navy frowned upon. And—Poindexter's eyes narrowed—she was so plump as to be almost overweight. All these, however, were to be expected of the navy's experimenters. The rumors about her singing in the rare times that she was not talking to either her computers or their ghosts he dismissed as unimportant.

However, her Officer's Evaluation Reports followed a disturbing pattern as she moved from post to post: always they started off warm and glowing until, as time passed, her superiors slipped from praise to insult and innuendo. Such OERs could be read two ways: either Trudeaux's ineptitude was hard to discern immediately or she was so brilliant that her commanders sought to discredit her. Poindexter had seen both. What was unusual, however, was Trudeaux's continued requests for combat duty or command, preferably both. More alarming were her superiors' refusals on the grounds that she was "too valuable in her present position" to let her go.

Even more unusual was the fact that she was nearly one billion kilometers from her post. That fact prompted the court-martial papers now lying in plain view on Poindexter's desk, and this preliminary investigation.

"They tell me that the *Dasher*'s right engine is mere shrapnel somewhere back in Jovian orbit, and that the left engine has fused," Poindexter began, civilly. He saw her relax somewhat and chided himself, barking: "You've set back the navy's Matter/Anti-Matter propulsion project a good ten years! Explain!"

Margaret Trudeaux winced, clearly upset and uncertain.

"*Dasher* was ambushed." Maggie began.

"Ambushed!" Poindexter roared. "Ambushed! *Dasher* has the best stealth electronics in the navy!" He spluttered: "Ambushed!"

"Ambushed," Margaret maintained icily. Good! Poindexter thought to himself, pleased that his antagonizing tactics had worked. He raised an eyebrow to indicate that she should continue, reminding himself that he was supposed to be the hard captain, intent only on the facts.

"They took out the right engine, combustion chamber, and feed lines, in the first bolts. They also hulled

the ship. In the next, they got the communications
gear and the Reaction Control System."

"And just where were you when they attacked?"

"I was indisposed." Trudeaux replied.

In response, Poindexter slammed his finger on a
naval-issue voice-recorder. "I want every detail."

Margaret Trudeaux nodded slightly, closed her eyes,
and remembered.

Dasher was the Navy's test ship for MAM, Matter/
Antimatter, propulsion systems. It was a modified courier, unarmed, relying on its incredible speed and
unsurpassed stealth electronics to protect it. It had
been the test ship for the Polarized Radiation MAM
engines until two pilots had died from gamma radiation poisoning, and now it was the Navy's Chaotic
Flow Chamber MAM test bed. CFC had proved a
winner: computer-controlled injections of a secondary
propellant (hydrogen) had not only given the *Dasher* a
specific impulse of 0.05 c but had produced a control
room that was absolutely free of any radiation other
than space-normal levels. And it was so safe "Even a
woman can drive it!", as Dr. Brenschluss had crowed.
Margaret had refrained from giving the professor a
chance to examine his heart firsthand, in order to be
selected as the female to prove his boast. The old
Prussian had done it to needle her, resentful of the
breadth of her engineering skills.

Dasher had already made three flights from retro-
grade Sinope to Amalthea, the satellite most blind-
ingly near to Jupiter, and the test results had been
perfect, the test pilots almost boring in their praise of
the reliability of the engines and the handling of the
modified courier. The most intriguing episode of the
three flights had been one pilot's recounting flying
straight through an enemy fleet without causing the
slightest blip on their radar; *Dasher*'s stealth electronics and hull coating were the best the navy could
boast.

So Margaret Trudeaux, test pilot, chief engineer,
leading and only architect of MAM combustion cham-
bers, was selected for the fourth and final flight of the

Dasher before it was replaced by a larger ship equipped with a production version of the CFC MAM drive—the drive that would give humankind, particularly U.N. humankind, the stars.

In mis-response to Margaret's outrage at being chosen to fly *Dasher* only when it was proven safe—those were *her* engines, dammit!—the chief test pilot, "Red" Nelson, a relic from prehistoric times, had consoled: "Don't worry, it'll be a milk run." A milk run! She had hoped she would not be bored silly, and prayed that Red was merely displaying his usual cultivated calm.

In fact, Margaret Trudeaux was in the galley trying to figure out how quickly to eat her ice cream when the enemy ships attacked. A sudden savage lurch of the ship was immediately followed by tearing noises and the hiss of vacuum. She clapped her hand over her mouth, with no time to swear as she leaped up and lurched to the control room. The air in the control room was fogged with water vapor condensed by the sudden pressure drop. She strapped herself into her chair and saw a sea of red lights glaring balefully on the control panels. First, hull integrity was gone. Ship's internal oxygen lines were functional. Margaret turned her seat, grabbed a facemask, and slipped it on, pulling the straps over her head and tightening them. She set the regulator and was soon breathing pure oxygen. As a precaution, she located and started charging the portable oxygen system. With the regulator set at a mild overpressure she could work until the ship's own pressure dropped below two percent of standard. After that she would have to don a hardsuit.

"Let's see what we've got here," she said to the ship's computer in her best "pilot's calm." Another blast shook the ship.

Margaret checked her radar: two destroyers were hot on her tail. A quick look forward showed only Jupiter. Another scan of the panels showed no new major damage. Outside, the stars were visibly moving in response to the roll of the crippled ship. The brighter

star, Margaret guessed, was Amalthea, not that it would
do her any good. The navy kept no ships on that tiny
dustball.

"They've got you pegged," she said to the computer, expecting it to plan evasive actions. Somehow
they must have found out about the *Dasher* and the
navy's experiments and simply waited until a reliable
engine had been developed. Now they wanted to steal
it.

"No way, José," Margaret swore, shaking a chubby
fist at the distant enemy. How did they find me, she
wondered. Margaret glanced over to the stealth electronics panel. It was still functional. She sucked her
teeth in consternation.

"Oh my god, they've countered to our stealth gear!"
This information was probably worth as much to the
navy as a working MAM engine was to the enemy.
The computer still had not responded. Margaret checked
its panel and found that the main unit had been destroyed in the second attack. She frowned, fingers
poised above the destruct switch for the stealth
electronics—if she was wrong, she was destroying her
only chance—and pressed. The panel glowed brighter
and then went dark.

Committed, Margaret switched her attention to the
engines. The panel showed that the starboard main
engine was scrap. Maggie's fingers moved quickly to
stop the hemorrhaging of valuable fuel, a loss which
had made *Dasher*'s course an erratic heloid and probably had saved her from being further assaulted or
boarded by the enemy.

The left engine was functional at reduced power,
but *Dasher* relied on the twin thrust of the left and
right engines. Using only one engine would put the
Dasher into fast right turn. Attitude-control thrusters
could counter some of this. Maggie gave a gargled
groan when she noted that the attitude Control System
was so much junk. Either the enemy had been incredibly lucky or it had known just where it hit *Dasher* to
immobilize her. Margaret decided that it was not luck.
But it hadn't gone all their way: *Dasher*'s roll about its

long axis meant that she could thrust the left engine by itself and wobble in a path that was mostly forward. She would have to be careful with her motions, though: the laws of energy conservation were such that a roll about the long axis would try to convert itself into a yaw about the center of gravity, just like a top falling over to its side. One of the early Explorer satellites had done just that.

"Don't bother checking the com gear," Margaret told the defunct computer, then shrugged when she realized her mistake. With a dismissive wave she responded to herself: "Doesn't matter, they probably took out the main antenna and, besides, you don't have enough power with just one engine to punch a distress call back to Sinope."

She reviewed her options: the enemy wanted *Dasher* intact, Margaret herself would be an added bonus; she had only one engine to use but it was fully functional; *Dasher* had no armaments, relying on speed and its now-destroyed stealth gear. She was not far from Jupiter.

Jupiter! "Period, period, what's this goddamned rotation period?" Maggie chanted to herself. She locked her eyes on a bright star that could have been Amalthea and counted *Dasher*'s roll rate at three revolutions a minute, more or less. Margaret plotted a thrust that would vector her toward Jupiter.

"How much can that chamber take?" she asked herself, hoping that as the designer she might know and knowing, as the designer, that she had never bothered to calculate it—*Dasher* had never been expected to make even one-G thrusts. "Never mind that, Trudeaux! Just get moving!" she ordered.

Maggie fired the engine manually, the computer being hopeless. She set the matter and antimatter flow rates to produce first one half gee, then one gee and finally, in a mixture of devil-take-all abandon and sheer desperation, five gees. She cut the engines quickly and tried to determine how fast the ship was turning. When she thought it was just about aligned for Jupiter, she thrust again, countering the turning moment. Then, aligned to head toward the huge planet, she started a corkscrew towards the leviathan of the skies.

"What's your speed? You've got to go faster, Trudeaux, you've got to *run* away from the enemy!" Maggie barked aloud, forcing herself to play hard captain. She was disappointed to admit that she could think of no easy way to calculate *Dasher*'s speed. Dasher had been on a trajectory designed to swing around Amalthea and back towards Sinope but, as Sinope moved other-clockwise around Jupiter than Amalthea, Margaret and *Dasher* would have to execute a very fuel-costly direction reversal that few chemically fueled ships could do—one of the reasons that the navy felt orbits between Amalthea and Sinope were safe. In order to facilitate the maneuver, *Dasher*'s trajectory was arranged so that the ship would be traveling at the lowest possible velocity when the reversal in direction was made.

At Perijovian, the lowest point of her orbit, she would have had the same speed as Amalthea—slightly over thirty kilometers a second. To get into a low Jupiter orbit she would need a speed of just over forty-two kilometers per second, a difference of twelve kilometers per second. And she wanted to get to Jupiter fast.

"Two gees?" Maggie asked herself, taking the time to review the panels in front of her. "Let's see: t equals delta vee over a; at two gees, nineteen point six-two meters per second squared, delta vee is twelve thousand, t is about, uh"—she glanced nervously about for a working calculator or *something* that could do simple math and swore when she found nothing. "Call it twenty meters per squared second, that's six hundred seconds—ten minutes at two gees!" She mulled the figures over.

"Maybe it'll shake 'em. It'll sure give 'em a rough ride!" Her captain voice agreed, adding: "Won't be too easy on you, either!" Maggie crouched onto the command chair for extra security, set the flow controls, and fired. The enemy were taken by surprise. It was a long thirty seconds before they fired off in pursuit of her.

Maggie spent the long minutes en route to Jupiter alternating between checking the enemy, pulsing the one engine, watching her fuel, and wracking her brains for a way out of her predicament. Just outside the atmosphere she stopped her two-gravity thrusting, waited a quarter of a corkscrew, and made another thrust, a wrenching, bone-jarring six Gs. She countered it ten seconds later with another agonizing six Gs. Now *Dasher* was in the pull of Jupiter's gravity and on a course deep into Jupiter's clouds.

"How much pressure can this hull take?" Maggie wondered scientifically, continuing captainly: "Can it take more than they can?"

Under more normal circumstances Margaret would have addressed these questions to the ship's computers, but there was no computer to talk to. Then she remembered that the ship was holed—the internal and external pressures would both be Jupiter's. Her ship could take more pressure than theirs. The question was, could she?

Switching from the chair's oxygen to her portable supply, Margaret made her way to the suit locker. With much grumbling she managed to pull her deep-space suit over her shipsuit. With it she could take more pressure but would lose dexterity. She returned to the control room and found to her disgust that she could not fit herself into the command chair and was bouncing out instead. Abashed, she remembered that she had to activate her magnetic soles.

Now she said to herself, *the question is, how much can this suit take?*

"One way to find out!" Maggie waited until she figured the good engine was almost above her, fired another four-second burst, counted to six and repeated the operation, plunging *Dasher* deeper into Jove's thin air.

She glanced at the displays: *Dasher* was ten kilometers inside Jupiter's atmosphere. The enemy ships were following her with no difficulty: the atmosphere was mostly opaque at this depth. Navy manuals did not take into consideration mad dives into the Jovian atmosphere; it took Maggie quite a while to guess a depth she was willing to risk her life with.

"Even if you can go lower than them, Maggie, they'll just wait until you come up for air," she noted tactically.

"You've got to sucker 'em into letting you get away," she decided captainly. She thought about it as Jupiter's atmosphere thickened from tenuous to visible. She forced herself to glance at the hull temperature gauge—it was already edging into the red. *Dasher* was not supposed to make atmospheric entries—no one had ever envisioned *Dasher* trying to smash its way through the Jovian atmosphere.

"You can outrun 'em if they don't knock out the other engine," she advised with her engineer's tone, noting that she had over twenty kilograms of precious antimatter contained in the ship's magnetic bottles. Then she sighed: "Won't work, Maggie, they'll just radio ahead. You've *got* to lose them somehow."

Whatever happens, she continued silently, they can't get this ship. She smiled as that dark thought led her through a darker series to an image of *Dasher*'s antimatter evaporating through the magnetic containment in one vast explosion. Twenty kilograms of the stuff would probably shake up ol' Jove himself, she mused. Pressure was rising rapidly in the spaceship. Vibrations through the floor plates and groans in the thin air warned Margaret that, even holed, *Dasher*'s hull was feeling the increased pressure. Margaret was glad when *Dasher* passed below the ammonia ice clouds, the thinnest of Jupiter's clouds: it gave her the first little something to hide her ship under.

Later, at a pressure of slightly over six atmospheres, under the rusty orange of Jupiter's ammonium hydrosulfide clouds, Margaret made two rapid firings to keep *Dasher* from descending further. When *Dasher* groaned threateningly against the light thrust of the MAM engine, Margaret hastily reduced the thrust and increased its duration. She understood the tiny ship's predicament: movement in her hardsuit was laborious, and several times she had had to stop herself hyperventilating from the fear that her suit was leaking or, worse, buckling. Overriding the suit's controls, she increased the internal pressure to five atmospheres—adding nitrogen, as she knew that oxygen at this pressure would literally cook her from the inside out. The increased internal pressure reduced the difference between outside pressure to one atmosphere. Margaret hoped that the suit would handle the one atmosphere difference; she was depending on it.

She checked radar. The two destroyers were over ten kilometers behind her and seventy-five kilometers above her—high up where the pressure was less than one atmosphere. *Dasher*'s speed through the thick atmosphere was heating the ship up at an alarming rate. From the cockpit Margaret could see the near-white glow from *Dasher*'s nose. The temperature inside her suit was also rising. Maggie started sweating profusely, and cursed the fact that the extra pressure of her suit made her sweat just stick to her skin.

"Drink your water, Trudeaux," she growled to herself and suited actions to words, squirming in her helmet to drink from the water nipple. Dehydration in these circumstances would be fatal.

"Damn, now I'm hungry," she complained. "Low blood sugar," her scientific side noted.

"Well, the ice cream's melted for sure," she told herself flippantly. "Probably spoiled, too." She checked the pressure gauge: it was dropping, telling her that *Dasher* had started its ascent from its roller-coaster plunge through Jupiter's air. Gratefully, she vented some of the excess pressure in her suit.

"About time, too. Now you've got two choices: continue up and surrender or stay down here. Either way your goose is cooked." Her stomach growled at her poor choice of words.

As if in response to her stomach, the quart of ice cream she had left in the galley chose that moment to waft serenely over her head and bounce sickly against the forward viewport. With a sense of irony Maggie noted that the outside was liquid, something she had been trying to accomplish when the enemy had first attacked her only—she glanced at the chronometer—twelve minutes before.

"Well now, Trudeaux, you've got two riddles to solve: how to get away from two enemy destroyers before you burn up and how to eat ice cream under six atmospheres!" She noticed that her words were somewhat slurred now, and that made her worried that her suit might be leaking. A quick glance at her inboard monitor panel reassured her; she decided that her tongue was feeling the effects of the extra pressure.

Or is it because you're starving, she wondered. Now what was it they had said at the Academy? "When you have several problems, sometimes the best solution is to combine them into one large problem and solve *it*."

So where did that leave her? Nowhere. The two problems were separate.

Well, Maggie, she thought to herself, you always wanted a combat job! She snorted. "How could you have guessed that your only weapon would be ice cream!"

How do you get away from two enemy destroyers using only ice cream?

"That's simple," Margaret voiced, "throw it at them." She pursed her lips while she pondered the possibility. If she just kicked the ice cream out the door, it would continue on in the same orbit until she thrust *Dasher* away. The differences in velocity between the ice cream and the destroyers would pick the ice cream up on radar long before it was a danger and vaporize it. But if the destroyers did not know it was ice cream and did not detect it until it was too close, say a kilometer, then the destroyers would have to make a massive orbit change to avoid the mysterious projectile. And if any of the ice cream did actually hit—Margaret frowned as she worked the numbers through in her head, and sighed—all it would do was make a loud noise.

"Now all you have to do is shoot the ice cream at them and make it invisible," Maggie muttered aloud. Well, shooting it wasn't difficult: stuff the ice cream in the airlock, tight against the outer door, override the mechanism enough to force the airlock to open only to the diameter of one of the ice cream containers and—whoosh!—out they fly at a fair clip. Maggie worked the numbers out and found that her airlock thrust chamber would give her a respectable 700-meter-per-second velocity difference. She calculated the impact energy for eleven two-kilogram objects and grinned. "Now to make 'em invisible!"

With part of her next problem solved, Maggie focused on the present and examined the control panels, noting that hull temperature was well within limits. Through the viewport she could see that she was passing through Jupiter's ammonia ice clouds. Soon she would be outside of Jupiter's atmosphere and a good target for the destroyers.

"Time's almost up, Trudeaux," she told herself. "Think! You've got to make them blink."

"Let's see: they're going to see the ice cream liquid or solid. The containers will hardly make a blip, but they haven't got any mass and no one's going to jump away from something they can't see." Maggie shook her head. "The only chance is to make a hot radar blip when they aren't expecting it. They know you've got antimatter aboard, so a quick blip on their screens would probably scare 'em all the way out to Pluto."

Maggie sighed, looking out the viewport in an effort to distract her consciousness from a problem best left to her subconscious. The last wisps of Jupiter's clouds were passing off to one side. Maggie thought about those ammonia ice crystals and how they must look as they fell, warmed on the outside, solid ice cores surrounded by liquid. "That's it! They'll light up like Christmas trees!"

Radar beams going through the liquid ice cream at a distance would probably produce a very weak or nonexistent return, just faint enough to convince the enemy that they were nothing to worry about. And radar beams going through solid ice cream would only produce a slightly greater return. But while neither liquid nor solid were much on radar, a liquid-solid boundary layer was a fantastic radar reflector. If she managed it just right the enemy would suddenly see incredibly powerful returns on radar and think she had unleashed some secret weapon. No telling what they would do. "But they'll certainly blink!"

Now, how to deliver that heat when required? She glanced around the cabin and made her way to the rear. Because *Dasher* was an experimental ship, lots of spare equipment was left aboard for ease of use.

In the rear of the craft, strapped in or magnetically attached, were all sorts of measuring equipment. There were thermo-couples, ohmmeters, magnetometers, vibration transducers, all sorts of useful equipment for dealing with the effects of an enclosed matter/antimatter unit. But Maggie could see nothing that could be used to *generate* heat.

As her search grew more frantic the rear of the cabin became a dangerous constellation of flying discards as Maggie flung them away in disgust at their inability to meet her simple needs.

"Just one radio-controlled heating unit," she begged. "Even one would do the job!" No good. She had completed her inspection and reinspection as castoffs floated back in and out of her vision. A glare at the control panels assured her that she didn't have the time to make one.

"Face it, Margaret Trudeaux, you're licked." She shook her head while saying it, as if her body were in revolt against her mind's conclusion. It was her first command! And she didn't have anything that could even *scare* the enemy! An idle, detached part of her mind noted that soon the enemy would be in range again, they would finish the crippling of *Dasher* and board her, their magnetic boots clanging on the hull. They would cycle the airlock and they would find Maggie there. . . .

"Singing!" Maggie exclaimed. She scanned the scattering debris of her earlier search with renewed energy. Margaret was looking for only one thing: a vibration transducer. It was nothing more than a microphone that was attached by suction or magnetism. The microphone would pick up the noise of unwanted vibration and transmit it back to the receiver. Margaret whooped for joy when she found the receiver—it was a transceiver. Often it was desirable to not only record the vibrations of a test item but also to induce vibrations. The gear on board *Dasher* could do both: it could receive the vibrations picked up by the transducers or it could transmit vibrations through the transducers. And vibrations would produce heat! A resonance, the ice cream would heat up fastest and produce the required thin liquid layer. It did not have to be much, less than a tenth of a millimeter would do nicely.

Margaret picked up the box of transducers and the transceiver and brought it back to the galley. She left the box in the galley and brought the transceiver forward to the control room. Up in the control room, she secured the transceiver by its magnetic clamps and reviewed the positions of the enemy through her radar. The two destroyers were now closing upon her, the range about forty kilometers. Another twenty kilometers closer and the enemy would be within firing range. A couple of flashes on radar indicated that the destroyers were willing to try for a lucky shot even at this range. Margaret cursed them and hoped that their weaponry would blow up. For her plan to work the enemy would have to get a lot closer. She would have to let them within ten kilometers of *Dasher* before she could launch her gastronomic artillery.

Margaret kicked the circuit breakers, plunging *Dasher* into darkness and cutting all power from the batteries. The emergency lights snapped on, as did her helmet light, and *Dasher* was illuminated in the baleful red of a dying ship. Margaret hoped that the enemy would decide that the strains of Jupiter had been too much for the small courier, that all power was lost. She wanted them to think that *Dasher* was dead and not bother to fire on it. The superconducting magnets could contain *Dasher*'s antimatter forever, if need be.

Decision made, Margaret went over to the airlock and used the emergency override to open the inner door. She checked the monitor and was glad to note that it showed no signs of leaks in the airlock. If the enemy's blasts had hulled the airlock, Margaret's plan would have been doomed. She went back to the galley, opened the refrigerator door, and pulled out the remaining eleven quarts of ice cream.

"The things I do for the Service," Maggie groaned theatrically, placing the transducers on the tops of the ice cream. She turned on each transducer and checked it for functionality. Satisfied, she carried the ice cream over to the airlock.

She placed the quart containers one on top of the other just at the seam between the outer airlock door and the airlock itself. That done, she stood back in the airlock and inspected her work. Satisfied, she left the airlock, closed the inner door, and pressurized. Then she spent time overriding the standard airlock cycle. Instead of evacuating the air in the airlock before opening to space, the airlock door would pop open under the pressure of one atmosphere just enough to allow the quarts of ice cream to be forced out.

"Of course the airlock'll be useless after this, you know," Maggie noted with the hurt tones of an engineer about to damage an artifice.

Back inside the cabin she checked her suit's chronometer: four minutes to go. Of course, the enemy could have accelerated to overtake her—in which case all her plans were useless. Relentless, Maggie tore off the cover to the propulsion control panel and started tinkering with the injector controls. There was no way that she could use the antimatter in its hyper-strengthened, shielded containers for offensive purposes, but she could rig a dead man's button that would force the MAM engines to full acceleration; even if the stresses did not splinter the courier all over creation, the resulting thrust would certainly kick *Dasher* well out of the Solar System.

She checked the CFC controls and tied them into the dead man's stick, so that not only would *Dasher* accelerate at inhuman speeds but the thrust chamber would be irradiating gamma rays in all directions instead of photons directed only rearward—making *Dasher* too "hot" for anyone to get near ever again. She was very pleased with the dead man's switch itself;

she had rigged it to monitor her heartbeat: a second after her heart stopped beating, the dead man's switch would trigger.

Satisfied but made even more apprehensive by her precautions, Margaret watched the seconds tick away on her chronometer. To take her mind off the wait Maggie worked out the thrusts she could use to get back to Earth; she was certain that *Sinope* had been infiltrated by spies and might even have been destroyed. Earth! With only twenty kilograms of propellant! No, she corrected herself, forty kilograms of propellant: twenty of matter and twenty of antimatter. *Dasher* was a light ship, massing only one thousand kilograms, one tonne. The destroyers behind her were ten times more massive. With forty kilograms of propellant, *Dasher* had a mass ratio of 1.040. Burning all that fuel between Jupiter and Earth would result in a measly 1.4 percent gee and take nearly fifty-two days.

"Rats!" Margaret snarled. If the thrust efficiency could be brought up, if she could up the specific impulse, then she could get back to Earth faster. She knew a few ideas she'd been wanting to try but Professor Brenschluss had *nicht*ed her. She leaned back into the Chaotic Flow Controls and tinkered. Changing the beat frequency to just below the first resonant frequency of the thrust chamber should produce the same effect as twice the hydrogen damping, which would halve the hydrogen being kicked overboard merely to protect the chamber and increase the specific impulse accordingly.

"Of course if you're wrong, Maggie me dear, you're going to get cooked for sure," her engineering side warned her scientific self as she checked her handiwork. Her detached side wondered why she was always making food jokes. She glanced at her suit chronometer. "Cripes!"

Ten seconds. She raced back over to the center control panel, one hand poised over the radar circuit breaker, the other over the radar gain.

"Eight . . . seven . . . six . . . five . . ." she counted. "Lights, camera, action!"

She punched in the circuit breaker and the radar screen warmed up. The test lights blinked on the radar display and then the central tube starting glowing brighter.

"Come on, come on!" she implored. Finally the tube was fully on. She changed the gain, searching for the enemy ships. Twenty kilometers, fifteen kilometers . . .

"Bingo! You boys stay tight and you'll win the prize!" The two ships were close together and ten kilometers behind *Dasher*. She switched axes and took an azimuth reading. The angle between the top of *Dasher*'s control room and the ships was about one hundred and thirty degrees—forty degrees from the airlock. Margaret raced to the lock, counting seconds to herself. "Three . . . two . . . one—oh shit!" She was still rushing to the airlock when the time passed! *Dasher*'s airlock was not pointed at the enemy!

"Count Maggie, count!" she exhorted, terrified that the enemy ships had noticed her radar. "You have to count down until the 'lock is lined up again!"

"Nineteen . . . eighteen . . ." A bright sear appeared in the ceiling to her right. The enemy was firing. A shiver of fear lanced up her spine.

"Sixteen . . . fifteen . . . c'mon! . . . fourteen . . ." Another bolt tore into the hull to her left. Maggie jumped to the right. "Twelve . . . eleven . . ."

The ship made a horrible groaning noise. "*Please*, not the left engine!" she shrieked, right hand poised over the airlock override, left hand coming up to her emergency suit vent—if they boarded, she'd blow her suit open and when the air ran out . . . well, hypoxia was a great way to go.

"Eight! Seven!" Her voice rose in anticipation. "Six! Five . . . four . . ." Another bolt glanced on the hull. "Three . . . two . . . *Now*, you bastards!" She hit the lock override. Alarms flashed and klaxons sounded noiselessly in the vacuum. The airlock pressure blipped out to zero. Rushing to the control panel, Maggie started counting again.

"Twelve . . . eleven . . . ten—oh god, what's the

frequency?" She stopped, horrified. "What's the resonant frequency for the ice cream?" Terror and visions of cold death beat at her, her breathing doubled and her sweat turned to ice as she imagined the next bolt searing through her suit and her body.

"Think, Maggie, think!" she shouted uselessly in brash military.

"Time! Time!" she shouted scientifically. Her heartbeat was racing and she was hyperventilating.

"*No*! No, Maggie not now!" she told herself. "Breathe slower! Control!" She took a deep breath, held it, and let it out again slowly in iron-tight control.

"Again!" she ordered herself. The second breath was more controlled. She willed her breathing back to normal.

"Okay, time," she said quietly, desperately. She flicked the broadcast switch on the transceiver, linked in the input to her suit mike's output.

With a bittersweet grin Maggie remarked, "It's not over until the fat lady sings," and started singing.

" 'Johnny could only sing one note and the note he sang was this: Aaaaah!' " Maggie checked the radar while singing: still two blips, closing fast. She peered a bit closer and thought she could just detect the smudges outlining the containers, but it might also be space dust. She switched songs, going to Wagner's "Valkyrie," tearing up and down the scales as fast as she could. There! The radar showed spots! They were getting brighter. She sang up the scales, zeroed in, and held it.

Blips—seven, eight, eleven—burst into brilliance on the radar screen. They were practically on top of the first destroyer.

"Now!" she told herself, singing the word. She punched the controls, fired the left engine, spun the ship, countered the spin, and punched up a steady five gees.

Looking back at the radar she watched the tiny blips disappear, merging with the first destroyer. Nothing had happened. She took several deep breaths to retain her calm. The two ships were pursuing.

"Wait a minute!" she exclaimed, straining against the five-gee thrust to get a better view.

"Alllllll right, Maggie!" she yelled. "Way to go!"

Her shrieks filled her helmet and resounded achingly, but she kept them up nonetheless. The two blips merged, became one larger blip, and separated again into many smaller blips.

"Jeez! Have they got egg on their face!" she cackled. "What are they going to tell the base commander?"

Then she sobered up. "What am I going to tell the base commander?"

The office was cool but Margaret Trudeaux was hot as she finished retelling her story. Captain Poindexter had stopped his irritable finger-drumming somewhere through her account and was now scribbling numbers on his notepad.

"So I shaped orbit for Earth and got here as quickly as I could," Maggie finished. "I rigged up a simple com circuit on the way back and called in as soon as I was near base." She made a rueful face. "They had to cut away the airlock, it was so badly warped." He looked up momentarily when he realized she was silent, then returned to his scribblings. Margaret started to feel more uncomfortable. She could not tell that Poindexter was using those moments to regain the calm, detached manner of an investigating officer—her account was pure naval history. Finally, Poindexter laid down his pen.

"You got here in a little under six days?" he asked. When she nodded, he continued: "That's a specific impulse of just over forty-two percent of the speed of light."

"Well," Maggie began slowly, "I explained about the changes to the CFC, didn't I?" For the first time, Poindexter noticed how hoarse her voice was. He nodded sharply for her to continue.

"Well, sir, I did figure out another way to get more thrust from the chamber." She hastened to add: "It would have been a long trip unless I could figure out a way to get better performance, so I tinkered a lot."

She had hummed to herself quite a bit after her victory over the destroyers, and had quickly decided that she wanted to hear other music than her own. The audio-video gear was still functional but the speakers had no air to vibrate.

"So I rigged the speakers to the hull and then I got the music from the vibrations through my suit," Margaret explained.

"What does *that* have to do with increased performance?"

"Everything! The vibrations traveled through the hull to the combustion chamber and influenced the chaotic flow. I experimented a lot, tried everything. Finally, I found that if I sang along with one particular song, I got a tremendous boost in performance."

When it became apparent that the lieutenant would have to be enticed, Poindexter raised an eyebrow encouragingly. Maggie swallowed before saying: "Beethoven's 'Ode to Joy': the soprano line. I'm afraid that only a woman can sing it." She added hastily: "Though doubtless further experimentation would allow a mere recording to suffice."

"Doubtless," The captain agreed. He turned to the tape recorder and flipped it off. "Lieutenant, as you know this was a preliminary investigation for your court-martial."

"Yes, sir." Margaret's voice held neither hope nor regret.

"I have reached my conclusion." With elaborate motions, Poindexter collected the papers listing the charges against her, and tore them to bits.

Then, to Maggie's great surprise, intense elation, and overwhelming joy, he solemnly rose from his chair, held his body rigidly erect, and with steel-precise movements brought up his right hand into a perfect salute and held it there for a long, long, long time.

Jupiter Station

Nothing is more useful in a war than neutral ground. Jupiter Station had been the first orbital scientific station orbiting the gas giant. Established as a joint project by both alliances, it was also the first permanently manned station outside the asteroid belt. By 2056, after thirty-five years of service, Jupiter Station had grown far beyond its original structure. It now housed almost a quarter of the non-military population of the Jovian system. Its value and erratic orbit enabled the platform to maintain a very uneasy neutrality throughout the Jupiter War.

The shape of Jupiter Station's elliptic orbit meant that this unique facility passed near each of the planet's moons at least once per Earth month. This made it the ideal location for the refining units that were necessary to purify the ore for the long plunge back toward Earth. Since both sides needed the Jovian rare earths, the station was able to parley this dependence into a form of independence from both combatants. Both the U.N. and the Feds maintained "offices" on the Station, but neither dared claim jurisdiction over it. Whenever one side exerted too much pressure on the station's administration, the other was appealed to.

Even at the peak of the war, neither side was willing to risk attacking Jupiter Station. To do so would likely have resulted in the platform's destruction, either in the assault or by the other side if successful. Doing this would have alienated the hundreds of independent miners who were less concerned with politics than accumulating riches. This also would have destroyed the only location they had for R & R within two months travel. Eventually the station also served as the location of the truce talks, but not before the war had run for five years and cost fifteen thousand highly trained lives.

By 2057 each side had replaced most of their lost ships, and ship-to-ship combat changed from an exception to the rule. Two attempts were made to occupy enemy land bases by force, one by each navy. The attack on the Tirner compound on Ganymede proved a major embarassment to those U.N. SEALs involved in that fiasco. The Fed attack on the Europa mining complex never even reached the defense perimeter due to their loss of control of the space over the moon during the action. Isolated and bombarded from space, the Federation marines were eventually forced by a lack of oxygen to surrender or suffocate.

During the Jupiter War the social climate of the orbital station resembled that of any neutral city, if that city were a wide-open mining camp as well. Jupiter Station had always been wide open, a place where money spoke louder than morality. Most of the regular residents, many having been born and raised on the station, saw the war simply as an opportunity for quick profits. It soon became a hotbed of espionage and counterespionage. This situation resulted in the arrival of so many intelligence officers from each side that the Jupiter Station actually gained population during the most violent periods of the war. This is not to say that life on the station was without hazard. Agents tended to have a short period of usefulness and no need for a pension plan. Disposing of a body when surrounded by vacuum and so close to Jupiter was never a problem. Nor was identifying the opposition— not that the opposition was always from the other side.

GOLD-DIGGING
by Jody Lynn Nye

Myessa Rosarita Casales y Fuego watched as the
stevedores unloaded the crates of her possessions from
the vast freight container out onto the loading dock
inside Jupiter Station. Inside those crates were the
mattresses for twenty-six brass beds, the frames for
ten airbeds, a gross of lamps, mirrors, desks, futons,
roll-away couches, works of art, fifteen crates of cos-
tumes and other clothing, and a hundred cases of the
best liquor to be found anywhere in the Confederation
capital of Buenos Aires. There was more; cases of
gourmet provisions were down being vetted by the
Agriculture Bureau, and would be delivered later. They
were—Myessa smiled—for the only officially commissioned regiment of hookers in the entire Confederation military.

"Where shall we put these, ma'am?" one of the
boys asked, easing a handcart of priceless brandy
through the service door of the Club Mardi Gras. His
voice was respectful, but his eyes considered the possi-
bilities of what was before him. The club's proprietor
was wearing a skin-tight dress of silver-trimmed mid-
night blue, which reached to her ankles but provided a
pretty good topographical map of what was inside it.
The young man and his companions certainly found
the package appealing. Myessa counted on that little
extra oomph from workers who found visual aids helpful, and always dressed accordingly when she was having repairs done in her establishments or moving from
one place to another. It was one of the little bonuses
that made her memorable as an employer, the next
time she needed work done.

Myessa had had a successful business on Earth, in her native Argentina. Her impulse to move to Jupiter Station came at the same time as the letter from the local authorities urging her to move along out of their district. The next elections were coming up, and a government that permitted, or rather winked at, a house of prostitution in the constituency stood little chance of reelection in this day and age of renascent morality. Myessa knew them all, and knew them for hypocrites, but she understood that it paid her nothing to antagonize them. Before she told them of her plans she wheedled out of the Council a promise not to make her go until she was ready, as long as she wasted no time.

Relieved to have their problem solved without legal proceedings, they agreed, and Myessa considered the matter settled. Now openly, she sent out queries to her real estate agent, a charter service, and suppliers of food and drink, as well as those seeking official sanction for her journey. To her surprise, her applications for space travel, conveyance of personal property, business permits, and purchase of residential space on Jupiter Station began to come back to her marked REFUSED. Puzzled, she resubmitted the paperwork, and instructed her lawyer to bring the documents to the right authorities in person. She was once again denied permission for everything except the permit to "convey personal household goods, but only if they are accompanied by the owner or owners." That was no good to her without the other papers, so the forms went back a third time. One more document, that applying for a permit to purchase and occupy residential space on the station, arrived marked "APPROVED," this one in the company of the tax man, who wanted a form filled out detailing the source of the money with which she would be paying for it. This was another annoyance; Myessa kept her tax records well up to date, because that was the first thing that crusading politicians always brought up to try to run her out of town.

Naturally, Myessa called her *abogado* to demand an

explanation. As he was the most expensive legal representative in Buenos Aires, he must be able to pull some strings with those of influence. The locals were starting to get hot, what with the date of the election approaching, and no sign of Myessa's departure. Her lawyer called one morning and asked her to attend a meeting in his office, which, he promised, would immediately settle the problem one way or the other.

Miguel Guillermo Boscaverde de Gutierrez was not easily discomfited, but it was clear to Myessa that this was one of those rare occasions when life had caught him with his pants around his ankles. She sailed into his private sanctum past the bowing attorney, touching him familiarly on the cheek with two fingers, and sank gracefully, if theatrically, into one of the rich, leather upholstered chairs Miguel kept in front of his desk for visiting clients. The explanation for his nervousness he articulated solely with a nod of his head toward the other chair.

Its occupant, a man with ebony-black skin and black, red-shot eyes, nodded a barely courteous greeting to Myessa. He was an officer of the Confederation forces, with his hat still on his head despite the recent entry of a lady into the room. Myessa didn't keep up to date on the badges and symbols of rank, but the number of medals on his dress tunic spoke of long service. She had nothing against servicemen—some of the finest skirmishing she'd ever known was under a captain of the marines—but if this stuffy-looking individual was the man holding up her applications she wanted to know why.

Miguel made introductions, his upper lip under the pencil-thin mustache twitching nervously. "Señora Myessa Casales y Fuego, may I introduce to you Colonel Charles Njomo, of Inteligencia Militaridad."

Myessa inclined her head courteously.

The square-jawed colonel regarded her without expression. "I will come directly to the point of my visit, señora. You wish to go to Jupiter Station?"

"Sí, of course. Jupiter should be a good place for my business." Myessa set her hand down on the desk, palm first. "Let me come directly to the point, too, my colonel. I wish to establish my business, not merely live there. It isn't uncommon for houses like mine to open in frontier mining posts like Jupiter. In fact, it would be uncommon if they did not. It is from those women of the past that the term *gold-diggers* comes. There are certainly other independents already operating in the cylinders and in the space stations. The government knows what I do. Surely they wouldn't be preventing me from opening my house there. Unless the government is creating its own . . . service corps?" she asked coyly. "I would hate to be in direct competition with the Confederation."

"Señora Myessa, are you a patriot?" Colonel Njomo asked.

"Of course I am a patriot. But that usually means someone wants me to do something for free. I don't work for free. Now that you know that, tell me. As a businesswoman, how may I serve the land of my birth?"

Njomo smiled, and the whiteness of his teeth contrasting with his skin surprised her, attracted her. "We would never consider asking for free service. I always question the motives of those who don't want to be paid. Your proposed move to Jupiter Station coincides brilliantly with a need which we of the Secret Service want fulfilled. Let me outline to you a small idea which we are tossing around. If you refuse, there will be no difficulty, but I must ask that you not discuss it with anyone. There could be loss of lives—Confederation lives—if you let it slip. And naturally, carrying our secret, we couldn't let you leave Earth."

"Señor, that sounds most unfortunately, and I am certain, unwittingly, like a threat. I have kept secrets during my twenty years in business that would still embarrass half the heads of state on Earth."

"Excellent. My intention is not to threaten you, but to bring to your attention a matter which we consider to be most serious. The Confederation lags far behind the U.N. in information-gathering services, and it is telling on us in the war effort. The battle is escalating. We are far behind the U.N. in resources. We could lose all our small stake in the mineral rights of the outer planets, not to mention the lives of many citizens of the Confederation. Perhaps you have experienced the openness that exists between consenting adults in an intimate situation?" Myessa, listening politely, nodded. "Men and women who live stressful lives are willing to talk about almost anything if they are comfortable enough. We know about your previous . . . houses. You provide the kind of atmosphere in which tired men and women would reveal to you intimate or classified secrets. On Jupiter Station, we want you to listen to the pillow talk when those tired officers and executives of the U.N. speak to you, and pass your gleanings back to me. Help us. Help the country of your birth and its allies."

Myessa threw back her head and laughed. Her pretty voice held the tinkle of amusement when she spoke. "Nicely put! So this is the kind of gold you want my people to dig for! Why not?"

"Naturally, you and your employees will be given commissions of honorable rank, and shown every courtesy and advantage in . . . ahem! . . . setting up shop."

Well, she took the offer. Myessa didnt mind in the least being a major of the Intelligence Service, especially not when she would answer directly to the handsome Colonel Njomo. It was one more thing to add to her memory book, a tome that would have filled many volumes and been a scandalous best-seller had it been in print. She went on gathering her handpicked stable, and organizing the sale of such belongings and valuables as she would not take with her to the stars. This was her opportunity to offer employment to such bedroom artistes as she had met and admired in the past, but hadn't dared to steal away from rival establishments.

The armed forces made a frustrated attempt to put the regiment of prostitutes through basic training while they were staying in the Rio de Janeiro isolation camp awaiting the date of departure. Myessa just laughed at the drill sergeants, who came to her furious with the ladies and gentlemen of the evening who just turned

over and went back to sleep when roused at dawn.
The shouts of the DI's had been audible through the
window of her bedroom, but she pretended that the
noncoms had awakened her when they entered to
present their complaints. She refused to discipline her
employees, citing instead, with a small grin, their priv-
ilege as a special services unit. The sergeants were
invited to join them somewhat later in the morning,
when over half of her "regiment" participated in
warming-up Tai Chi exercises and dance classes to
keep the muscles limber. Myessa's "regiment" also
eschewed the standard army fare and ate instead in
the spaceport hotel restaurant, at the military's expense. Soon, they would be setting up shop on Jupiter
Station. Rio would be glad to see them ship out.

She was happy for the extra help in doing what
she'd always wanted anyway. "Never count the teeth
of a gift horse," she said. "Replacement prosthetics
are cheap." The colonel didn't understand why there
had been a smile on her lips from the time he'd made
his proposal. Myessa understood that they needed her,
and she could make some currency or, more useful by
far, "convenience" out of that fact. Currency they'd
have no problem raising once they got going.

The estate agent had come through like an angel.
The nascent Club Mardi Gras was to occupy a cube-
shaped space forty-five feet on a side inside Jupiter
Station, enormous for a private company. Myessa's
office was to be at the heart of the cube, with a
devious escape route built in beyond the chamber for
those who needed to enter and leave the club discreetly. The director of the space station, a neutral in
the dominance battle between the U.N. and the Federation, was only too happy to give Major Casales y
Fuego anything she needed. Water recycling and air
systems hookup were scheduled for the moment the
construction work was completed. The grumbling
plumbers and architects, who had been pulled off of
other jobs to work on the club, assumed it was because Myessa was running a whorehouse, and she let

them think so. To assuage the disgruntled foremen, the proprietor promised them each a one-time freebie in the club, once it commenced operations. "But only if you bathe, my sweethearts. My artistes must not have their senses impaired."

"If we can use your water systems, it's a deal," the electrician grinned. "I've got a daily allowance of thirty ccs."

Myessa had allowed herself a generous stipend for water. She liked to provide many amenities that the clients could not get at home, and was well aware of the tight rein that had to be kept on such precious commodities in space as clean water and oxygen. So long as her expensive recirculators held out, she could afford to be generous. The workmen came out of their encounters raving about the airbeds and the shimmering silver walls of some of the rooms, which helped the small cubicles seem bigger while at the same time providing a pleasant sense of slight disorientation to cap the effects of the liquor and euphorics. Words of praise sufficient for the talent of her staff, naturally, were beyond mere technicians.

So far, the director was the only outsider who knew the actual status of the employees of Club Mardi Gras. As for the employees themselves, Myessa trusted them implicitly or she wouldn't have hired them.

When they weren't working, her ladies and gentlemen generally congregated in the common room, joined by a nearly invisible double door to the communal dining room and kitchen on the main floor, and the stairs to the storerooms below. Flor and Feliciana came from Brazil, tall women with marvelous skin and perfect asses, which were on display under the string bikinis the ladies wore nearly all the time in the common room, accepting the stares they attracted as their legitimate due. Both were dancers who spent hours every day limbering up and riding the stationary bike to keep their leg muscles strong. They gave skillful demonstrations of native dances for special occasions. To complement them Myessa had three supple young men, one also from Brazil and two from Borneo, who were sword- and fire-dancers. Among the rest were handsome men, both young and not so young, who were just the debonair kind of date that lonely space-women were looking for. She also had hired girls from southeast Asian countries who had learned pleasing arts as well as bedroom skills.

Myessa preferred her prostitutes also to be musicians, performers, and dancers, rather than be—she excused the expression to herself—one-trick ponies. Without other accomplishments one could become very dull. Addicts she would not employ; they tended to be dishonest, both in behavior and in giving fair measure to the client. Each artiste was assigned his or her own room, which could be decorated to taste so long as taste was employed. Myessa hated red and black velvet drapes, and forbade any displays that included real weapons. Her own apartment had diaphanous draperies and artfully placed mirrors that diffused the light, making it seem larger. Though she wouldn't admit it she suffered slightly from claustrophobia, and hated anything that made a room feel small.

The rest of the staff—housekeepers, technicians, and a pair of decorators—lived in rooms on the top floor of the club. With the exception of the kitchen staff and her communications technician, Myessa had no objections if these took free-lance work outside in the station itself. Myessa didn't want meals interrupted and she didn't want Sparks, the communications tech, off somewhere else if something went wrong with the Panic Button emergency system. It was intended to provide silent security for the artistes if a client became uncontrollable and help was needed. In Myessa's experience, the alarms sometimes went off by themselves.

Jupiter Station was officially neutral in the battle between Confederation and U.N. having been built in the spirit of cooperation that existed between the governments of the world when the mining project had begun. It was old. Maintenance was the first priority of operation.

It was also the biggest of the cylinders in space. It held a Trojan orbit around Jupiter itself, balanced in the elipse of Ganymede's revolution. The troubles endemic because of its very size put builders off attempting another such; all the following capsules and cylinders were markedly smaller, and functioned more efficiently. Jupiter Station was always having oxygen leaks and breakdowns in the clean-air delivery systems. Every business and residence on board had to have emergency equipment handy, and each person was required to have some training in its use. Water and waste main failure was the next most common problem. Sensible residents made sure to donate heavily to the Watermen's Fund, either officially or unofficially, and to stay current on station charges.

Myessa got the rundown on the station workings from the owner of the equipment repair shop next to her club. While other residents of the station had shown few signs of welcome for her and her employees, Jack Conroy was glad to see them.

"So far, you've increased my walk-in custom about three hundred percent," he grinned, sitting over a cup of coffee with her the morning before the club opened. "I serve mostly the independent miners. They come in one day, drop off their troubles, go and have a bath and a few drinks, pick up their goods, and you don't see them again for seven years. You can see where we're fixed, far down G Corridor like this. No one walked by much when your space was empty. Everyone wants to know what's going on, and give me their opinions on same. Not everyone's happy, but I'm sure that doesn't bother you. Well, it all helps to pay the oxygen bill."

Myessa also made friends with the portmaster, who gave her schedules of arriving ships with projected lengths of stay. That day, a U.N. ship was arriving, joining one already docked. A freighter was expected in the middle of the late shift.

About 2000 hours, the first clients entered the club between the bouncers' posts, and were shown into the foyer, where they were met by Myessa herself. The financial arrangements were handled quite frankly up front. Too well she knew that if she waited until the

customer was ready to leave he or she might not be
inclined to talk about money, or even in any shape to
do so.

A few of the men and women who entered were
merely curious. Myessa served them drinks and chat-
ted with them. Yes, it was a brothel; she had nothing
to hide. No, she did not hire interested amateurs.
Would you trust someone's nephew to fill your tooth?
The scantily dressed Brazilians performed a wild, graceful dance, earning them the immediate interest of two
of the men newly arrived from the U.N. military ship.
They retired to their separate cubicles with panting
clients in tow, leaving Niko, a Javanese girl, to perform delicate *koto* music for those still in the common
room.

"Anyone can have taped symphonies," Myessa said,
grandly. "Here, all you see is real. May I offer anyone
another brandy?"

She was pleased with the way the first evening was
going. One of her older gentlemen, a real hidalgo
from Guadalajara, Jose Maria Veracruz de Rojas, was
in the corner with a female officer, chatting over a
rosé and a glass of her priceless cognac. Few women,
including herself, Myessa reflected, could resist the
soulful black eyes and silvering temples of such an
attentive gentleman. He made them feel beautiful,
unique. Jose Maria was the escort of choice for respectable young ladies, especially officers. He was very
presentable, even at formal functions. Myessa had
questioned taking him on, wondering why a former
high-placed executive would seek employment in a space-
bound house of prostitution. Jose Maria had swept
her a sardonic bow, and replied with a twinkle in those
deep eyes. How better for an aging gentleman to see
the outer planets than by having women pay him to
have sex with them? The proprietor liked him. They
were not far apart in age; she wondered if she could
be so honest about her own motives.

There was a loud cry and a crash from the stairs on
the upper floor. One of the U.N. marines threw himself out of the door of the cubicle, followed by Flor,

clutching her abbreviated costume to her breast. He
shoved her backward and stormed down the staircase,
yanking his tunic on over his head.

"I'm paying you to screw, not babble," he yelled.
" 'Specially not in that foreign lingo! I thought you
were Northern—your skin's pink enough. You trying
to pass for respectable?"

"What is going on here?" Myessa demanded.

"Aren't there any *Northern* women here?" the marine demanded, casting a furious glance around the
room. "No. Not even you." He pointed at Myessa's
ivory complexion, dismissed it with a scornful gesture.
"You're all Fed trash, with your 'yatata-yatata' lingo.
This looked like a classy place, but it's full of scum!"

Myessa looked around at her other guests, who
were becoming agitated. "Please calm down, sir," she
began.

"Calm down?" the young man almost squeaked.
"I'm sure it's a violation of some law you're here; I'll
see to it you're shut down! You lure us in here . . ."

A large, brown hand reached over Myessa's shoulder and took hold of the marine's arm, twisting it
slowly. It was Arsène, one of the French Guianan bouncers. "The lady asks you to calm down, m'sieur. If you
wish to talk quietly, we can go outside."

The boy wrenched out of Arsène's grasp and threw a
punch at him, missing by yards. Myessa ducked out
of the way. The burly bouncer grabbed both the marine's wrists. With his advantage of height, he hoisted
the boy up into the air, yanking his feet off the ground.
Kicking, the young marine shouted for help, and other
heads popped out of cubicles on the upper floor and
from comfortable seats around the common room.
Before Myessa could stop them marines in various
stages of undress streamed down the stairs to defend
their comrade. One man dashed into the fray carrying
an inverted wine bottle, the mouth of which still drib-
bled wine, as a club. Two of the sconce lamps on the
staircase were pulled down and shattered as a handful
of marines attempted to yank Arsène and the other
bouncer, Columbe, up the steps where they could beat

them. Jose Maria's lady extracted herself from the love seat near the bar, and piled into the brawl, shouting for attention.

"Quiet! Tone it down!" she yelled, both hands raised above her head. It was too late. Battle was joined. On one side, the club's employees were trying to separate the combatants and throw out the brawlers. On the other side were marines, spoiling for a little action on the neutral station, whatever the excuse. In the middle were Arsène, the young marine, and Flor, who, just before the crowd shoved her backward, Myessa could see scoring the face of her erstwhile boyfriend with her nails. She ran for the station security alarm and pushed the button. In a moment she was connected to the office, who assured her help, and the shore patrol, were on the way.

It took less than ten minutes for Arsène to fight his way through the crowd and throw his burden out of the door into the corridor. The bloody-faced marine landed with a thump in front of the security force's open-topped car. Twenty minutes later the fight was over, and the marines who showed signs of having been in the fight had been removed from the premises. All the other clients had fled when the brawl began.

"Lousy Fed dirtbags," one of them spat as the shore patrol pushed him out of the door. "Here just to spy on us."

Myessa kept her expression dignified as she closed the door on him, but she was quaking inside. What if their cover had been revealed? "What brought that on?" she demanded of Flor, who was sitting on the carpet amidst the ruined furniture, sucking at a slash on her wrist.

Flor looked up at her sideways, trying to seem innocent. "Just asking him questions about his work, *mamacita*." The cut began to bleed again, and the dancer dabbed at it with the edge of her costume.

"Don't be so obvious, *ninita*, if you love your life! What if they knew why we want to know?" Myessa grabbed the girl's arm. "Your blood would boil away so prettily in vacuum, like a red cloud. They do not spare spies."

Proudly, Flor rose to her feet. "I meant no harm. I will be more discreet."

"For your life's sake. For ours. Now come with me. I shall bandage that." Myessa led her to the office. "You others, begin to clean up this mess. I will join you in a moment."

The next morning, two members of the shore patrol called to retrieve the rest of the young marine's garments and other possessions. A silent Flor led one of the officers up the stairs to her room while the other interviewed Myessa.

"We've heard Private Edmundsen's side of the story, Señora," the muscular female sergeant said, showing her a statement on her clipboard screen. She was a Northerner, but didn't seem to hold Myessa's nationality against her. "It sounds like an over-eager boy shot his bolt too quickly and blamed it on the girl. She offered him another round on the house. Embarrassed, he became abusive. He starts a fight. End of story. Do you wish to press charges?"

Relieved that there was no mention in the young man's narrative of Flor's clumsy interrogation, Myessa shook her head. "Where is he now?"

"Spent the night in the brig sleeping it off. His face is a mess, but apart from that I don't think he remembers much. I would guess he's out now policing the general area for wrappers and beer cans, or swabbing latrines. That was his lieutenant here last night. She saw the whole thing."

"A night in the brig I am sure has done all that I would have done. Thank you for responding to the call so quickly, sergeant." The other sergeant appeared, carrying the boy's undergarments in a bundle under his arm. Myessa smiled at both of them, and dipped her lashes playfully. "Stop by anytime, officers."

She called her artistes together in the common room for a talk on discretion, and thereafter things ran much more smoothly. "There is no need to get a full curriculum vitae from each contact," she chided them. "I understand that you wish to do the best job, and the most quickly, but hold back. One misunderstanding, one man or woman who comprehends what it is you are doing, and we will never see Earth again. Do you understand? Little facts, little rumors which we can gather up and check, which they will never know they dropped in your lap, is what we want. They believe you are here to give them pleasure. Never let them think you have come for any other purpose."

It wasn't possible to record the information her artistes picked up into computer files. Such things were too easily infiltrated. Myessa chose instead to record them in a code of tone and rhythm, tucking them into one of the sixteen tracks of her personal library of audio compact disks, a different track on each. When it was time to transmit a report she had the song transmitted back to Earth, as part of an audio letter to Charles Njomo, pretending that he was her lover waiting at home for her.

"Send me more music, my darling," she wrote, wickedly picturing Njomo's expression of amazement. "I want to know what you are thinking of me today."

Slowly, the data trickled in. Myessa realized as she compiled rumor here and revelation there, that she was hearing more now every day about the world outside the cylinder than she had heard in any amount of gossip over the weeks the club was being built. Joao, one of her lithe sword-dancers, brought her the titbit that the U.N. had managed to make their new jetpack work, but his source hand't seen it himself yet. Myessa held that piece of information until the Thai girl Narntil told her that the fact was confirmed. She had slept with one of the pilots who tested it and, she confided, he was as much of a rocket as his jetpack.

Not every report went into the mail circuit on a music disk. Once or twice she arranged to have the data etched in bar code onto the plastic surface of a disk mailer, with a hint in the nondescript message inside that it was there, and sent to the base on Ganymede, addressed to a nonexistent friend. Very occasionally, when Fed personnel were in Jupiter Station, she had the opportunity to pass on a report directly.

One morning she had the pleasure of presenting her data face to face with an MI colonel, or face to ear, while she buttered toast for him in bed. She handed the bread down to him as he lay with his head propped against her breasts. Colonel Esteban Cordon ran his hand up and down the skin of her thigh as he digested both the toast and the report.

"*Muy bien*," he said, glancing at her upside down. She kissed his forehead. "I take it this room is soundproofed."

"Sealed against audio devices. If anyone is looking in on us, they see a woman and her satisfied customer speaking words of insincere love after a night of mutual enjoyment."

"The customer is very satisfied, Myessa. The colonel will be pleased with you, as I am." His eyelashes dipped slightly, inviting her to share the humor of his remark. "I am pleased not only because this is a breakthrough—your girl has established a 'friendship' with the pilot?"

"Oh yes, I think so. He has already returned once. His ship leaves in twenty-seven hours."

Esteban nodded, smiling. "This is also the only decent food in the quadrant, as you must know. *Dios mio!* You should open a restaurant, with your cook and baker."

"So sorry, but they're a team—and for what you don't want to know. They make a hundred times in bed what they could in a kitchen."

Esteban slid reluctantly from the sheets and began to put on his uniform. "I should go. The pleasure was all mine, dear lady major."

"And mine." Myessa leaned forward and ran a gold-edged fingernail delicately down into the cleft between her breasts under the neck of her satin shift. "Come back again anytime, Colonel."

With a sweeping gaze that summed up and stored

her most attractive image for his memory, Esteban Cordon bowed himself out of the room.

There were more brawls in the club's common room in the ensuing weeks. Whenever a Confederation ship was in port at the same time as a U.N. ship there was trouble. It usually resulted in bruises and broken glass, but occasionally there were more serious injuries. After taking one of her young men to the infirmary with a badly broken arm, Myessa brought her problem to the director of Jupiter Station in hope of a solution.

"Can't you ask them to take shore leave at different hours?" she pleaded. "One shift for each, and the third dark so my children can get some sleep?" Myessa knew she was beginning to look haggard. Her mirror had told her that her complexion was suffering from the sleeplessness. She was vain of her smooth skin, and didn't like to reveal weaknesses. Cosmetics could only hide so much.

"I can't," the director said mournfully, clenching his hands. "I can't openly suggest that there's anything wrong between the two factions, though it's obvious to anyone who listens to the news. The war is heating up."

"Every day now there are fights in my common room. I have hired two more bouncers but it won't be enough."

The director bowed his head. "I'm sorry. I don't know how long I'll be able to continue the station's policy of neutrality. It can't be long before someone makes me declare for one side or the other, and then goodbye, Jupiter Station!"

Myessa patted his hand. "It is in their better interests to leave you alone. But if they don't, I beg that you give me notice so I can get my people away. Whichever way you declare, there's bound to be more trouble for me. If you declare for the U.N. we're targets, and we had better leave quickly. If you declare for the Confederation all right, but the U.N. will attack us because we're vulnerable. We need to be open for our clients," she explained apologetically, "or their support fades as quickly as their memories.

Our long work day makes the club an easy target for terrorism."

The director began to bite his nails. Myessa took his hand out of his mouth and set it firmly back on the desk. "I am scared, too, but do I mutilate my hands? No. Why don't you come back with me? Have a relaxing massage, my cook will make you a meal fit for a gourmet, and one of the girls will be nice to you, eh? You look like you could use the break."

Gratefully, the director followed her back to the club. The strain was indeed beginning to tell on the residents of the station. Columbe let her in hastily, and directed her to the third floor, where Arsène was mediating a dispute between one of the girls and a client. Sighing, Myessa put the director into the capable hands of Kytera, one of her ladies, and hurried up to handle the argument.

At the top of the stairs, a U.N. officer was shouting and waving his arms. Matching him for volume and vituperation was Yao Pei, a tall Chinese girl whom Myessa had spotted waiting tables on Earth. Normally, Yao Pei was the most placid of creatures, patient with even the most obstreperous clients. What kind of crank was this officer to set off her temper?

"Excuse me," Myessa shouted, when both of them had paused for breath. "There are others who wish to enjoy the day without excess noise."

"You're the owner? Your girl—" the officer indicated Yao Pei with a sharp gesture.

"Not here," Myessa interrupted him, as Yao Pei started to shriek that she had done everything the officer had asked. "Come to my office. Stay here," she directed the girl. "I will talk with you later."

"No!" the U.N. man growled. "I want her to hear everything I have to say." He seized Yao Pei by the hair and pulled her down the stairs ahead of Myessa. "Which way?"

Something in his manner frightened Myessa, but she kept herself erect and formidable. The officer hauled the screaming girl into Myessa's office and threw her down on the floor.

"I demand my money back. She's a cheat!"

At that declaration, Myessa recognized a typical cheapskate. He'd been satisfied, all right, but decided halfway through that he could get his money back. "Very well, sir," she said soothingly, counting out into his hand vouchers totaling one hundred and fifty percent of what he had paid for Yao Pei's services. Released, the girl scrambled to her feet and fled the room, sliding the door shut behind her. "I am including an honorarium over and above that price for your disappointment. I lose by this, because I won't let my girl starve just because you didn't like her. You may have a refund just this once. If you make such an accusation a second time with a different girl, I will have to assume that there's something wrong on *your* side, and our association is at an end."

Myessa eyed him suspiciously when, instead of storming out or assuming a pleading mien, a slow smile spread across his face. After all, she had just insulted him. "You handle yourself well, madame. I'm impressed."

"Thank you. Now, if you'll excuse me, I have work to do." Hands on hips, she indicated the door with her chin.

The man shook his head. "I want to talk with you. This was the only way I could arrange a private meeting."

"What?" Myessa shrieked. She reached for the security call button set into the key pad on her desk.

"There's no need to call your muscle men," the man said smoothly, deflecting her hand from the control before she could press, and flipping a card embossed with a chip out of his pocket. "Here's my identification. I am Captain van Owen of Military Intelligence. I have a job for you."

She eyed the card. It seemed genuine, but only hooking up the card to an ident unit would prove it. "The only job we do here is to pamper the sexual mores of lonely men and women, Captain. That's all I want to do."

"Oh, but I think you can do more." Van Owen

pulled up the lush visitor's chair and loftily gestured
across the desk. "Sit down, please."

Myessa crossed her arms. With one toe, she pushed
the stud under her desk that triggered the recording
devices Sparks had hidden in the walls. "I will stand.
Say what you have to before I grow tired."

"As you please. I've been watching your club for
many weeks now. I observe that many Fed spacemen
and businessmen, er . . . sleep over. I want to know
what it is they tell your girls and boys."

"Pillow talk, such as it is, is private," Myessa said,
with a patient smile. "My clients usually talk about
themselves and how lonely they are."

"I know that is not true, madame. I have sent
operatives into this house, and they spoke freely of
potentially classified material with your employees,
who seemed eager to listen."

"That's their job," Myessa interrupted. "To seem
eager, even when the body and mind are growing
tired. As I am. Are you finished?"

"You are playing with me, madame, and I'm not
that patient. I want your girls and boys to listen when
they hear information, and to pass it back to you, for
collection by me. Or . . ."

"Or what?" Myessa said, narrowing her eye at him.
"Or else? I've been threatened before."

"Or this: you have had a peaceful enough season
here thus far, but it can end like that!" Van Owen
snapped his fingers. "There will be brawls every day,
problems with waste control, annoyance in the form of
official interference from the Space Station Authority,
and if those do not move you, madame, problems with
water and air supply—or perhaps you would like to
find one of your girls or boys outside on the surface of
the capsule, breathing vacuum?"

"And what if I go to the U.N. and the Space Station
Authority and request protection from you, citing what
you have told me today?"

Van Owen lowered his voice until it was a chilling
whisper. "Then you might have a terrible personal
accident, and your employees of this establishment

would begin to suffer fatalities right away, once you are helpless to prevent it." He smiled. "Or, I could simply ruin you. If I let it become known that there are incurable diseases here. I could introduce IDs, and let a U.N. soldier discover it the hard way at his next physical. You'd be sequestered until you could go back to Earth—if you can afford to go back."

Myessa shuddered. ID, Incurable Disease. There were plenty of them in the Earth community. Each of her people had been screened over and over again during a period of three months on Earth and for the weeks before the club opened in the station. Some very good performers had been left behind because they suffered from progressive calcium disease. The ailment was more or less harmless to atmosphere dwellers, but it was fatal to spacers who had to metabolize calcium faster than they did, and it was highly communicable. Others had permanent venereal disease or other illnesses that required constant cleanliness to contain outbreaks, an impossibility where water was such a scarcity.

Never mind. Her own people had constant health checks, too. An ID would be detected before it could do too much damage; she couldn't hope that it would do none. Wait . . . The residents of the space station and the armed forces were all put through rigorous medical examination to arrest potential disease threats. Where would IDs be introduced without infecting someone first to give it to them? Any attempt to infect one of her people physically would be categorized as assault, and she *would* press charges with the World Court. "Get out!" she said furiously. "And do not come back."

Slowly, insouciantly, the officer rose to his feet and moved to the door. "I will leave now, madame. I look forward to renewing our acquaintance."

Two days later, Jose Maria stopped by Myessa's office. "May I speak with you privately, Myessa?"

She looked up. Her hidalgo was as dapper as usual, in a frilled-edge tunic that would have looked effeminate on anyone else, but he seemed troubled. "Of course, Jose Maria. Please, make yourself comfortable. May I offer you wine?"

The older man lowered himself into the seat as if his bones hurt, and stretched out his legs in front of him. "Thank you, no. The grape is an inviting hostess, but I fear that if I accept her hospitality I may overstay my welcome. I have information for you."

Myessa inclined her head and waited. For some reason, he was finding it hard to speak. "Please."

"The U.N. is bringing in many more ships, mustering them from Earth and every point they can. They are intending to make a massive strike against the Confederation. And there is something curious about those ships, but my source does not know what it is."

"But this is good news. Precisely what we need to know," Myessa assured him. Jose Maria sighed. "So, what troubles you?"

The hidalgo smiled and studied his feet sadly. "There is one who has touched my heart, the little lieutenant, Patty. I have been accepting information from her to give to you. I feel terrible. I am betraying her."

"It is our survival, Jose Maria. We must. If we do not, many of our countrymen will die unwarned. This way, the U.N. will arrive and there will be no one there to shoot at."

"Or it will become apparent that someone has given the information to the enemy, us. She could die a traitor's death, and that I cannot bear."

Myessa watched him carefully. "She is a good source." The man nodded, still not looking at her. "But we do not have to use every source."

For the first time, he smiled. "Thank you, *maestra*." He sighed, his chest expanding as if freed from a tight band. "I ought never to have become involved. Perhaps I should retire from the escort business. Maybe marry, or just retire and watch the grass grow at home on Earth. I have money of my own, from my days as an executive, and I have saved much here."

"You would be wasted on one woman, my friend, but as always, it is your decision. You are not betraying your friend. Information can be used as a preemptive strike, if I read Charles's instruction book correctly. You may be saving her life."

"*Gracias*. You are wiser than I." Jose Maria bowed over her hand, and left.

Such data could not wait for her weekly letter to Njomo. Even the minutes of delay in transmission seemed too long to her. She began to encode a letter to her "friend" on Ganymede, that would be beamed as soon as she could get to the portmaster's office. The code for urgency was the invitation to a party—but what a terrifying party, if it was not defused promptly. She was preparing the privacy seal of the message when there was a loud *bam!* It sounded like the impact of a heavy metal object falling on a metal floor. The lights through her bedroom door went out and there was a wash of terrible cold, followed by a powerful wind, sucking toward the bedchamber. Wafers and disks, and anything light, swept off her desk and flew through the air toward her door. As she got up to see what was wrong, disk recorder still clutched in her hands, the containment door swooshed across, blocking her. It clamped tight in its frame, and seeming to press inward. As soon as the door closed, the wind stopped. Myessa flew for her desk.

"There's a breach in the walls!" she screamed into her intercom. "In my room! The air is running out!"

"Did the door seal it, madame?" Columbe demanded. "Are you trapped? Can you breathe?"

"Yes, I am in my office, but my things, my clothes! It's so cold!"

"Wait there, madame. Do not attempt to enter. I will summon the repair crew."

Myessa slumped in her chair, stunned. The wall had broken, and the vacuum of space was invading her personal quarters, her home! She was trapped inside a tiny box in space, surrounded by the cold hostility of the universe. Overwhelmed, she began to cry.

Columbe and one of the new bouncers came in, massive in pressure suits, followed by Sparks, the slight Chinese girl who was her communications technician.

Others crowded the doorway, and Myessa looked at them miserably through a haze of smeared mascara. "Go to your rooms, children. It is dangerous here."

"Tch, tch!" Kytera, a large Kenyan woman, clad only in a short white silk shift, bustled in and sat down on the arm of Myessa's chair. She took one of the proprietor's hands and stroked it. "I heard the boom. I feared you were hurt. Was it a bomb?"

"I . . . I don't think so. If it was, it wasn't inside the station." Myessa looked up at her, wide-eyed, like a child. "A bomb, set on the shell by someone to kill us!"

"You shouldn't be saying things like that," Kytera chided her. "Things collide with us in space. See the face of Ganymede leading us in our orbit? Full of craters and holes."

Narntil crept in behind the two of them and undid Myessa's long fall of hair and began to brush it. Soothed, Myessa was soon in control of herself again.

The bedroom door slid open. Sparks had taken off the wall plate and activated the controls manually. Columbe and his partner slipped inside. Through the doorway Myessa could see the appalling debris left behind by the cyclone that the breach in the bulkhead had caused. Her mattress was pinned flat against the wall, and sucked halfway into the hole.

"It saved your life, madame," Columbe called. "Phrang, as I move it, throw the patches at the breach. Quickly!" The big man heaved at one edge of the mattress, and the cold wind swept them again until the patch was in place. The door slid closed past Sparks, who exclaimed under her breath and went to work again. She never swore. She was the quietest person in Myessa's entire stable.

Strictly speaking, Sparks wasn't in the stable. She'd had a try at hooking, didn't like it, wasn't very good at it, but she could make a single transformer think it was the whole Very Large Array and perform accordingly. Myessa hired her at a bargain, because she was insufficiently appreciated in the Chinese family-dominated small company from which she'd come in old Hong

Kong, and gave her unlimited control and a generous budget sufficient to fund personal experiments.

"Where is the maintenance crew?" Myessa demanded.

Repeated calls to the repair facility confirmed that a crewman had been sent out. Myessa was at first in a state of panic, and at last angry when the man finally appeared. He was youngish, probably on the underside of thirty, and smiled nervously at the mob of frightened people who greeted him at the door of Club Mardi Gras and hauled him and his bag up to the second level.

"Madam Casales? I'm sorry. I was held up waiting for official channels to clear me through to you. I hope no one was injured?" He shook her hand and looked around the room. Columbe, still in his suit, waited by the temporary patch, watching it for new breaks.

"Official channels! *Christo mio!*" Myessa exclaimed. "I will never love bureaucrats. They told me you were sent out already, half an hour ago. But since we cannot just walk away from them in vacuum, we must deal as best we can. Here," she slipped the embarrassed handyman a credit voucher. The sum was generous, but she wanted to make a point with him. "Next time, don't wait for the official word, I beg you."

The man looked at the bill in his hand and turned red. "I'm so sorry, ma'am. I . . . I was ordered to wait to respond. I guess I owe you to know that."

He tried to return the voucher, but she closed his fingers on it. Myessa thought she could guess the identity of the person behind the repairman's conflicting orders. "Keep it," she insisted, "and remember you owe me a favor sometime. Now, fix."

All that night, Myessa lay awake in the dark, listening to the air-recirculation unit and worrying about her safety and the safety of those who depended on her. She owed them her protection, for what tiny measure of security that was worth, here in the shadow of mighty Jupiter. It was not possible to run away. There was no place to go or to hide. Outside of this metal

box were millions of miles of cold vacuum, and it
could gain admittance to the box so easily. It niggled
at the back of her mind that she shouldn't have taken
the job for the intelligence colonel. Surely she shouldn't
have involved forty other people, whose lives could so
easily be snuffed if someone chose to interfere with
the precious station life-support system. Yesterday's
inaction by the maintenance staff had proved that. If
she gave in to that U.N. blackmailer, she realized, she
would be more vulnerable than ever. But how best to
regain the advantage? He wielded fear as his weapon.
In its face, mere bravery wouldn't serve. She still
could die horribly, and all her employees with her,
swept away by another such accident. But what about
bravado, concealing wit? Certainly that was one of the
things for which the colonel had employed her.

She sat over her desk the next morning reading but
not comprehending the financial report that her computer had spat out. Her aching head felt like a nova
about to go super. There was a clatter from the intercom, and Arsène's voice announced van Owen was
here to see her.

"Admit him, but stand by."

"Oui, madame."

Myessa pulled herself upright and hoped she didn't
look as wretched as she felt. The door slid into the
wall and van Owen strode in, looking fresh and arrogant. Myessa longed to slap his face.

"I hope you are well today, madame."

"You find me in health, thank you."

"I wonder if I find you any more cooperative than I
did three days ago?" Van Owen raised an eyebrow
expectantly. "They say that adversity brings out the
best in people."

She knew what he meant, and scowled at him. The
lives of her people were at stake. "I don't do anything
for free. I'm here to make a living. I'm not greedy, but
I'm not a fool, either."

"Madame, you are in a precarious position."

"I am in a just barely legal profession. I'm *used* to
being in precarious positions. Nino, you can go ahead

and ruin me. I never gamble the rent. My bank balance is fat enough to fly out of here first-class. I'll go home to Earth. Health tests are a matter of public record there. I'll just go back into business. Or maybe I'll retire and raise chickens." With an effort, she wiped all expression from her face and waited.

Van Owen broke first. He must really have felt that he needed her as a conduit. He was dangerous, but he was vulnerable, too. "Very well, how much?"

"I can be reasonable." They dickered. Myessa watched him out of narrowed eyes as she rejected one offer after another, and made her counter-offer. This man was failing to respond to all the sensual signals she was firing at him. Either he took it as his due as a hotshot, or she wasn't what he liked. It might help her to understand him more if she could find out what he did like. She'd parade her group through next time he came and spot the best choice for later analysis.

A price was agreed upon. "Now," the U.N. man went on, rising to his feet, "I'll be back on a regular basis for your reports. I wish you a good day. Oh," he stopped at the door, "sorry about your girl, Yao Pei. She was just fine."

Myessa had already heard Yao Pei's side of the story. "I know. Don't expect free love next time you come. You'll pay, just like everyone else. *More if I can help it, chico*, she thought, as the captain left.

Naturally, the report of his whole visit went in the next message to Colonel Njomo. Her people received their new instructions with disbelief. Two of them asked to be excused from the duty even if they heard something, and she gave them her permission.

"He won't know what we don't tell him, right?" Myessa said at a meeting, after Sparks had swept the room for stray listening devices. "I can't force you to betray your countrymen, and it would be unwise to make up data. I'm waiting to hear instructions from Earth."

It was a terrifying three weeks until she received word that Njomo had her message. During that time, Myessa closed down several of the rooms, complaining that there was structural damage caused by the breach, and gave some of her people a paid furlough, so there wasn't much going on to report either way. Captain van Owen came back in the second week for his report, and threatened her because she didn't have so much as the location of a remote mining stake to give him. In a dudgeon, she took him to the blocked-off rooms and showed him the damage caused by the break in the wall, some of which had been artificially made worse by Sparks and the two decorators.

"The Space Station Authority thinks it may have been a meteor, but I suspect a stray shell from the battles, or deliberate sabotage," Myessa said pointedly. "I am losing money every day until this is repaired. I will give you data when I have it. I have agreed. Come back later. The Executive Officer of the *Simon Bolivar* has an appointment with two of my people at the beginning of second shift."

When van Owen had gone she sorted out declassified information from a training handbook Colonel Njomo had given her, and gave that to van Owen. It gave him the official strength of the *Bolivar*, months outdated, but she guessed he wouldn't know that.

When he returned, she gave him the disk. The U.N. man put it into Myessa's desk reader and turned the hooded screen toward him as she stood watching. His eyes flickered as they scanned the text. "Very nice," he murmured, scrolling down the short page. "Yes, not bad. Not a lot of information, but we will save this, awaiting further confirmation. Your payment, madame."

He put a credit voucher down on the desk. From where she stood Myessa could read the denomination, and picked it up disdainfully with finger and thumbtip. "What's this, a tip?" she demanded.

"Your remuneration. I think it's adequate. You can't expect full payment for such a morsel of information."

Myessa dropped it at his feet. "I certainly do. If I perform, no matter how the customer responds, I get *paid, hijo.* Go ahead. Call in your ID. Call in your brawlers. I guarantee I won't be on Earth two weeks before I've got a new shop. I'll send you my change of address letter."

Angrily, he retrieved the voucher, keeping his eyes locked with hers as he knelt and handed her another voucher, this time for the full amount. "If I don't get more satisfaction for my money the next time, there will be trouble."

Myessa tucked the voucher into her cleavage. "I can't give you what I haven't got, señor. You'll just have to wait, as we do." She smirked as he left the room, though she was quaking inside. He might cause her more trouble, as a warning, if she didn't come through soon with real data. But where was her backup? Njomo had assured her that she would have the support of the Inteligencia Militaridad. Where was it? She issued a quiet order to the others never to go walking alone, and to stay away from her visitor if they saw him in the corridors.

The mail packet arrived from Earth on a scientific shuttle that called at Jupiter Station before proceeding to Tito Two, a U.N. research vessel. There was a box for Myessa, four inches square by a foot long. Inside were two dozen new sixteen-track CD's, with a note. "Apologize for the delay. More complex and wonderful music than any ever written is what sings in my mind when I think of you. Can't wait to hear from you again. Your adoring Charles." There was nothing further in the box, but Myessa suddenly felt safer. He had read her messages and understood the danger. She kissed the note. "I adore you, too, Charles. Thank you."

Within a week there was word from the portmaster, notifying her that there were three Confederation ships bound for Jupiter Station.

"One of them is all the way from Earth," the portmaster informed her. "Carrying a consortium of executives from the ice-mining companies, the passenger list said. Be nice to 'em. That's where the money is."

Club Mardi Gras's fame had obviously spread to the crews of the *Cristobal Colon* and the *Emperor Akhito*.

As soon as shore leave was permitted, the common room of the Club was filled with Confederation sailors and marines. The ladies and gentlemen of Club Mardi Gras were overjoyed to see so many of their old countrymen and improvised a party of welcome, complete with dancing and music. The cook and baker outdid themselves for a buffet spread.

"I was beginning to get a Northern accent," complained Feliciana, opening a bottle of the best rum in the liquor stores for a Peruvian geologist from Nippon Enterprises. "All these Canadians and Germans. I love to hear a good South American voice again."

Some of the visitors stayed in the common room to sing and drink, but most of them were eager for friendly company after the long journey from Earth.

Myessa herself entertained a high-level Egyptian executive from Confederation Pure Water, Incorporated. Fouad Fatah was a small, square-shouldered man with glasses, who bowed deeply and gratefully when she led him to her private shower room and threw the taps on full. He disappeared into the spray while Myessa prepared herself.

When he emerged from the shower room, wrapped in a robe made of toweling, hair damped down to his skull, Myessa was waiting for him, in a flame-colored silk shift and peignoir of nearly invisible gold chiffon. She settled him on the bed and gave him the "big strip tease." It was a cross between a dance and a disrobing, which ended with her loosing the shoulder straps of the shift so that it slid down her hips to the floor, leaving her naked, with skin aglow in the silken light of the silver room. Fouad never moved throughout her dance. The man must have had iron control. Normally, the client was across the room with his head buried between her breasts by the time her shift hit the floor. It wasn't that he wasn't interested. Myessa could see his flesh straining against the fabric of his robe. He must like to have the lady do more of the work. Very well; she always did what would please the client best. She glided across the room to him, and knelt at his feet.

"Madam, I hardly deserve such treatment, when I am but a humble servant of the corporation, a mere bookkeeper."

"You have come all the way from Earth to visit me," Myessa purred. "That makes you honored guest enough."

"I am but a tool of NPW. It is the movers who command me to calculate the value of the dark side of Io on behalf of the Federation. It is for one of them that you should make such efforts."

Alarms rang in Myessa's head, and she worried about listening devices. "Dear sir, shouldn't you keep that kind of information private? That sounds so very confidential to me."

"Oh, but I want to tell you. You're so sympathetic. I can't see that there would be any harm if I do."

Bingo. It was just the barest trace of a wink, a lowering of the eyelashes of his right eye, which could have been an involuntary twitch. There were no other signs. This man, who was legitimately a senior executive and deserving of all the hospitality he eschewed, was very good. Myessa smiled at him, and dropped a kiss on his knee. She wanted to see how he'd perform in the boardroom some time.

"Of course, dear. Let me order some wine, and we will enjoy it together while you tell me what you'd like me to do for you."

When Fouad slept, Myessa went back to her office to record her newly received information. Kytera was waiting for her.

"If I don't talk to you right this minute, I'm going to burst in a shower of sparks."

"Save it for the clients, *querida*, they might like that kind of thing. What is it?"

"Privacy?" asked Kytera, looking around.

"Of course." The Club owner activated a small device under her desk, installed by Sparks, which effectively scotched any listening device. "But the effect is temporary. We do not wish it to be detected."

"Major," Kytera began, and broke into hysterical

giggles. "I can't call you that! It's too funny. Listen, I had a corporal in bed with me last night. Almost put me through the bulkhead, he had so much energy. I calmed him down some, and we stopped for refreshment. He paid for the wine, said he's celebrating. Well, somewhere between the cork and the glass, he tells me the news. The U.N. has developed a new kind of space drive: matter/antimatter. It's an honest breakthrough. Dangerous, but they got it to work without killing anyone."

"That's the finest news I've heard in a Jupiter year," Myessa said, smiling broadly, and glanced back at her bedroom door. "Nearly." A low beeping interrupted them. "We're public again. Of course, you deserve a bonus."

"Put it in my credit," Kytera requested, winking. "I paid for a bottle, too. He was not bad."

The next time van Owen appeared, he proved well satisfied with the report Myessa had for him. "A mission to the dark side of Io, eh? We have a substantial interest there, as well as a large base. Those scientists and so on will be very surprised that that seat, so to speak, is already taken."

Myessa was disgusted that he would gloat so openly before her. "You know I'm from the South. I'm spying on my own, you bastard."

"Life is hard for the small businesswoman, madame."

And man, she thought, smiling to herself. Sometimes one had to settle for a batch of ill-made goods. There had been an amazing number of Confederation visitors: military, scientific, and commercial, and all amazingly talkative. She was sure that was Charles's doing, and certain also that much of the information these talkative clients gave them was bad.

She thought she had it nailed down, which of her stable would easiest attract the son of a bitch. It was down to Joao, a slim, dark, sword-dancer, and Sparks, her communication technician. So, this time the U.N. man came, she had Sparks interrupt them.

Sparks came in at that point, looking pale and interesting. She had a pouch of common gear slung by a long strap over her shoulder. The strap defined her small breasts and the narrow bones of her upper body. Van Owen devoured the sight hungrily as the small woman bent near him to repair a split wire, her black hair swinging over a perfect, white-jade cheekbone. Yes. The way van Owen looked her up and down, there was more than interest, there was lust. This was his favorite prey—skinny, dark, gentle, and afraid. He was into big power trips, that Myessa knew from the way he tried to bully her, but he liked to dominate Sparks's and Joao's kind. Well, the denoument couldn't take place in the House, that was clear.

Aha, I have the key to your soul, hijo mio, Myessa thought. "Well, Captain, what'll it be? You feeling happy? I'm generous. Today we're running a special. You've paid me for one . . . service, I'll throw in another. You name it."

"What about her?" Van Owen aimed a glance at the kneeling technician.

"She's not on the menu, *ninito*. Reserved for one rich hotshot who comes in about once a month." Myessa had long since given up explaining to uncomprehending fools that not everyone who worked in a whorehouse was a whore.

"Then thank you, no. Some other time."

"Why are you so certain that I am passing on this data to you straight?" she asked van Owen as he prepared to leave. "Why are you so sure I am not doctoring it?"

"I just know," he said with that little smile that never failed to infuriate her. With a careless flick he tossed her the credit voucher, and left with her disk tucked into his pocket.

"You don't know," she said to the door after he had left. "You are arrogant, and that is why you will lose the war."

It was only a matter of time before he discovered that the information was bad. Myessa needed to disarm van Owen somehow, and get him off their backs.

His confidence in the continuity of their data told her that he must have a way of checking up on it. The usual method was to plant a mole among her employees, but Myessa didn't hire from the local talent and van Owen couldn't have suborned anyone. He never stopped to pass the time of day with anyone working for the club. The second method must be the one: the rooms were tapped. Myessa had Sparks do a sweep for foreign listening devices. The girl assured her the place was clean.

Van Owen appeared four days ahead of schedule and slammed the disk on her desk. "This data is bad, dammit! Why didn't you check to see that your contacts were telling the truth?"

"How am I supposed to know what is good and what is bad? Am I inside High Command's head? I give you what I get."

"Goddammit, can't you check?"

"No! How can I? Do you want me to tell them I'm a spy and give me references?"

They glared at one another, at an impasse. Van Owen left, furious, and Myessa worried that they would have to do something about him before he did something about them.

That night, while she was walking about on the top floor of the Club, she caught sight of a slim figure sneaking through the corridors. Calling for the bouncers, she gave chase.

Arsène cornered the intruder near the disintegrator, and held the figure there until Myessa could catch up. It was Sparks.

"She was trying to shove this in the disposer," Arsène said, passing Myessa a bag. It was full of electronic components, which Myessa recognized as eavesdropping devices.

"I am not responsible for them. I found them in the ceiling and walls. I removed them, and I am destroying them, I swear to you!"

"Who put them there?" Myessa barked.

"I don't know!" the girl shrieked, struggling in Arsène's arms.

"Why didn't you tell me you were finding bugs in the Club?"

"Because I was sure you would think it was me."

Myessa opened the bag. The bugs were of a design she hadn't seen before, but she understood the little spokes with suction cups affixed at the bottom of each one. These could "walk" to a preset destination, and fasten themselves to a support. It was unlikely that Sparks, who had access to every square centimeter of the station, had created these. "I nearly ordered you spaced just now, *chiquita*. Next time you tell me, and let me judge. Don't you think I'm fair?"

"Oh yes, Myessa!"

"Then trust me. Help me. This is a matter of life and death to us, to our home nations. We can discredit this monster, van Owen, so you can find all the equipment you want and it won't help him, no matter what he hears."

"Anything."

"Solicit him."

"No, please, Myessa. He terrifies me!"

"Well then, you must be his mole. I'll turn you in, but first I let Arsène take you for a walk to the airlock."

"I'm not his mole!"

Myessa took Sparks's hand. "My child, I am desperate. You are the one he wants, so you are the only bait I can use. I promise you won't have to sleep with him. Is that good enough? All I want to do is discredit him."

The girl was weeping. "Yes, Myessa. I'll do it. I would never be disloyal! You know what I owe you."

"It's all in your head, my child. You owe me nothing. Everything you have, you earned. Now here is what I need you to prepare, and how I want it done."

"Captain van Owen, you have been accused by this woman of attempting to molest her," the director of the space station said sternly.

"I saw the whole thing," put in Jose Maria Veracruz. "They passed in a corridor. She spoke to him, he spoke to her, and suddenly, he seized her to him, kissed her, and . . . how may I put it delicately?"

"I was with Señor Veracruz," put in the slim lieutenant. Patty, Myessa remembered. She was pleased to have been able to inform him that though the covert operation would be on Europa, not Io, the U.N. would be alone in the midst of that cold and dreary landscape. No lives would be lost. She offered to break the news of Jose Maria's second employment to Patty, but the hidalgo told her it wasn't necessary. "My observations are the same as his." Jose Maria looked at Patty fondly, and she squeezed his hand.

"He said that I was a Fed whore. He told me if I didn't go to bed with him, he would have me executed as a spy. He tried to rape me."

"This is a serious charge, Captain. What is your defense?"

The captain's fair-skinned face turned purple. "The bitch solicited me! She offered me her body for money because she was tired of her usual client."

"This woman is a technician only " Myessa put in, setting a disk on the table. "I have her employment records here. She does not work in the bedrooms of the Club. Clearly you can see that she is terrified of him. Why would she approach him outside, when he visits my club regularly once a week?"

Van Owen sat silent throughout the arraignment and the statements. Myessa sat next to Sparks, one hand placed protectively on the girl's arm. Her "regiment" was performing brilliantly, and she was proud of them.

"I see," the captain spat, when the director left them alone. "You've concocted this story to try to discredit me."

"I think we have done so," Myessa said with satisfaction. "Your service rank is no longer secret, so your profile is much too high to be a receiver of stolen secrets. Perhaps they will find you a job tapping wires elsewhere."

"Not only did I outsmart you, my Captain, but I outrank you." She laughed at the puzzled expression on his face. For an intelligence officer, he was remarkably ignorant. "Never try to teach a gold-digger how to dispose of dirt."

The Convoy

By late in 2059 the forces deployed by each side in the Jovian system were at near parity. Back on the Earth, the Confederation was losing the war of production. The U.N. nations, with their larger industrial base and greater experience at spaceship construction, were producing almost twice as many ships as the Southern nations.

This had actually been the case since late in 2058, but at first this excess production had not affected the balance of forces. The reason the extra ships had no impact was the work of one man, Kinyetta Kimoyso. Captain Kimoyso commanded a squadron of Confederation commerce raiders that had managed to ambush and destroy almost a third of all the ships dispatched to the war zone by the U.N. While his existence was officially denied by the Confederation on all levels, the efforts of his eight ships had staved off their defeat for almost a year.

In May 2059 Captain Kimoyso reported a strange lack of U.N. shipping. It provided his exhausted crews with a badly needed rest. This respite was brief, for in mid June the reason for the break became apparent. The U.N., having earlier rejected it as too cumbersome, had finally adopted a convoy system.

Accompanied by two cruisers and a carrier, a convoy of twelve merchants arrived on Europa with the loss of only one ship. This compared favorably with the forty percent loss rate the U.N. had suffered over the preceding six months. Encouraged by this success, the U.N. began accumulating ships. By late August over two dozen newly commissioned capital ships and thirty-one heavily laden merchants had gathered at Ceres Station. On these merchants were enough fighters to completely restock all nine U.N. carriers already in the Jovian system. This mass of material constituted almost six months of United Nation's output. If it had arrived intact, the balance of power around Jupiter would have irrevocably swung in their favor. Its loss would have been a powerful incentive to a negotiated peace favorable to the Confederation.

Confederation intelligence first learned of this super convoy from a leak on Jupiter Station. Before it could be confirmed, the convoy had left. A courageous attempt to delay the departure cost Kimoyso two of his ships and resulted in less than a six-hour delay. The Confederation Central Command realized this was to be the key battle of the war and ordered the convoy stopped at all cost.

Plans were made for the Fed ships in the Jovian system to attempt to intercept the convoy when it was still a week out. The U.N., its intelligence service proving equally effective, soon learned of their intent and was less than two hours behind the Fed fleet when it departed. Trapped in open space between the two forces, the Confederation Admiral ordered full acceleration. He was aware that the convoy could neither deviate from its set course or even cease decelerating without creating a massive delay or missing Jupiter System entirely. She was also aware that she also could now not slow down, for this would allow the U.N. ships to catch up. If that happened it was likely that the convoy would pass completely unscathed while her ships fought an even battle with those of the U.N. Jupiter Force.

The first shots of this decisive battle were actually fired by Kimoyso. Half an hour before the convoy and Fed force met, he lead his six remaining ships in an attempt to destroy or even draw off in pursuit some of the convoy's escorts. Outgunned, he lost three more ships in this courageous action and severely damaged one cruiser and three freighters. When his remaining ships retired, they were not followed.

The rest of the battle was a matter of brute strength and speed. It lasted slightly less than seventeen seconds. As both forces approached each other at a relative velocity of several thousand miles per hour, each ceased accelerating and fired ahead of itself everything possible. Fanning ahead of both sides was a curtain of smart missles and shrapnel. Several of the lightly armed U.N. freighters actually jettisoned ball bearings and small-arms ammunition while continuing to decelerate, though, since it was easy to dodge, the effect of this impromptu barrier was slight.

During the short period between the time each side encountered the other's ordnance and when they had flashed past, each lost almost half of their ships. The lightly armored freighters suffered considerably more damage than the warships involved. The Confederation fleet then swung in a large arc and returned to tier bases. The U.N. ships met the convoy an hour later. Less than half of the freighters survived the encounter. Three of those that did had to be towed in. In the sense that they had decisively diminished the effect of the convoy's arrival, this battle was a Fed victory. They had achieved their objective, but the cost had been high. The Confederation fleet had been cut by a third, and the originally equal U.N. fleet had not even seen action. When the surviving warships from the convoy's escort were added, the U.N. now had an insurmountable numerical advantage.

Of course, the next day this no longer mattered. Only the losses were of any concern—though not for the reasons anyone had expected.

THE WAY HOME

by Michael Reaves & Steve Perry

Dan Corbin knew he was going to die.

He could sense the impending doom, feel the primal, screaming fear it roused in the deepest reptilian areas of his brain. He felt the *wrongness* of it even before the instruments began chirping and flashing their urgent warnings. He wanted to yell something, to warn Baedecker and Tyne, but what would be the point? It was too late—they couldn't exactly slam on the brakes, turn around and go home. Besides, the gut-wrenching torture of the Jump itself made it impossible to speak, an effort even to breathe. Whatever was going to happen was going to happen.

He recalled when one of the techs, attempting to describe in layman's terms the theories of what the Jump would feel like, had said it would be like trying to pour a full-grown man through a magna-key slot. Corbin usually put little stock in techs' opinions, but this time he had to admit that they had been entirely too close to the truth.

The only thing that could be said in its favor was that it didn't last long. Almost as soon as it began, it was over. Corbin inhaled long, shuddering gasps of air, feeling the inside surfaces of his suit sticking to his clammy skin. He no longer was being pulled apart by wild animals while being simultaneously squeezed in the fist of a maddened giant—the sensations of the Jump demanded mixed metaphors.

Something had gone wrong, but at least he was still alive.

Now all he had to do was find out what the problem was.

Whatever had happened was bound to be bad. There are certain scenarios in which no mistake is a trivial one, and the first test Jump had to be a dictionary definition of that. Corbin began checking the readings, noticing via the slightly distorted peripheral vision afforded by his wrap-helmet that his two companions were doing the same.

The die had been cast, now they had to see what number had come up.

Life-support systems were green. Power systems were green. The computer link to the displacement engines blinked alternately amber and red. He hit the reset switch, but the lights failed to go cool. Not good. The Jump engines weren't taking calls.

All the other systems were green. How bad could it be?

He remembered, incongruously, how annoyed Dainbridge had always been at the use of the word "Jump" by the media and many of the team personnel. He had preferred "displacement." Actually, there had been a lot of argument over a word that would work best to help popularize the process while remaining accurate to the science involved. No one had really been able to suggest one, and so Jump it had stayed.

Corbin stared at the readouts before him. How bad could it be? Real bad. They were a long, long way from home. No man had ever been farther. Don't like 'Jump'? I've got a word for it, he thought grimly. The perfect.

Suicide.

He had never set foot on a planet in his whole life, and he sure didn't want to. His mother and father had been quite clear in their reasons for choosing to be among the first wave of immigrants to the tube-worlds that floated serenely at the LaGrange points between Luna and the Earth. The home-world that Dan had never walked was polluted, overcrowded, and generally bereft of any sort of opportunity. You couldn't even go outside without risking UV burn, unless you slathered your skin with sunblock. Dan had seen holoproj documentaries—the crime-ridden cities, the underdeveloped countries full of disease and war . . . no thank you. He might be only nine, but he already knew he never wanted to take the long slide down to the purgatory at the bottom of that gravity well. He would weigh twice as much on the planet, and that was a pretty bad feeling. Once in edcom they had made everybody strap on weights to see what it felt like to be a dirtwalker. Dan couldn't believe how hard it had been to do anything—to sit up, walk, even eat: it took everything you had.

Nakawashi Station was a much better place to live. The name meant "inside the eagle," and Dan knew that an eagle was a big bird native to Terra, bigger than any that flew free on the station. That was a neat thought, to be flying up above it all. A rotating cylinder approximately five klicks on its long axis, the station sustained its population of thirty-five hundred perfectly. It was a clean, compact, and small town. You could play in the open parks and streets of the main level with a comfort and security not known on Earth in over a hundred years. And one other thing about life on the station that pleased his parents particularly: it was nearly impossible to get lost here.

On a planet, how could you ever expect to find your way around?

"All right," Baedecker said, holding the hard copy in one gloved hand. "Here's the bottom line. The good news is, we made it. That big bright star seven degrees off starboard is Proxima Centauri. We're less than one-point-five AUs from it. So the Dainbridge Displacement Drive works, and we're the living proof."

"For how long?" Tyne muttered.

Corbin stared at the other two crewman. Baedecker was from Earth, a big, powerful man who probably outweighed Corbin by forty kilos. The Commander had thick shoulders and arms, and although he wore his black hair buzzed tight in a spacer's cut like the rest of them, he had body hair all over him that was almost like fur. He was physically a throwback to some earlier time, but mentally he was strictly a rules man. Tyne liked to joke that Baedecker couldn't go to the toilet without taking a copy of the Space Regs with him to tell him how to do it properly.

Tyne was more like Corbin in build, since he had also been born on a tube-world, but where Corbin was fair, with light brown hair and pale skin, Tyne was dark, with kinky hair and a complexion that was somewhere between *café au lait* and strong tea. Baedecker was a hot pilot in anything that could fly; Tyne was the copilot, but his real talent was that he could run and repair almost any machine he touched. Corbin's primary responsibility was as navigator and com officer.

Baedecker ignored Tyne's muttering. "We've covered over four light years in a little less than four minutes. The bad news is that the displacement generators are nonfunctional. I've no idea why, and neither, it seems, does the computer."

There was a long silence in the wake of this. Corbin felt a fluttering in his stomach that had nothing to do with freefall. They had all known what the dangers of this test mission were when they volunteered; still, to face the reality of dying so far from home—it wasn't easy. He looked at Tyne. "Can you fix it?"

Tyne shook his head. "I ran all the tests. It's not a machine as much as it is some kind of metaphysical gobbledygook. I don't know where to begin."

"So," Corbin said finally, "the operation was a success, but the patients die—is that it?"

"Not necessarily," Baedecker replied. "Because there's also some news that might be good or bad, but in any case it's extremely interesting. We've known for decades—ever since the Belt telescopes became operational—that Proxima has a planetary system similar to our own, with at least one planet theoretically capable of supporting life.

"Well, the displacement drives may be down, but the ion subdrives and our Em-rockets are still operational. And we're within four days of that planet."

It took a moment for Corbin to understand what Baedecker was suggesting. When he did, it took him a moment longer to believe it. "You're suggesting we make planetfall?"

Tyne began to shake his head. "Oh, man," he said quietly, over and over. He moved to one of the viewplates. He touched a control, cleared the plate, and stared through it. Corbin followed his gaze; sure enough, there was the planet in question, a steady point of reflected light barely visible against the harsh glare of Proxima.

"Absolutely," Baedecker was saying in response. "Mass interferometer and spectroscopy readings indicate a world very close in size and atmosphere mix to Earth. There're no readings that indicate civilized energy output, so we must assume it's a primitive world; if there is life, it's animal or pre-tech intelligence. Still, we might be able to survive there, and that's our primary duty."

Corbin stared at Baedecker in disbelief. He had always thought the man cold and emotionless, a real by-the book rocket jocket. He hadn't realized how right that estimate was. Here he was talking about landing on an alien planet as if it would be a holiday picnic in a theme park. And babbling about duty as well.

"Maybe we could," Corbin said slowly, "assuming we don't catch something fatal or get caught by something big and hungry. But even so, what's the bloody point? Are you seriously suggesting we become *castaways?*"

Baedecker looked at him levelly for a long moment. "Is there an alternative? Our air will give out in a week, two if we do emergency coldpross. We will certainly die inside the ship in a maximum of another sixteen days. We have to send back our ship data as best we can, but we can also add to humanity's knowledge of this planet."

"Yeah," Tyne said, "maybe they'll even name it after us. Fools' World."

Corbin shook his head. "This is not an atmosphere ship. How are you going to get it down? It has the aerodynamics of a brick!"

"Better to attempt the unlikely than the impossible," Baedecker replied. "Unless you know of a way to eat space dust and breathe vacuum, the only chance we have is on PC-Prime."

Corbin stared at the viewplate. Choke to death slowly, or burn up during atmospheric entry, or crash-land the ship. Great choices.

Most of the station was as familiar to Dan as his own cube; he had been all over with his friends. Almost all over. There were restricted areas, of course: the fusion plant, the smelters, and the waste recike-and-dispose section. Children weren't allowed to roam around in the restricted sections.

Except . . .

Except there was a way to sneak into the waste section. Two of his friends, Skinny Bill and Tooey Champion had done it. A circ vent went from Level One all the way down to Level Five, where waste was, and it was just big enough so somebody about nine could use it.

"Oh yeah," Tooey said, as he and Dan sat near the main fountain on One, watching the water arc up and fall back. "It is too mean, you know? There's these big, *big* titanium tanks full of goop, and huge shuntpipes that gurgle like boogs in the night. And there's drones running back and forth like entcom police dragoons, watching for leaks and stuff. Mean, mean, *mean*!"

Dan grinned. "I gotta see it. When you wanna go?"

"Aw, I'm stuck doing base ed makeup until day after tomorrow. My father'll scream if I don't get it done. I can show you where the vent is, but you'd be afraid to go by yourself."

"Earth I will! I'm not afraid!"

"Bet you are."

"Bet I'm *not*! Show me the vent."

Tooey grinned. "I'll show you, but you'd better wait for me. You can get lost down there."

Dan laughed. "Lost? C'mon!"

"I heard that it happened to a guy once. First-term guy named Teek Chin. Right after the station was finished and everybody moved in. Teek went down and never came back. They never found him."

Dan's laugh was as loud as before, but a little forced. "You're making that up."

"I swear on my spit. His ghost is supposed to still be down there."

"Well, I'm not afraid. I'm going."

"When?"

"As soon as you show me the vent."

"You'll need a light."

Dan pulled a small induction lamp from his tunic pocket and waved it at Tooey. As long as he was inside the station, the lamp would draw power from the 'casters.

"Show me the vent," he said.

The automatic broadcasts from the *Argo I* had been going on a tight-beam back toward the Solar System all along, telemetry and cabin recordings and other basic black-box info, but each of the three crewmen kept a personal log whose broadcasts were optional. Corbin hadn't intended to send any of his back, but he had relatives who would want to know more than the official dry stats, should he die. And since it seemed that his death was approaching fairly rapidly, one way or another, he decided it was time to speak to it.

"Hi, Mom and Dad and Susita, this is Dan, calling from that pinpoint of light to your left to say hello— and maybe goodbye. Seems that this seventy-billion-stad experimental toy is broke. It's a long walk home, so we're going to try to land on PC-Prime and do a little camping. Drop by next time you're in the neighborhood. . . ."

Corbin faltered, and the personally coded VA recorder shut off and waited for him to speak again. He was trying to make it easy on them, show them he was in good spirits despite the problem, but he didn't feel like being light and funny. If he sent the message off now it would be four years before it would get home. Four years. By then, he could be nothing more than radioactive dust settling through the air of an alien world; or, if Baedecker somehow managed to miraculously put the ship down in one piece, probably dry bones bleaching under an alien sun.

He started again, speaking quietly so that the other two men wouldn't hear him. "Look, things are bad and by the time you get this, I'll probably have been dead for years. It's okay. I wanted to come, wanted to be the navigator on the first ship to break light speed, wanted to be the one who would bring it home. I think you know why. I knew it was a risk. It's been too many years since I had the nerve to try Level Five, and win or lose, I'm glad I came. I love you all. Remember that I did my best."

"Dan?"

Corbin turned. Tyne was floating there. He had removed his suit and wore only his thin, pale-yellow synsilk coveralls.

"Hey, Leon. You're out of uniform."

"So what's Baedecker going to do? Put me in space jail?" He smiled. "We get the *Argo* down in one piece and we are going to have to start breathing the local fluid sooner or later. If we don't . . ." He shrugged.

Corbin untabbed his own wrap-helmet, pulled it off, and reached up to scratch his nose. "Ahh. Yeah, I guess you're right. Anything more on starting the Jump engines?"

"I got it narrowed down some. The diagnostics say all the links are fine, but the slavecomp down there doesn't want to talk to the mainframe. The slave is alive, it's putting out tac and sensor data, I can get to the auxiliary storage disk, but that's it. I can't tell if the problem is in the slave or the engines. Doesn't make much difference."

"So much for triple backups. Could we maybe go down there and do an eyeball?"

"Sure, if you want your eyeballs fried."

Corbin knew that the radiation danger was high inside the Jump engines. "Maybe we could draw straws? If we could fix it, might be two of us could get home."

"Nice thought, but the slave is smack in the middle of the hi-rad cross-channel. Without a class-four radiation suit a man would last, oh, maybe forty-five seconds. It'd take that long to remove the inspection plate. We need a drone. I tried to tell them, but they didn't want to spring for the extra mass."

"Well, now you can say 'I told you so.' "

"That's not exactly what I had in mind telling them."

Corbin laughed. Tyne smiled back at him.

"Uh-oh," Baedecker said.

Corbin and Tyne swiveled to look at where the Commander sat watching his comp screens.

" 'Uh-oh?' " Corbin said. "I don't like the sound of that."

"Check your screens," Baedecker said. His voice was tight. "Doppler Two."

Corbin swiveled his chair and punched up the appropriate channel. Tyne watched over his shoulder, holding onto the back of the chair with one hand to keep from floating away.

They were still a day away form making even a high planetary orbit, but the globe loomed large, filling the viewplates and the ship's bioelectronic sensors. They could see cloud weather, pick up ionization bands and magnetic fields, tell within a hundred meters the depth of the three main oceans. They had already determined that the atmosphere at sea level was mostly nitrogen/oxygen, with about sixteen percent O_2, so if they got that far they could breathe it, though it would be a bit thin. Co_2 was at a level consistent with fairly extensive plant growth, and there were some forest-like green patches. There was enough methane to postulate animal life.

But for Baedecker to say what he'd said meant something new had been added to the scenario.

When the doppler channel came on-line, Corbin saw what it was. Dop II was tied into the heatscan infared viewer.

"Holy shit!" Tyne said.

Corbin punched in the computer augs and asked for an enhanced pix with peripherals. What he saw stunned him.

There were four continents on PC-Prime: Two of

them were polar, both irregular pancakes, slightly larger at the north pole than the south; the third continent was a sprawling, almost diamond-shaped giant that straddled the equator and was fully half of all the land mass on the world, and possessed of a lot of mountains. The fourth continent was a mostly flat, squarish island probably close to the size of Australia. They'd taken to calling it "Square Land." The planet's rotation had brought this last continent around so that it now faced the approaching crippled ship.

Square Land was on fire.

The computer-generated pix ran a number crawl up the sides, along with sliding graphs to show temp scales, and there were large fluctuations across the land, but the average temperature was over 300° C. The whole damned *continent* was burning! Already the smoke from it was blotting out the sight of the fire, and threatening to cloud over the entire eastern hemisphere.

It was hot enough down there to melt lead.

Tyne shoved himself through the cabin toward his own control panel and began operating his comp console.

"What the hell could do that?" Corbin whispered.

"Split screen to Record I," Tyne said.

Corbin dialed the screen to split and tapped in the command for the recording channel. The picture showed the same continent, but looking the way it had last time Corbin had seen it.

"That's last revolution," Tyne said, answering the question before anybody could ask it. "Check the clock."

"Jesus," Corbin said. Between the time the planet had taken the square continent around the other side and brought it back, *something* had set the whole thing aflame. No natural phenomenon Corbin had ever heard of was *that* violent. And anyway, the landmass didn't show any signs of previous volcanic activity; that was all on Big Diamond. Hundreds of thousands of square kilometers of land didn't just spontaneously combust!

And would a natural fire be able to burn that hot with the oxy that low?

On a hunch, Corbin flipped into his com board and scanned the radio bands. What he heard confirmed his suspicions.

"Listen up," he said. "Opchan is catching wiggles from right on top of us."

Tyne shook his head. Opchan—operations channel— was alive with old signals, of course; radio beams from the Solar System that had left the region for years past, but these were different. He looked at the readouts. "Jesus and Buddha, they're bleeding all over five different bands." He turned up the gain. "Listen to that!"

The comp speakers rattled off a series of liquid whistles and hums, interspersed with harsh cackles.

"What is it?" Baedecker asked.

"Not what," Corbin said, "but *who*. We've got company out here, only . . ."

"Only what?"

"It's not anybody we know."

The vent was easy for Dan to negotiate. There was only one tight turn anywhere in it, and it had been simple to wiggle around that. There were no side vents big enough to get into, so you couldn't take the wrong one. Once you were inside the thin metal walls you had only two choices: up or down. Up was Level One, down took you to Five. Simple.

He wasn't afraid of enclosed places, not many people on the station were, and anyway he had his light, so it was no big deal. It was a little hard to keep enough tension on the tube's walls with your feet and arms to keep from slipping, but Tooey had told him about that, so Dan had his thick-soled running slippers on and bands cut from the old scooter tire around his elbows for padding and added friction.

It took around ten minutes to make it to where the vent came into the ceiling of Level Five. There was a glasfiber filter and bird grate over the end to keep the swallows out, but it was on a hinge just like the one on the top had been. The vent opened right over one of the big tanks, like Tooey had said, and it was only half a meter below, an easy slide.

The tank rang hollowly when he stepped down onto it, and Dan grinned as he shut the lamp off. Oh, this was mean, mean, *mean*!

Climbing down from the tank was a bit tricky, but there was a pipe you could use that ran almost all the way to the top. In a minute, Dan was on the floor between two of the three-meter-high holding units—in a new world that was his to explore.

"Shut down the ion engines!" Corbin commanded.

Baedecker looked at him as if he'd suddenly sprouted wings. "What?"

"Kill the drive, now! Hurry!" Corbin was busy with his own controls, stopping their automatic radio transmissions back to the vicinity of Sol.

"You've lost your mind—" Baedecker began.

"We don't have time to argue. Tyne, get that drive off! And everything but life-support while you're all it. Hurry!"

Tyne hesitated a second, then moved to obey.

"Stop!" Baedecker roared. "Touch those controls and I'll have you brought up on charges!"

Tyne laughed, a short, sharp bark. He lifted the cover and flipped the old-style mechanical switch that kicked off all but emergency life-support.

The battery lights kicked on, dimmer than the regular lighting, and the vibrations of things mechanical inside the *Argo I* rumbled to a stop. The silence that followed was profound.

Baedecker came up from his chair and started to hurl himself at Tyne, who was closest.

"Hold it, hold it!" Corbin yelled.

The Commander hesitated.

"Look, let me explain. Thirty seconds, and if you still want to tear somebody apart, don't pick on Leon, you can have me."

"You can't abort ship's functions like that!" Baedecker

said. Breaking regulations was to him what breaking a
spiritual law was to a religious fanatic.

"We'll die if we don't," Corbin said.

Baedecker glared at him, but the words sank in.
"What are you *talking* about?"

"Look, Tony, what do you think cooked Square
Land?"

"I don't have any idea. Neither do you."

"Yes I do. Hear me out, okay?"

"Go on."

"I think," Corbin said, "that there are alien ships
on the other side of PC-Prime. I think they just got
through using Square Land for target practice."

Both Baedecker and Tyne stared at him.

"Look, we don't know of anything natural that can
do what we see down there, right?"

"It's a new planet, Corbin—"

"Physics is physics, Commander. Think about it for
a minute. One day down there and the continent is
peaceful and cool; the next and it's barbecue city. If
there was anything alive down there, it's cooked crisp."

"Granted. So?"

"So all of a sudden I'm getting coherent signals all
over my com bands in a language like nothing we've
ever heard. The computer doesn't recognize it and
field strength says it's in the neighborhood. Something
on the other side of Prime did that"—he pointed at
the unseen planet through the wall of the ship—"and
nobody lives there who's got radio or weaponry capable. That means ships. More than one signal, and
talking to each other in those glottal stop whistles.
Where'd they come from? They aren't native; nothing
else in this system could possibly field life as we know
it. We've got *aliens* over there!"

Baedecker shook his head, disbelieving. "All right.
Suppose you're right. Why turn our ship off?"

Tyne cut in. "Yeah, I see. He's right, Commander.
If they are there they're probably in orbit, and maybe
they'll swing around to this side. If we're spewing ions
and radio, they'll see it."

"Exactly," Corbin said. "I don't know what kind of

sensor gear they might have, but they do have radio so they might hear us; our beam has some spill."

Corbin took a deep breath and let it out, trying to calm his voice. "Tony, if they can fry a continent from off-planet, what do you think they can do to our unarmed ship?"

Baedecker wasn't convinced that there was anybody on the other side of Prime, but he was willing to wait a few hours to see. They were still heading toward planetfall at a good clip, even without the engines, and if there was anything at all to Corbin's theory it might be a good idea not to attract attention.

Tyne said, "Look, if there *are* aliens over there, there's no reason we have to assume they're hostile, is there?"

"You saw Square Land, didn't you?"

"Come on, we don't know if there's any life down there except trees and bugs, if that."

"We don't know that there isn't, either. Besides, anybody who would destroy an entire continent where life *might* evolve probably wouldn't think twice about taking us out."

"Your logic is flawed," Baedecker said.

"We're a long way from home, Commander. Do you want to take the risk? Follow my flawed logic for a little while more. If they aren't locals, then where did they come from? More important, how did they *get* here?"

"You said that yourself—they have ships."

"Right. They must have FTL ships. They have the Jump, and likely their version is in a hell of a lot better working order."

"I fail to see—"

"My god," Tyne said slowly. "If these *are* unfriendlies, they're within spitting distance of Sol!"

Corbin nodded. "Exactly. And if we can hear voices from home, so can they."

Baedecker got it, finally. "We've got to warn the System!"

Tyne said, "If those jokers are staging here to hit

the Solar System, they'll be there a long time before our radio signal gets home. We're fucked, and so is Earth."

Corbin became the devil's advocate for a moment. "Look, I know I said all this, but there's an off chance that maybe these guys aren't hostile. There could be another reason why they melted Square Land, something we don't understand."

"So what are we supposed to do?" Tyne asked.

Corbin looked at him, and saw that Baedecker also was waiting to hear the answer. The book had failed the Commander, there was nothing in it to cover this situation. Nobody had planned on the first Jump ship running into aliens who could destroy a continent from space. "There's nothing we can do but wait and watch." Corbin said. "We need to know more before we make any decisions."

Dan wandered around the tanks, watching the tiny, box-like robots—the drones—as they scurried back and forth on their little plastic tires, scanning pipes and containers with their UV lasers, looking for problems. The drones ranged in size form about that of a shoe package all the way to the repair models with patching tools that stood near Dan's own height.

He walked for what seemed a long time before he ever looked at his chronograph. The timer on his wrist warned him that it was nearly time for him to be home for the evening meal. Better start back.

After a few minutes, he was a little worried.

After half an hour, he was scared.

After an hour of searching for the vent and not finding it, Dan was in a full-blown panic. He remembered what Tooey had said about the boy who disappeared into Level Five, never to be seen again. He remembered about the ghost. But he couldn't remember where the vent was. He darted about, the fear covering him like his nervous sweat, his mouth too dry to do more than croak for help. He was lost!

He couldn't find the vent.

He couldn't remember the way to get home!

*   *   *

"Son of a bitch," Corbin said softly. He was watching the high-res doppler scan on his screen.

"What?" Tyne said.

"There they are. Coming over the pole."

Baedecker and Tyne got busy at their own boards. They were too far away for direct visual, except maybe as tiny pinpricks of light, but the ship's sensors had eyes that could see a long way.

"Oh Lord, there are dozens of them. Hundreds!" Tyne said.

Even Baedecker forgot the book. "Look at the sizes! The smallest is ten times as big as we are! The big ones . . ."

Corbin nodded, not speaking. The largest ships were *huge*. As big as a tube-world.

Though they couldn't see them, the computer was able to construct pictures. The smallest ships were winged and looked capable of dipping into an atmosphere and flying; the larger vehicles were rod-shaped, long and cylindrical, obviously meant for deep space.

"Their lowest ships are in orbit at nine thousand, six hundred klicks," Baedecker said, back in control. "Unless they've changed it, their weapons are effective at least that far."

Corbin nodded grimly.

"Can they see us?" Tyne asked.

"I hope not," Corbin answered. "Not much we can do about it if they can."

He began tapping controls on his com board.

"What are you doing?" Baedecker asked.

"They're using a fairly wide VHF band to communicate between the ships, more than they need for voice radio."

"What does that mean?"

Corbin shrugged. "Could be sending computer data. Or maybe visual. I've got a signal at around a hundred megahertz, I'll see what our computer can do with it."

The alien ships continued their north-to-south orbital segment.

"I make it a hundred and fifty ships exactly," Tyne

said. "Looks like they are broken up into three big squads."

The computer began to decode the alien radio beam. It took a minute. Corbin touched more controls and spoke to the VA pickup to hurry the bioelectronic brain along.

Then, suddenly, he knew what they had here. "Television!"

"What?" That from Tyne and Baedecker together.

"Punch up com three," Corbin commanded. The computer lined in his own flatscreen as he spoke.

"Oh, *man!*"

What the computer gave them was a picture of one of the aliens.

"What is it, a reptile? A mammal?"

Corbin looked at Baedecker, then back at the image on the screen. "I don't know. I'm not a zoologist."

What the three men saw was the head and—for want of a better term—shoulders of the alien. The head was squarish, with thick brows and deepset eyes, and it had flat nostrils over a long gash of a mouth. The jaw was underslung, bulldog-like, and wired to knots of bunched muscle on the top rear of the skull. The neck was long, but thick in relation to the head, and there seemed to be four long ropes of muscle that inserted under the jaw, coming up from four bony protuberances at the top of the torso.

It had no arms.

Behind the thing were two elephant trunk-like appendages. Corbin couldn't see where they were attached to the creature—the torso? Were they tails? Each of the trunks had three fingers on the end, one of which opposed the other two.

Corbin was aware of saying something softly, but he wasn't sure what it was.

The signal broke up but the computer managed to drag in another one, a slightly different view of the alien. There was nothing in the background to give a size comparison. But this picture was smiling. Or at least showing its teeth.

"Oh shit," Corbin said.

"What?" Baedecker stared at the image.

"Look at the teeth."

The thing had long and pointed eyeteeth, and shorter but similarly shaped fangs on either side of the big incisors. The row of teeth inset into the bottom jaw were shorter, but tapered to tiny points. There were no molars in sight.

"So they have teeth, so what?"

"Those are not cud-chewers," Corbin said. "That's the dentition of a predator."

"I still don't see what—"

"It's a killer," Corbin said, cutting him off. "A killer in a ship that can throw a rock more than nine thousand kilometers to nail its prey."

"Oh, man!" Tyne said again.

Exactly, Corbin thought grimly. Man was in deep trouble.

"We've got to do something," Baedecker said. "We've got to get the Jump drive operational and get back to warn the system."

Corbin stared at him. "How?"

Baedecker was really upset. He removed his helmet and wiped at his perspiring face. Strictly against regs.

"I'll go down and examine the malfunction."

"Won't work," Tyne said. "You'd be cooked before you could get a good look at it, much less repair it."

"We have to do *some*thing!"

"I suggest that we get into a matching orbit and stay on opposite sides of the planet from those guys," Corbin said.

"What good will that do?"

"It'll keep us alive a little longer. Alive and working on it is better than dead and not."

Nobody argued with that.

Going over the south pole they nearly hit a big chunk of spinning rock twice their own size.

"Jeez, look at that!" Tyne said.

The sky ahead was filled with debris, some of it as

small as the house-sized boulder they'd just missed, most of it much larger.

"Where'd all this crap come from?" Corbin wondered aloud.

"Asteroids? Maybe Prime had a moon and the monsters from outer space blew it up," Tyne said. "What do you think, Commander?"

Baedecker was adjusting the ship's course so it wouldn't plow into a city-sized rock rapidly approaching. "I'm busy."

Halfway around the back side of Prime, the three got another surprise. The comp-aug enhanced picture showed them another piece of flying real estate, this one four or five klicks long by half that wide. Upon this moonlet was some kind of artificial structure. It was roughly dome-shaped and covered with a reflective material like silvered mylar. As they got closer, the computer told them there were large mechanical devices in operation both within and outside the dome.

"Some kind of mining operation," Tyne said. "Those are diggers and crushers. Bet there's a smelter and gasworks inside."

"Makes sense," Baedecker said. "A fleet that big would have to have some way of generating supplemental supplies. Air to breathe, water, other essential gases."

"Is it manned, you think? Or *alien*ed?"

Baedecker shrugged. "Could be. Could be automatic. Tyne?"

"Probably automatic. That kind of stuff is easy to program, assuming their technology is only as good as ours. What difference does it make?"

Corbin bit at his lip. He had the glimmerings of an idea. It was iffy at best, but they were certainly at the stage where any idea was better than none. He looked at Tyne. "You suppose they have the equivalent of drones down there? Small ones?"

"Probably."

Corbin grinned. "You think you could figure out how to take control of an alien robot and make it do what you want?"

Tyne cocked his head to one side and considered that. "Maybe, if their technology wasn't too different." He smiled as the thought took him.

The mining operation flashed by as the ship sped along in its orbit. Baedecker said, "What are you two talking about?"

"Commander, do you think you could rendezvous with that rock being mined?" Corbin asked.

"Yes, of course. What would be the point?"

"Getting home."

Baedecker looked at Tyne and Corbin. "What the hell are you trying to say?"

Corbin and Tyne exhanged glances, and then Corbin told Baedecker.

"You're crazy, both of you."

"Better to die trying the unlikely, didn't you say?"

Baedecker rubbed at his mouth with one hand. "It will be tricky. We're doing one orbit every ninety-seven minutes. I'll have to start slowing well before we reach the mining operation. Even with the Em rockets, we'll only have a few minutes at best before the fleet circles around and sees us."

"You have a better idea?" Corbin said.

Baedecker sighed. "No," he admitted.

Whatever else you might say about Baedecker, he's one hell of a pilot, Corbin thought. After two more orbits, he brought the ship to a path parallel to the large moonlet and no more than twenty meters above it, then held the ship steady as Corbin and Tyne went OTS. Neither man wore a tether; they pushed off from the airlock and sailed toward the surface of the moonlet in a cloud of frozen air. There was some gravity, not enough for walking, but Corbin felt a slight bit of tug as he reached the surface.

They were just inside the terminator line on the dark side of Pc-Prime. Corbin saw a bright flash of yellow-white light erupt against the dark planet. He pulled himself along the ground and tapped Tyne on the shoulder. They touched helmets so they could talk, not wanting to risk their suit radios.

"What was that light?"

"Falling rock burning up, most likely. These orbits are probably decaying pretty fast."

"Yeah. You don't suppose this one is going anytime soon?"

"I doubt it. Be a waste of mining gear."

"I hope you're right. Let's get moving."

The two space-suited men flew over the ground, pulling themselves along with their hands, and correcting with their CO_2 guns when they drifted too high. It only took a minute to reach the dome.

"Where's the hatch?" Corbin asked.

"Fuck the hatch," Tyne said. He pulled a wrench from his tool kit. Holding onto one of the dome's external support struts for stability, he hit the fabric with the wrench. The thin stuff tore, and a blast of yellowish gas flared out from the rip and froze into a crystalline fog. Using their hands, the two men opened the small hole until they could fit through it. The gas froze around them and clouded their helmets, and they had to wipe it away.

"You think this is what they breathe?" Corbin asked.

"Probably not. This is probably just to keep the machines running right. Maybe a byproduct of smelting or something."

Inside the dome it was dark. If the machines needed to see, they did it in a spectrum outside man's range. Corbin and Tyne flicked on their torches and widened the halogen beams.

"We've got ten minutes left," Tyne said. "Come on."

It was eerie, floating around in the dead-quiet darkness through the still-running machines, many of which Corbin could not begin to identify. The escaping gas tended to pull the two of them back toward the hole they'd made. Every time they would let go of the ground or a machine, the breeze would blow them toward the tear in the dome.

In the end, it was that tear that saved them.

"Look!" Tyne said.

Corbin followed the pointing finger and saw a box about the size and shape of a suit's air tank rolling on a kind of wide tractor tread toward the rip in the dome's fabric. The box was hung with three jointed arms, each of which ended in a different hand-sized device. The two men followed the drone and watched as it found the rip. The drone clamped two of its arms to the vertical tear and pulled the edges together; with the third arm, it began to seal the edges together with what appeared to be heated glue.

"How about that? It's a little tailor drone. Come to Daddy, son," Tyne said. With that, he grabbed the drone and pulled it away from the fabric. He pushed himself through the rent, and Corbin was right behind him.

"I'm taking us out of orbit," Baedecker said. "The alien ships will be right on top of us in a few minutes. We'll never get up enough speed to stay ahead in the same plane."

Corbin pulled himself down into his chair and strapped in. "Affirmative, Commander."

"Will the drone work?"

"I don't know. If anybody can do it, Tyne can." Corbin grinned, but the smile faded as he looked at his screen. "Company. I've got blips coming up behind us."

"I'm kicking in the rockets. Prepare for acceleration."

"Tyne, you strapped down back there?" Corbin yelled.

From the workroom, Tyne yelled back: "Affirm that."

"Go," Corbin said.

Baedecker hit the Em rockets and an invisible hand pushed Corbin into the hardfoam seat. The pressure grew stronger.

"Kind of heavy there, aren't you, Tony?"

"We're only eight thousand klicks ahead of them," Baedecker said. The *Argo I* moved off at a right angle directly away from Prime, emergency rockets on full.

"Think they'll see us?" Corbin asked.

"Better hope they don't," Baedecker replied grimly.

Apparently their luck was holding, for the alien armada stayed in orbit as the *Argo I* sped out toward deep space. After the last alien had circled from sight, Corbin went to check on Tyne.

"How's it going?"

Tyne had the alien drone partially disassembled, with pieces velcroed to various surfaces in the work area. "This guy is really built," he said. "They've got a plastic that is as strong as stacked carbon but twice as flexible. And a battery that's three times as efficient as anything we've got. Look." He held up a disk about the size and shape of a small coin. "This powers the whole unit. I can't even begin to tell you how it works."

"This is all wonderful, Tyne, but can you use the drone?"

"What? Oh yeah, sure. I can't figure out how it sees, but I've cannibalized one of the hull video pick-ups, that'll give us eyes, and I'm wiring in radio-control circuits for the arms. This arm can be modified to use a Phillips screwdriver, see? And this one will mount a socket, if I can borrow a small motor from somewhere. . . ."

"How long will it take you to get the drone operational?"

"Four, five hours."

"Good. If we can stay out of the gunsights of the aliens for another three orbits, we'll be in business."

Baedecker, despite Corbin's protests, had turned the ion engines back on. The rockets were used up, and he wanted to put as much distance between them and the aliens as possible.

"All we know is that they have a minimum effective firing range of nine thousand-plus kilometers," he said. "Maybe they can reach twice that far. We don't even know what they are using."

"All done," Tyne said, floating into the cabin with the drone under one arm.

"Will it work?" That from Baedecker.

"Should. The little tailor here is capable of popping the hatch on the slave comp. We still don't know exactly what the problem is, though."

"Let's find out."

Tyne moved to his control board and began tapping in commands. "Put the drone into the engine access shaft," he said.

Corbin hurried to do that.

"Can it move in zee-gee?" Baedecker asked.

"I put Velcro on the treads and the shaft is lined with it for our own service drones. It should work. Once it gets there, I can use the arms to pull it into place."

Corbin moved back to his station to watch the monitor, trying not to let his nervousness show.

"There's the problem," Tyne said.

Corbin looked at the screen. "Where?"

"See that bank of biogel, to the left?"

Corbin saw it. The hard plastic cover over the bluish gel had ruptured, and the electronic molecular substance had oozed up through the hole and shorted out a circuit board next to it.

"That's not supposed to happen," Baedecker said.

"So send the computer people a nasty note." Tyne tapped in commands on the keyboard.

"Can you fix it?" Corbin asked.

"Not from here. Our little tailor is good, but we don't have the spare parts."

"Shit," Baedecker said. "That's it, then."

"Not necessarily," Tyne replied. "There's one last thing to try. I can dump the core program from here."

"What does that mean?"

"It means if we wipe out about half of the mainframe's current memory, I can reprogram it to run the Jump engines."

Corbin found himself filled with hope where before there had been none. Even Baedecker was smiling.

"Soon as our little tailor can open the modem lines, we're in business." Tyne's fingers danced over the keyboard.

Corbin glanced up at his external monitors. "How long, Leon?" His voice was tight.

"Another twenty minutes. Why, we in a hurry?"

"Yes. Company."

On the doppler, three of the alien ships were leaving the formation in orbit around Prime—and heading right toward the *Argo I*.

"They will be in range in ten minutes," Baedecker said.

"Shit!" Corbin said. "Tyne, can you hurry it up?"

"No. I download this file wrong, I'll dice up the main computer. Wipe out stuff we have to have to run the ship."

Corbin sat staring at the screen, watching the three alien vessels close.

"Seven minutes," Baedecker said. "And we'll need a minute of that to put the main engines on line before we Jump."

"I'm going as fast as I can!"

"Four minutes."

"Leon . . ." Corbin said.

"I can't do it. I don't have the space."

"*Make* the space!"

"Three minutes," Baedecker said.

"Tyne!"

"All right, I've got most of it in. I'll have to wipe a file."

Corbin heard the clicks as Tyne's fingers flew over the keys. The copilot started talking, kicking in the VA input. "Take out nearest ROM, ten to the fifty bytes."

"*This will destroy essential operating data,*" the computer's voice chip said.

"Override! Do it, now!"

"Two minutes. We're about out of time," Baedecker said.

"It's in. It'll either work or it won't. But I don't know where it will take us," Tyne said. "Because I just wiped out the navigation program."

Corbin jerked around to stare at Tyne. *"What?!"*

On Level Five, Dan Corbin sat next to one of the big tanks, sobbing. He was lost. He didn't know how to get home. He was going to die here because he had been stupid!

He was still sitting there when the maintenance supervisor found him. The drones had alerted him to the small crying intruder, and the man smiled at Dan when he bent to pick him up. "I guess you'll know better than to do something like this again, won't you son?"

Dan nodded, the tears flowing. He would never, ever go anywhere again without knowing the way to get back.

The ship shook as Baedecker put it into the tightest turn he could manage on ion power.

"Jump engines on line," Tyne said.

"It doesn't matter," Baedecker said. "We might find ourselves in the middle of a star if we Jump. Or lost forever!"

"They're shooting at us. My sensors show a beam of charged particles just missed us by less than half a kilometer," Tyne said. "I guess that means they don't want to be friends. So do we fry or Jump blind?"

Corbin shoved his panic down. His fingers danced over his keyboard. The coordinates flowed from his hands into the board and into the computer.

"What are you doing?" Baedecker asked.

"Taking us out of here."

"How?!"

"I remember the coordinates."

"That's impossible! You are talking about more than fifty coded numbers in sequence!"

"I memorized them. Habit I developed, from something that happened to me as a kid. I don't like to be lost." Corbin tapped in the last number. "Do it," he said.

"If you're wrong . . . !"

"We're history either way! *Do it*!"

Baedecker took a deep breath and jabbed the activation sense pad.

They Jumped.

When Corbin opened his eyes, his screen was blank. But his radio came to life with familiar calls in languages he knew.

"We did it!" Baedecker screamed. "That's Sol, we're back in the System!"

Tyne launched himself from his seat and flew into Corbin, nearly knocking Corbin from his chair. The copilot hugged him. "You did it! Sonovabitch, you did it!"

Dan Corbin grinned. Yes. He had done it. He had remembered the way home.

At last.

(0451)

PERILOUS DOMAINS

☐ **SHADOWRUN:** *NEVER DEAL WITH A DRAGON:* **Secrets of Power Volume I by Robert N. Charrette.** In the year 2050, the power of magic has returned to the earth. Elves, Mages and lethal Dragons find a home where technology and human flesh have melded into deadly urban predators. (450787—$4.50)

☐ **SHADOWRUN:** *CHOOSE YOUR ENEMIES CAREFULLY:* **Secrets of Power Volume II by Robert N. Charrette.** When magic returns to the earth, its power calls Sam Verner. As Sam searches for his sister through the streets of 2050, he realizes that only when he accepts his destiny as a shaman can he embrace the power he needs for what waits for him in the final confrontation. . . . (450876—$4.50)

☐ **THE CHRONICLES OF GALEN SWORD, Volume I:** *Shifter* **by Garfield and Judith Reeves-Stevens.** Rich, New York City playboy Galen Sword is on a quest to recover his lost heritage—to return to a parallel universe where he had been heir to a powerful dynasty. First he must conquer his enemies, terrifying shape shifters who fear the power Galen doesn't know he possesses . . . (450183—$3.95)

☐ **THE CHRONICLES OF GALEN SWORD, Volume 2:** *Nightfeeder* **by Garfield and Judith Reeves-Stevens.** Galen Sword's search for the First World made him the focal point between warring clans . . . and his very survival rested with that most dreaded of legendary beings, an adept whose powers could only be fueled by the blood of the living. (450760—$3.99)

Buy them at your local bookstore or use this convenient coupon for ordering.

NEW AMERICAN LIBRARY
P.O. Box 999, Bergenfield, New Jersey 07621

Please send me the books I have checked above. I am enclosing $_____ (please add $1.00 to this order to cover postage and handling). Send check or money order—no cash or C.O.D.'s. Prices and numbers are subject to change without notice.

Name_____

Address_____

City _____ State _____ Zip Code _____

Allow 4-6 weeks for delivery.

This offer, prices and numbers are subject to change without notice.